LEGACY

By D. K. Mamula

Edited by Rosalind Winton

onevoiceliteraryagency.com

© Copyright 2015

ISBN 978-0-9966515-0-9

The story within these pages is a story about family and friends, heartache and loss, fear and courage, romance and music... but most of all, it is a story about a boy who grew into a young man and along the way, learned about the strength of the human soul and the power of love. It's possible that by reading his story, you may learn something about yourself. I know I did.

D.K. Mamula

Many angels have moved in and out of my life over the years. I would like to take this opportunity to acknowledge a few of them.

Chuck Dillihay

You were my first best friend. We had so much fun growing up together, using our imaginations to create wonderful worlds where anything could happen. I remember the nights when we would lie awake in our beds and talk to each other through the open doorway between our rooms and how we laughed until we cried. I guess that's where my vivid imagination came from. You've always been there to cheer me on in everything I do. You are the best big brother a little sister could ask for. I love you with all my heart!

Justin Dillihay

You are my child, the light of my life. You are the very best part of me. You never cease to make life interesting. Your independent spirit inspires me and the sound of your sweet laughter warms my heart. Thank you for choosing me to be your mother. I will always be proud of you and I will love you eternally.

Willis Mamula

My sweet, wonderful husband. You are my soul mate and the love of my life. I have always said you were the most tolerant man in the world and every day you continue to prove me right. I truly appreciate everything you do for me and for our family. Thank you for putting up with me and all my eccentricities. I love you more than you'll ever know.

Judith Lee East

Having someone who believes in you—really truly believes in you—can change your life. That's what you did for me. I honestly believe that we were supposed to find each other that night at the Riverside. There were forces at work that night that are greater than we could ever imagine. Over the last 20 years we sang, we danced, we laughed, we cried, we gained some great friends… and we lost some great ones, too… but through all of it, we kept going and we're still going to this very day. I love you, Doodie.

Rosalind Winton

How do you thank someone who has helped you realize a dream? Through one mutual interest, the Universe brought us together and sparked a creative fire that burns brighter every day. For all your invaluable advice, all your publishing prowess, the endless hours you've spent editing my manuscripts and every proverbial kick in the arse you've ever given me…

I love you and I thank you.

There have been many, many angels who have helped to guide me along the way… some I knew well, some I didn't… and there were some whose influence I hadn't noticed until I looked back through my memories. There are even a few who are completely unaware that they had any influence on my life at all. To all of my angels—past, present and future—and to anyone who has ever, even for the slightest second, believed in me, you have my sincerest gratitude.

D.K.M.

This book is dedicated to two very special women.

My mother,

Betty Rosalie Garrison Dillihay

(1934-1992)

You were the woman who went above and beyond to make the 'two-story chocolate-brown brick house' into a loving home. You taught me about hard work and perseverance, dignity and grace....and courage. You are the strongest woman I have ever known. We may not have had much, but we had family, we had a home, and we had love. As it turns out, that was all we really needed.

You are my hero.

I miss you terribly and I will love you eternally.

And

My elementary school music teacher,

Mrs. Gloria Morris

(1921-2013)

You were the first person outside of my family to encourage my interest in music and performing. One of my fondest memories was the day you let me bring my autoharp to class. I sat in a desk at the front of the room and you sat next to me and held my music book. I played 'Oh, Susanna' as the rest of the class sang. It was my very first solo performance in front of an audience. Teachers have so many opportunities to make a difference in their student's lives....
You definitely made a difference in mine and I will be forever grateful.

Thank you.

~ ~ ~ ~ ~ * ~ ~ ~ ~ ~

"Papa?"

"Yes Davey?"

"Why do you sing songs all the time?"

"Because it makes me happy."

"It makes you happy when you sing songs?"

"Yes."

"Even when you sing sad songs?"

"Especially when I sing a sad song."

"But how can you be happy if you're singin' a sad song?" Daniel sits down on the step next to his young son.

"You know how sometimes you get really sad?" Davey nods. "I mean really, really sad, way deep down inside?"

Davey nods again, "Uh-huh."

"And sometimes, you get so sad that you just know you're gonna cry. Have you ever been that sad, Davey?" Again, Davey nods. "What did you do about it?"

"I cried."

"You did?"

"Uh-huh, do you cry, Papa?" Daniel nods. "Is that why you sing sad songs, so you won't cry?"

"Sometimes."

Davey leans against his father. "Papa?"

"Yes son?"

"Do I make you cry?"

"No, you make me happy."

"Is that why we always sing happy songs together?"

Daniel smiles. "That's right. We sing happy songs together because you make me very, very, happy."

Davey smiles brightly. "I love you Papa!"

Daniel hugs the little boy tightly. "I love you Davey!"

~ ~ ~ ~ * ~ ~ ~ ~ ~

Casey McCallister was small and slender with a petite figure. Her hair was long and silky, a deep velvety brown. The soft brown of her eyes matched her hair and her smile was as bright as a sunrise.

Casey had studied dance since she was a small child and many of the graceful, flowing gestures had become part of her natural movement. David loved to watch during rehearsals as she leaped and bowed and twirled around the room as if she was floating on air, reminding him of a music box dancer spinning around on her tiny stage. It was Casey who gave David the courage to share his talent with the world and in his heart, he knew there would be no show without her. The love he felt for her overwhelmed him.

David never understood what Casey saw in him. He was a mere five feet three inches tall and, in his opinion, average looking and rather boring. He often wondered what it was that made her stay.

"Look in the mirror," she said when he asked her.

"Look in the mirror?"

Casey smiled as she bent down and kissed him. "I gotta run, I'll see you later."

As she scurried off, he thought back to the time he first laid eyes on Casey McCallister.

PRELUDE - PART I

Murray Ackerman walked briskly along the sidewalk, stopping briefly at the corner to watch for cars before crossing the street. It was a beautiful Friday in May and he had decided to go out for lunch so he could enjoy some of the warm sunshine. As he stepped up onto the curb, he heard a familiar ring from his cell phone.

"Hello Beautiful!" he said sweetly into the mouthpiece, "I was just thinking about you." Murray continued to walk as he listened to his wife's voice on the other end of the line. He entered the Market Street Plaza and began working his way through a crowd that had gathered around a large platform stage. Soon the choir on the stage began to sing and Murray had to press his hand against his opposite ear in an attempt to block out the sound. "Marge, can I call you back? They're having some sort of show here on the plaza and I can't hear a thing… what?" He paused as she repeated her response. "Okay, I love you, too, bye." Murray turned the phone off and dropped it back into his pocket as he slipped into the door of the sandwich shop on the alley corner.

"Murray," the owner shouted, "long time no see!"

"Hey, Frank," Murray said as they shook hands, "how've you been?"

"Oh, I can't complain."

"Don't let him lie to you Murray, he does plenty of complaining!" a woman's voice interrupted.

"Ms. Liza!" Murray greeted her as he held out his arms to hug her, "I sure have missed your pretty face!"

"I've missed you too, honey!" she told him as she kissed his cheek. "What can I get for you?"

"How about one of those warm corned beef sandwiches on dark rye that you used to make?"

"With Swiss cheese and sweet honey mustard?"

"That's the one!" Murray grinned.

"Give me five minutes and it'll be ready to go!" She hurried back to the kitchen.

"So," Frank said, "how's the music biz treatin' ya?"

"Oh, I can't complain," Murray replied as they laughed.

"Still got that office in that big fancy building down on Twelfth Street?"

"Yeah, still got it."

"Have you found that golden ticket yet?" Frank teased him.

Murray smiled and shook his head. "Not yet."

"Lookin' for a diamond in the rough, huh Murray?" Liza inquired as she handed him a brown paper sack.

"Something like that." Murray laid a twenty down on the counter. "Keep the change," he said as he turned to go.

"Well, thank you kind sir!" Liza said.

"You know there's some kids singin' out there today. Maybe you'll find your diamond!'"

"You never know Frank, you never know!" Murray called back with a wave and a smile. He walked out onto the plaza, opened the sack and inhaled the aromas of the spicy corned beef and sweet honey mustard as they mingled together. A smile spread across his face as he folded the top of the bag closed. His cell phone rang, disturbing the perfection of the moment.

"Hello? I was just heading back April. I should be there in time for the meeting." He paused to let the secretary speak. "I'm sorry April, can you say that again?... We'll have to discuss it when I get back to the office, they're having some kind of...." His voice trailed off for a few seconds as he glanced in the direction of the stage. "They're having some kind of concert..." Again, he stopped mid-sentence. He moved the phone away from his ear to listen to what was going on in front of him. "April, cancel my appointments for this afternoon. I'll be out of the office for the rest of the day... no, I'm fine, I just remembered something I need to take care of..."

Murray ended the call and tried to navigate through the crowd in an effort to see the stage better. Halfway through the multitude, he looked up to see a young man on the stage, knees shaking, looking out at the mass of faces staring back at him.

The teacher smiled as the pianist played the song the boy had chosen for his solo, 'Corner of the Sky'. It was a song his father had taught him when he was young and one he had always loved.

As the cue to start singing came again, the soloist closed his eyes, took a breath and silently prayed the words would come out when he opened his mouth. He could feel his heart pounding in his chest while he sang the final chorus. As the last note sailed through the loudspeakers, he finally began to relax... it was over, and he had survived. He took a step back from the microphone.

Murray stood silent while the audience broke out in an enthusiastic ovation. As he looked around at the smiling faces, applause, whistles and even a few excited teenage screams filled the air around him. Looking back to the stage, he noticed the young man had integrated himself back into the group. Murray's eyes searched through the pack of choir students, in vain, to find the face to which that voice belonged, but the young man that had caught his attention was nowhere to be found.

As the applause died down, the teacher thanked the audience and closed the show. Turning to her choir members, she spoke for a minute and then sent them off to meet up with their families. Murray felt a panic slowly creep over him as he watched the group of teens suddenly scatter every which way from the stage and the crowd around him began to disperse.

"His name," he thought out loud, "what's his name?" After scanning the crowd desperately with no luck, he made his way to the front of the stage where he found the choir director talking to some parents. "Excuse me, miss?"

"Yes sir, can I help you?"

"Yes, hello, my name is Murray Ackerman."

"Mrs. Gloria Morris." Murray stood staring at her as they shook hands. "Is there something I can do for you Mr. Ackerman?"

"Yes, I was just wondering… the young man that just sang…"

"Yes?"

"What's his name?"

"May I ask why you are inquiring about the names of my students?"

Murray smiled at her. "Of course, I'm sorry, I should have told you right off." He reached into the pocket of his blazer and pulled out a small silver case and after fumbling nervously to get it open, handed her a business card. "I work as an agent and personal manager for several entertainers who are based in this area and I wanted to see if I could maybe speak to that young man."

Mrs. Morris read the card over carefully. "I'm sorry about being suspicious Mr. Ackerman, but we have to be very careful who we share personal information with these days."

"It's not a problem Mrs. Morris, I completely understand."

"You were asking about the young man who sang 'Corner of the Sky'?"

"Yes ma'am."

"His name is David."

"David."

"Yes."

"Great." The two adults looked at each other for a moment. "Um… does he happen to have a last name?"

The teacher smiled at him. "I'm sorry Mr. Ackerman, I just don't feel comfortable…"

"Ma'am, really, I understand your concern – my wife and I have two daughters and we're very protective of them – but you see it's difficult to contact someone if you don't know their last name." Murray waited as the teacher tried to decide what to do. "Mrs. Morris, I simply want to talk to the young man about representing him professionally." Once again, he waited.

"Will you excuse me for just a few moments?"

"Absolutely," Murray answered. He waited patiently as she stepped a few feet away and spoke privately to a stern-looking gentleman. Murray secretly prayed he wasn't a police officer as he watched them walk back in his direction.

"Mr. Ackerman, this is Mr. Miller, the assistant principal of our school."

"Very nice to meet you sir." Murray stretched out a nervous hand. The other man shook it firmly.

"Your name is Ackerman?"

"Yes, sir, Murray Ackerman."

"It's nice to meet you as well Mr. Ackerman. Mrs. Morris tells me that you're an agent for entertainers."

"Yes, sir."

"And you're interested in representing one of our students?"

"Yes sir," Murray said, "very interested."

"Mr. Ackerman, you do understand that the safety of these children is our main concern."

"Yes Mr. Miller and I agree with that."

"Good," the principal said. Murray tried to stay as relaxed as he could.

"Mr. Ackerman, normally I wouldn't do this, but I have known Mrs. Morris for many years, and I trust her judgment. She feels that you're being sincere, so I'm going to make an exception this once." He paused and looked seriously at Murray. "I'm going to allow you to come to the school as a guest speaker and address the choir regarding your profession. Mrs. Morris will contact you tonight with the particulars."

"Thank you, Mr. Miller."

"You're welcome," the principal replied, "and Mr. Ackerman?"

"Yes sir?"

"Don't make me regret this decision."

"I won't sir, thank you." He watched as the two educators went back to gathering their belongings. "Yes!" he said in reserved celebration. For several seconds he stood there taking it all in. He could feel his excitement growing as he turned to leave and soon, he was running across the plaza. When he reached the sandwich shop, he threw open the door. "Frank!"

"Murray!"

"Frank, I found him, I found him!"

"Who?"

"My diamond, Frank! I found him; I found my diamond!"

"You found him?"

"I found him!"

"Woo hoo!!" Frank yelled, punching the air with his fists. Murray left the shop and headed back to his office as Frank and Liza cheered after him.

PRELUDE - PART II

"Good afternoon sir," the secretary said as she walked over to the counter, "can I help you?"

"Yes ma'am, I have a one o'clock appointment with Mr. Miller."

"And your name?"

"Murray Ackerman."

"Please have a seat Mr. Ackerman and I'll let him know you're here."

"Thank you." The secretary headed back toward the maze of smaller offices. He sat down in one of the chairs that were lined up along the front windowed wall of the school's main office and quietly watched as random students came and went.

"Well, I see you found the school without too much difficulty Mr. Ackerman," Mr. Miller said as he walked out to the reception area. Murray stood and shook the assistant principal's hand.

"Not too much, it's nice to see you again Mr. Miller."

"You, also. Ready to meet your audience?"

"I think so, although I must admit, I've never really done this type of thing before. I usually wait in the wings," Murray chuckled.

"Well, you don't have too much to worry about. We do have a couple of students who get out of line now and then, but the majority are good kids." Mr. Miller motioned toward the door and allowed Murray to exit the office ahead of him. At that same moment the bell rang, and the two men became engulfed in a sea of energetic teenagers hurrying to get to their next class. "The choir room is just down at the end of this hall."

Murray followed him toward the north end of the building and through a dark brown wooden door. Inside was a long room filled with students, each with some type of musical instrument in their hands.

"This is the band room," he explained, "the choir room is right through here." Mr. Miller led him to another brown door on the south end of the band room. As he opened the door, a few students scurried past them in an effort to get to their seats before the tardy bell rang.

"Sorry Mr. Miller!" He shook his head at them. Murray smiled at him as they entered the choir room.

"All right folks let's settle down," Mrs. Morris waited for the room to go quiet. "Mr. Miller would like to talk to you for a few moments, so please pay attention."

"Thank you, Mrs. Morris. Good afternoon everyone. First, I want to tell you how much I enjoyed your concert last week, I know you all worked very hard on the songs and it really showed. You all sounded wonderful and did a great job representing our school, so give yourselves a round of applause for a job well done," he said as he began to clap his hands. The class cheered, whistled and stomped their feet in recognition of their accomplishment as the adults laughed. "Okay, okay," Mr. Miller smiled, "I have a guest speaker for you today who works in the entertainment industry. Let's make him feel welcome." The students applauded again as Murray stepped forward. "Thanks everyone, and thank you Mr. Miller and Mrs. Morris, for inviting me to your school today. My name is Murray J. Ackerman and as Mr. Miller mentioned, I work in the entertainment industry." Murray stood before them, nervous but determined. "I am employed by several entertainers and performers on the local and regional levels as their agent and personal manager. What that means," Murray said, pausing when he recognized David sitting silently near the wall on one side of the room, "is that I am the person who finds jobs for the performers, as well as helping to promote them and their work." Murray hesitated, a bit unsure of himself in this unfamiliar arena.

"Does anyone have a question they would like to ask Mr. Ackerman?" Mrs. Morris said from behind Murray.

"Yes," Murray said, "I'd be happy to answer any questions you might have." A boy in the back raised his hand. "Yes, young man?"

"What's the 'J' stand for?"

"I'm sorry?"

"What's the 'J' in your name stand for?" the boy asked again as some of the others snickered.

"Let's stick to questions about Mr. Ackerman's job Bobby," Mrs. Morris scolded.

"No, no, that's fine, it stands for James." The boy nodded quietly and sat back in his chair. "Um… anyone else?" A girl in the front raised her hand.

"Yes?"

"What kind of performers do you work with?"

"That's a good question. I work with many different types of performers."

"Do you work with circus performers?" another boy asked as the class laughed.

"Well," Murray said as he laughed with them, "I don't have anyone who walks on a tight rope or swings from a trapeze, but I do have a few professional clowns on my roster. Most of the people I represent are actors and actresses, bands, musicians and singers."

"Do you work with anybody famous?" another girl asked excitedly.

"Not yet, but you never know what will happen."

"Mr. Ackerman heard you all sing last week, and he was very impressed," Mrs. Morris told them.

"Yes, I was, especially with the solo performers." He glanced in David's direction, but David still sat silent and seemingly uninterested.

"Would any of those who sang solos on Friday like to sing for Mr. Ackerman today?"

"I will!" a young lady said.

"All right Monica," Mrs. Morris said, "come up here by the piano. Mr. Ackerman, would you care to sit down?"

"Yes ma'am, thank you." Murray sat patiently in a chair near the door and listened as Monica sang her solo. When she finished, the class applauded, and Murray stood and shook the girl's hand. "That was very nice Monica."

"Thank you!" she replied with a smile as she went back to her seat.

"Would you like to hear the other soloists from last week's performance Mr. Ackerman?" Mrs. Morris offered.

"I would love to!" He listened as the next two students repeated their solos, applauding and congratulating them as he had the first.

"And our last soloist on Friday was David," Mrs. Morris said. They waited as David sat engrossed in his textbook. "David?"

He looked up at the teacher. "Yes ma'am?"

"Would you come up and sing your song for Mr. Ackerman please?"

David looked at her and then at Murray, closed his book and laid it on his seat, then weaved his way through the snarl of chairs to the front of the room and stood by the piano.

"Ready?" Mrs. Morris asked him.

David nodded reluctantly and the teacher began playing as Murray listened expectantly. He couldn't put his finger on it, but something seemed different from what he had witnessed the week before. About halfway through the song, Murray stood and walked over to where David was standing.

"Excuse me Mrs. Morris, I'm sorry, but may I stop you for a minute please?"

"Is there a problem?"

"I'm not really sure," he answered, "David, can I ask you something?"

"What?"

"Do you like this song?"

"Yeah."

"Why?"

David looked at Murray for a moment. "I don't know."

"Well, do you like the music or the lyric, do you like the message it has, or do you just think it's fun to sing?"

"I like all of it I guess," David shrugged.

"I thought so, at least that was the impression I got when I heard you sing it last Friday. Do you think you could sing it that way today?" David shrugged again. "Mrs. Morris, could you play it one more time from the top please?" Murray watched and listened. He could feel the hairs on the back of his neck stand up. *That's it,* he thought, *that's the voice I heard at the concert!* When David finished, Murray joined him at the piano.

"That was much better David."

"Thanks."

"You have a very nice voice."

"Thanks," David repeated, "can I sit down now?"

"Yes," Murray answered with a smile, "you can sit down now." Murray's eyes followed David as he hurried back to his chair and sank down behind his textbook. He glanced at Mrs. Morris who just sighed.

"Well, thank you all so much for letting me visit with you today," Murray told the students, "and thank you for singing your songs for me." Suddenly, he saw a hand rise up. "Did you have a question?"

"Do you think any of us could be professional singers?"

"Well, I think you are all talented…"

"But do you think any of us could be stars?" another voice suddenly chimed in.

"You know, it's funny that you asked that," Murray said, "because there is actually one person here who, in my opinion, could do very well with a singing career."

"Who?" they all began asking, "Who is it?"

Murray gave quick glances to Mrs. Morris and Mr. Miller, then back to the students. "I don't think I should say anything else at the moment."

Mrs. Morris leaned over to him. "Isn't that why you came here?" she whispered. Murray smiled at her as he nodded.

"I'm curious as well, Mr. Ackerman," the assistant principal told him. Murray smiled again but hesitated as he looked out at all the questioning expressions, their eyes seemed to be begging him to say that they were the one.

"I bet it's me!" one boy said sarcastically. The class laughed at his comment.

"No way Bill!" another boy called out, "Everyone knows you lip sync!"

"I think it's Monica," a girl on the other side of the room guessed.

"So do I," another agreed as Monica beamed.

"It's probably Mr. Miller," another boy joked as the class erupted in laughter. Murray laughed along with them as Mr. Miller shook his head.

"I doubt it!" the assistant principle chuckled.

Murray looked around at the excited young faces staring back at him. He noticed that David seemed oblivious to what was going on in the classroom and had remained hidden behind his textbook throughout the entire conversation.

"Well Mr. Ackerman," Mr. Miller said, "are you going to keep us in suspense?" Murray glanced over at him.

"Everyone's dying to know," Mrs. Morris told him, "why not let us in on the secret?"

"Well, actually…" Murray began as his eyes scanned the room again, "it's David." The students gaped at each other as David slowly peeked over the edge of his book.

"You think *David* could be a *star*?" one girl asked.

"What?" David asked.

"Well, I don't know if I could guarantee that," Murray said, "but I do think he could make a name for himself as a vocalist."

David stared at him wide-eyed. "*Me*?" Murray nodded and David smiled as he shook his head. "No," he said with a small laugh, "not me!"

"Why not you?" David sat silent. He looked around at the others as they waited for his response.

"He's too chicken!" Bill said as the other boys laughed and made clucking noises. Murray watched as David retreated to the safety of his textbook.

"All right, that's enough," Mr. Miller said stiffly. Stepping closer to Murray, he smiled and stuck out his hand. "Well, at least you tried," he said, "it was nice to have you here Mr. Ackerman."

"It was nice of you to invite me sir."

"Thank you for letting us invade your class today Gloria," Mr. Miller said to the teacher.

"Yes," Murray added turning toward her, "thank you Mrs. Morris."

"It was my pleasure gentlemen."

The two men headed out of the choir room to the hallway and back to the main office. "I hate to cut this short Mr. Ackerman, but I've got some phone calls to make before the end of the day, you can find your way out all right?"

"Oh, yes sir."

"Well then, if you'll excuse me," he said, shaking Murray's hand one last time. He turned and headed back into the office leaving Murray alone in the empty hallway.

Murray stood wondering what he should do. He believed David had a real chance to make it as a singer, but it was obvious the boy wanted no part of it. Still, Murray had a strong feeling that he shouldn't let David walk away from this opportunity. As he stood pondering his next move, the bell sounded and throngs of students surrounded him like a tidal wave. He watched as groups of girls passed by him, gossiping and giggling and boys ran through the halls slamming lockers and causing mischief. Somehow in all the chaos, he managed to spot David walking alone. As the boy rounded the corner, he stopped at the water fountain for a drink. Murray realized this could be his only chance to really talk to him, so he quickly made his way to the water fountain.

"You didn't answer my question."

David looked up from his drink. "What question?" he asked, wiping his mouth on his shirt sleeve.

"Why not you?"

David smiled at him. "Um… thanks for what you said back there Mr… Mr…"

"Ackerman."

"Mr. Ackerman… but I'm really not interested."

"Why not?"

"I'm just not interested."

"You know, you've got a great voice."

"Okay, fine, I can sing, but I'm really not star material."

"I think you are."

"Man, you don't give up do you?"

"No, not when I really believe in someone."

David let out an exasperated sigh. "Look, I gotta go," David said as he started toward the stairwell.

"Will you at least think about it?"

"Yes, I'll think about it."

"Here, take this," Murray said as he stretched his arm out toward the boy.

David spun around quickly. "What is it?"

"It's my business card, it has my name and phone number. I would appreciate a phone call if you change your mind."

David took the card from Murray's hand. They looked at each other for a few tense moments before David disappeared through the stairwell door. Murray stood alone again for a minute in the silence, then took a sip from the fountain and headed for his car.

PRELUDE - PART III

David sat on the porch banister, his feet dangling above the sidewalk, as vibrant shades of red, yellow and orange marked the setting of the sun. Rose felt the coolness in the evening air as she leaned out to check on him.

"Davey, it's getting chilly, maybe you should come in."

"I'm okay."

"Do you want a jacket?"

"No thanks."

Rose took a sweater from the hook by the door, wrapped it around her shoulders and stepped out onto the porch. "The sunset's pretty tonight," she said looking at the sky.

"Uh huh," David replied without looking up.

"Whatcha got there?"

"A business card."

"May I see it?" she asked as she sat against the banister beside him. David handed the card to her. "Murray J. Ackerman, Talent and Personal Management Services." She paused as she looked it over, then handed it back to him. "Where did you get that?"

"He gave it to me."

"This Murray Ackerman gave it to you?"

"Uh huh."

"When?" she asked.

"At school today," David answered, "Mr. Miller invited him to come in and talk to the choir about his job."

"I see."

"We had to sing our solos again."

"So how did you do?"

"I thought I did all right," David said, "but he made me start over."

"How come?"

"He wanted me to sing it like I did at the show last Friday."

"And?"

"He said it was better the second time."

"Good," she said, "so he gave everyone his business card?"

"No," he answered, "just me."

"Why just you?"

"He said I have a great voice," he told her, "he thinks I could be a singer."

"You mean professionally?"

"Yeah. I told him I wasn't interested. He wants me to call him if I change my mind."

"Wow," Rose responded quietly, "that was a pretty eventful school day. Is that what you've been out here thinking about all this time?" David nodded again. "So, have you changed your mind?"

"I don't know, maybe."

"Was there something about this man you didn't like?"

"No, he seemed friendly."

"Someone else said something, didn't they?" Rose prodded.

David paused. "They said I'm too chicken."

"Well, are you?"

"A little, I guess," he admitted.

"There's nothing wrong with being afraid Davey, as long as you don't use your fear as an excuse for not trying." He sat silently staring at the card. "Would you like me to call him for you?" Once again, her question was met with silence. "Why don't we meet with him and find out what he has to say? You can always turn it down again if you want." David looked at his mother as she smiled softly; he tentatively handed it to her. Rose took the business card and stood up from the banister, wrapping her arms around David's shoulders. "I love you Davey," she told him, kissing his cheek.

David smiled. "I love you too, Ma."

Rose went back into the house and David returned his attention to the grass in the yard. He thought about what Murray had said to him in the hallway. "Me, star material." He laughed and shook his head at the thought as the sun disappeared behind the horizon.

The rain came down steadily as David stared out at the street in front of his family's home and watched for the car that was being sent to pick them up.

"Anything?" Rose asked as she looked over his shoulder.

"No, not yet," David answered, "Maybe they got lost."

"We're not that hard to find, are we?" she joked. David smiled. "They should be here soon," she told him, "I'm going to let your sisters know we're leaving."

David continued to watch as the raindrops tapped against the windowpane. It wasn't long before a dark shiny car pulled up to the curb. "Ma," he yelled, "Ma, the car's here!"

Rose hurried into the living room and peered over his shoulder again as the driver's door opened and a young man in a suit and tie emerged. He opened a large black umbrella over his head and began walking toward the front door of the house.

Rose nudged David out from behind the window curtain. "Get your jacket Davey," she instructed him. The driver knocked on the door and waited. "Quickly David," she said as she hurried him toward the door. Rose opened the door as the driver stepped back.

"Mrs. Steinman?" he inquired.

"Yes," she confirmed as he offered his hand to help her down the wet steps. David pulled the heavy door shut and wiggled the knob to make sure he had locked it before he joined Rose on the sidewalk.

"Right this way, ma'am," the driver said. He held the huge umbrella over them as he led them to the car and opened the door. Once they were settled, he returned to his seat behind the wheel. "Are you comfortable ma'am?"

"Oh yes, thank you," Rose replied, "We're fine." The driver nodded to them and pulled the car out into the traffic lane. Rose glanced at David as she reached over and patted his knee. "Pretty fancy, huh?" she whispered. He looked back at her and smiled, then turned his attention to the passing scenery while the rain streamed down the opposite side of the glass.

The car slowed as it pulled into the driveway that ran along the side of the brick building. Rose watched David as he stretched his neck to see past her through the passenger side window.

"Would you like to go first?" she teased him as the driver opened her door. David shook his head emphatically and sat back against the car seat. Rose smiled at him and stepped out of the car, followed quickly by her son as the driver waited with the umbrella.

"Right this way please." The man escorted them along the walkway and into the building's lobby.

"Good Morning!" the receptionist said cheerfully as she walked over to greet them, "You must be Mrs. Steinman."

"Yes," Rose told her, "and this is my son, David."

"I'm very pleased to meet you both! My name is April, may I take your coats?" Rose and David waited as April put their garments on hangers. "Why don't you have a seat and relax while I let Mr. Ackerman know you're here."

"Thank you," Rose smiled. April returned to her desk as the two of them settled onto a small couch in the lobby. David looked around the room at all the paintings and pictures, his eyes finally coming to rest on two large portraits on the wall opposite him. He studied them silently as the young girls in the pictures stared back at him. Rose followed his gaze. "They're very pretty aren't they?"

"Uh huh."

"Thank you," a man's voice replied from the other side of the lobby, "they're my daughters. You are Rose Steinman?"

"I am," she said as she stood.

"Murray Ackerman," he said, introducing himself as he reached out to shake her hand.

"I believe you've already met my son, David."

"Yes, hello David, it's nice to see you again."

"Hi."

"Well, shall we?" Murray offered as he led them down the hall to his office. David followed a few steps behind, examining all the doors up and down the hallway. Murray held the office door open so Rose could pass and waited for David to catch up to them. He watched the boy peek through the slender windows as he walked by each door. "They all lead to different types of studios," Murray explained, "I can show them to you later if you like." David looked up at him for a moment and then headed into the office without a sound. "Or maybe not," Murray said to the vacant passageway. He closed the door and sat down behind a large desk across from his visitors. "I was very happy to hear from you Mrs. Steinman."

"Call me Rose, please."

"I was very happy to hear from you Rose. I'm glad David changed his mind…"

"I didn't change my mind,"

"Oh, I'm sorry, I just assumed you'd called me because…"

"Mr. Ackerman," Rose interrupted.

"Murray."

"Murray, I called on David's behalf. We talked it over and decided to at least listen to what you had to say."

"I see."

"I understand you heard him sing in the school's program on the plaza in town?"

"Yes ma'am."

"So you liked what you heard?"

"Yes ma'am, I did, very much."

"And you think David could become a professional singer?"

"Yes Rose, I do."

"Well Murray," she continued, "what exactly do you have in mind?"

"I would be acting as David's personal manager and agent and would be helping him to develop his career," Murray explained.

"Mr. Ackerman…"

"Murray, please."

Rose smiled at him. "Murray, my late husband was a professional musician, so I am well aware of the responsibilities of a theatrical agent. What I meant was, what did you have in mind for David specifically?"

"Yes ma'am," Murray replied. He glanced over at David, who was staring at him blankly. "As I said, I would be working with him to help him develop his singing career."

"You would be working with him one on one?"

"Yes," he answered quickly. Rose stared at him for a moment.

"You would be willing to devote yourself to helping my son make a career as a singer?"

"Yes," he answered again, just as quickly.

"Why?" Rose fired back.

Murray let out a sigh as he sat back in the large leather chair. "Because I believe in him."

"Forgive me Mr. Ackerman, but I find it hard to accept that you could believe that strongly in someone you've only met twice."

"I can understand why you feel that way. If I were in your shoes, I would have trouble accepting it too." He leaned forward, placing his elbows on the desktop, the fingers of his hands laced together in front of him. "You have no real reason to trust anything I tell you. Now, I can provide you with the names and phone numbers of several references, both personal and professional, and you're more than welcome to ask them anything you like, but I have a feeling it won't make too much of a difference one way or the other what they say, because when it comes right down to it Rose, you're going to have to go with your gut, which is exactly what I'm doing." Murray stood from his chair and walked around to the front of the desk.

"Last week, I went to buy myself a sandwich for lunch. When I came out of that sandwich shop, I heard a voice that stopped me in my tracks. The longer I listened, the more I knew I had to find out who that voice belonged to. As it turns out, that voice belongs to your son." Murray sat down in the chair next to Rose. "I have represented a lot of very talented singers, but David has something they don't have. I don't know what it is… I don't even know if 'it' has a name, but whatever you want to call it, David has it. My gut instinct tells me he's the 'one'. I truly, truly believe that with the right support system behind him, David can…"

"Stop," Rose said as she raised her hand, "you don't have to say any more. I apologize for being so blunt with you Mr. Ackerman, but I've learned to be very cautious where my children are concerned. I can see you're being sincere with me and I appreciate that. If David decides to work with you, then he has my blessing."

Murray smiled. "Thank you Rose."

"You're welcome," she replied, "Now it's up to David, the final decision is his." The two young men looked tentatively at each other while Rose waited. "What do you think Davey, would you like to work with Mr. Ackerman?"

David looked from his mother to Murray and back again.
"What would I have to do?"

"That's a fair question," Murray answered, "I can give you a short overview of how the process usually works." He paused, waiting for a response. "First, I'd like for us to spend some time just getting to know each other and ask you some questions about what kind of things you like and don't like, what you're interested in, what your goals and dreams are and you can ask me questions as well. When you're ready, we would start going over some songs and you would pick out the ones you'd like to try. Then we would rehearse and rehearse and rehearse," Murray continued, "and then we would rehearse some more until you're comfortable with them, then we would go into the studio and record them."

"Then what?" David prompted.

"Well, we would do some photo shoots for publicity purposes and eventually the songs and photos would be put together into an album that could be presented to the public."

"That's it?" David asked.

"There would be public appearances and interviews."

"Interviews?"

"Sooner or later, we'd have to start scheduling some local performances and, if things go well, a concert tour."

David's eyes widened. "*Concert*?? I don't think so!!" he said shaking his head adamantly.

"That's way off in the future David, you don't have to worry about that for a couple of years at least."

"Years?"

"Well, yeah, it takes time to plan and rehearse and record and promote…" His voice trailed off as he began to feel a panic inside. The more Murray explained it, the more he could feel David backing off from the whole idea.

"Seems like an awful lot just to get to sing a few songs."

"You'd be doing more than just singing a few songs David. You'd be building your career. I'm not gonna lie to you, it won't be easy."

"Don't forget about your schoolwork," Rose added, "you'll have to keep up with that as well."

"I agree," Murray said, "we'll have to schedule time with a tutor, so you won't fall behind."

"No," Rose said suddenly.

"I'm sorry?"

"No, no tutors."

"I don't understand Rose, how can he keep up with his schoolwork without a tutor?"

"He won't have any problem keeping up because he'll be in school every day."

"But that would be impossible."

"Why?"

"Well Rose, as the wife of a musician, I'm sure you understand how important it is to be available…"

"And I'm sure Mr. Ackerman, that as a *parent* you understand how vital a good education is to our children."

"Yes ma'am, I do but…"

"Mr. Ackerman let me explain something to you. I have twenty children…"

Murray's eyebrows rose as he looked at her in surprise. "*Twenty children?*"

"Yes, twenty," Rose smiled at him, "Eighteen of them have already graduated high school and the nineteenth, my youngest daughter Sandy, will be graduating this year. David is my baby…"

"Ma!"

She looked at him and sighed heavily. "David is my youngest," she said, correcting her words to pacify the boy, "He only has three more years of school left after this year and I intend to make sure he finishes and graduates. Now," she paused, "you can find a way for him to take advantage of your generous offer while still attending school regularly, or you can wait until he graduates." Murray sat dumbfounded and speechless.

"Don't worry about it Ma," David told her, "I really don't think I want to do all this anyway."

"You're sure Davey? It really is a wonderful opportunity."

"Yeah, I'm sure. Thank you for the offer Mr. Ackerman, but I just don't think it would work. I mean, school is hard enough without adding on singing and rehearsing and recording and interviews and concerts… it's just too much."

Murray's heart started to sink. "But David, we can find a way to make it work."

"Thanks Mr. Ackerman, but no thanks. Sorry about wasting your time," he said, "Can we go home now Ma?"

"Sure," she smiled at him. The three of them stood from their chairs. "Good day Mr. Ackerman."

"Ma'am," he returned as he shook her hand. David held the door for Rose as they left the office. Murray walked behind the desk, dropped back into his big leather chair and let out a defeated sigh, drumming his fingers on the arms of the chair as his mind raced. "Come on Ackerman, think!" he said out loud, "There's gotta be a way."

As they reached the main lobby, Rose glanced out the window and saw the car that had brought them was still waiting in the driveway. David retrieved their wraps from the closet.

"It was nice meeting you April," she said to the receptionist.

"It was nice meeting you too, Mrs. Steinman."

Rose turned her attention back to David and, noticing that he looked sad, she reached over and touched his elbow. David looked up at her and could see the worry in her eyes, so he gave her a smile to reassure her that he was okay. When the driver saw them in the lobby, he hurried over to open the door for them and raised his over-sized umbrella to shield them from the rain as they walked toward the car.

"David! David, wait!" David stood up out of the car as Murray came running through the rain toward them. April grabbed a couple of umbrellas and followed him. "Just give me one summer!" he panted as he reached them.

David shook his head in disbelief. "Mr. Ackerman…"

"Before you say no, please, just hear me out," he pleaded as the rain dripped down his face. David was suddenly reminded of the conversation they had at the school the week before and how Murray kept trying to get through to him.

"Okay," he sighed, "I'm listening."

"Great, thank you." He smiled as David waited. "All right, here's the deal. You agree to work with me from now until the end of the summer. If, at the end of the summer, you decide you don't like it and you don't want to do it anymore, then you can quit."

"I can quit?"

"You can quit," Murray repeated, "but, if you decide that you like it and you want to take it further, then we'll revise the contract and keep working."

"What about school?"

"You can stay in school; we'll work around it." The two men stared at one another. Rose wondered who would be the first to give in.

"You're gonna work with me?"

"The whole time."

"Just me and you?"

"One on one."

"Through all of it?"

"I'll be there for *everything*," Murray assured him, "We can take this as far as you want to take it Dave."

Once again they studied each other. Rose did her best to curb her maternal instincts, deciding to let her young son handle this situation on his own.

"So it's only 'til the end of the summer?" David asked again.

"Only 'til the end of the summer."

"And at the end of the summer, if I don't like it, I can quit?"

"Yes, you can quit."

"I can just walk away?"

"Yes."

"No questions asked?"

"No questions asked."

David thought for a moment. "What about you?"

"I'll walk away, too."

"Just like that?"

"If that's what you decide you want," Murray said, "then I won't bother you again."

David looked hard at Murray as the pair stood silent again, then glanced over at his mother.

"It's not my decision Davey," she said.

He looked back at Murray. The look of anticipation on Murray's rain-soaked face made David laugh out loud.

"I'll give you one summer."

"Right," Murray answered almost automatically, but then he paused. "Wait, was that a yes?"

"Yes."

"That was a yes?"

David laughed again. "Yes."

Murray smiled brightly at him and looked over at April. "That was a yes," he told her.

"That was a yes!" she echoed back.

"Right, okay," Murray said as he tried to pull himself together, "why don't we all go back inside and we'll map out a schedule?"

"Yes," David smiled back at him.

"Yes." He took a couple steps back. "After you Rose."

Rose moved past him as the driver followed behind her with his umbrella. Murray stepped closer to David and held the umbrella over him as David closed the car door and turned to face him. A smile gradually grew across David's face and Murray finally began to relax. Without a word, they started up the driveway toward the front of the building as the warm spring rain continued to descend from the skies.

PRELUDE - PART IV

"I don't know Casey, there's an awful lot of people here," Adam McCallister told his daughter as their car entered the parking lot.

"It's an audition Daddy, there's supposed to be a lot of people at auditions."

"*This many?*"

"Yes."

"Are you sure you want to do this? I mean, you're probably gonna be here all day."

"Yes, I want to do this."

"Why don't we just get some take out and a movie and go home and relax?" he teased.

"Daddy…" She rolled her eyes; he smiled at her.

"Okay, fine, if you'd rather audition to dance with Donald What's-His-Name than hang out with your dear old dad…"

"You know I love spending time with you Daddy, but this is the chance of a lifetime," she told him, "and his name is David Steinman, not Donald."

"That's what I said," Adam said with a grin.

"There she is!" Casey said when she saw her friend, "You can let me out here." Adam stopped the car and Casey quickly hopped out.

"Do I need to pick you up?" he asked as she shut the door.

"No thanks. I'm gonna stay at Carrie's tonight."

"Okay, good luck sweetie, I love you!"

"Thanks, love you too Daddy!" She waved as he drove away.

The morning sun lit up the sky and warmed the air. As Casey and her friend waited in the long line for the audition process to begin, a black car pulled into the parking lot and drove up to the entrance; the driver hurried around to the passenger side to open the door for the vehicle's occupants.

"Is that him?" Carrie asked.

Casey shielded her eyes from the sun and stood on her tiptoes to see over the crowd. A tall man with a medium build and brown hair stepped out and quickly entered the building followed by two young women dressed in business attire.

"No, I think they're the people holding the audition."

"Do you think he'll actually be here?"

Casey felt the butterflies in her stomach fluttering around. "I don't know, maybe."

Soon after, the line they were in started to move. They passed through a doorway and into a short corridor, where one by one they gave their paperwork and headshots to the nice ladies at the reception table in return for a sticker with their name written on it. After being registered, they were guided into a large gymnasium and into single file lines to await further instructions.

"There sure are a lot of people here," Casey said, repeating her father's initial assessment.

"There sure are," Carrie agreed as they looked around.

"Carrie, Casey!" The two girls turned to see more of their fellow dance students coming toward them.

"Maggie!" Casey greeted her excitedly, "I thought you weren't coming."

"Well, I thought about it and decided I'd give it a try."

"Yeah," Kelsey chimed in, "what have we got to lose?" The four girls hugged happily.

"I'm so glad you decided to try out!" Casey told them.

As the girls stood and chatted, the tall man and his two protégés began walking up and down the lines of dancers. As they passed each one, the man would say "purple" or "white" and in turn one of the women would hand the dancer a small card of the corresponding color. They stopped when they reached Casey's group and the man looked all four of the girls over.

"Purple, purple, purple and purple," he said as he pointed to each one. Then they hurried on to the next group in the line.

"What do you suppose that was all about?" Maggie asked.

"Don't ask me," Carrie answered, "I've never been to an audition this big before."

"Well, it's gotta mean something," Kelsey said.

"This is your first *real* audition, isn't it?" the young woman behind them asked sarcastically; Casey nodded. "They're typing us."

"Typing us?" Carrie asked.

"Yes," the woman hissed back.

"What does that mean?" Kelsey asked.

The woman glared at her. "It means they are looking for a particular body type," she growled, "If you're not the right type, then they don't want to waste their time auditioning you." The girls looked at each other. "Look, one color means you're in and one color means you're out."

"Which one is which?" Maggie asked.

"They don't tell you until they're done, but in all the auditions I've been to, the dark color means you're out." She held up her white card. "Better luck next time, chickies!" she said with a nasty grin. The girls looked at the purple cards in their hands.

"So that's it?" Carrie asked.

"All this planning and practicing and we don't even get through the door?" Maggie asked in a defeated tone.

"Figures," Kelsey said, "Mom always says if something seems too good to be true, it probably is."

Casey looked down at the small purple laminated card in her hand. She ran her finger around the edge of it. *Purple is his favorite color.*

"Ladies, may we have your attention, please?" said a female voice over a loudspeaker, "We would like to thank you all for coming today and for your patience. At this time, would all of you with purple cards please remain where you are and those of you with white cards, please proceed to the exit on my left, that will be all for today, thank you." The four glanced around at each other, then looked at the snippy woman behind them holding her white card. She looked back at them angrily, snatched her bag from the floor and stomped off toward the exit.

"Okay," the voice began again, "those of you who are left, please take a seat around the outer edge of the room." After they were seated, they could see the two women who handed out the cards standing at the far end of the room.

"Hello ladies," the tall man said into the microphone. A scattering of 'hellos' were returned from the group and the man smiled. "Before we get started, you need to be made aware of a couple of things. First, this is not a one-time gig. This is a long-term job and by long-term I am talking about up to a year or longer. There will also be some traveling required, so if for any reason you know you cannot commit yourself to that type of schedule, please tell me now." The man paused for a few moments.

"All right then," he continued, "as you can see, we've had a rather large turnout for the audition today so we're going to be here for a while. There will be periodic breaks throughout the day and a lunch break a little later on for those who are still here. Are there any questions before we move on?" The participants sat quietly. He turned and walked back to a small platform with steps on either side. The two women went down each side of the room handing out a pen and a slip of plain white paper to each dancer.

"On the papers that April and Sasha are handing out, I want you to write your name, your age and how long you have been in dance classes." They waited as the participants wrote down their information. "Everyone finished?" The girls in the crowd nodded. "The next part of the audition is going to be an introduction. I want to chat with each of you and learn something about you by asking questions," he paused as a collective moan was heard, "Don't worry, I won't ask about anything personal or private, it's just a way for all of us to become a little more comfortable and a little less nervous about all this.

"Now, since I would never ask you to do something I wouldn't be willing to do myself," the man said as he stepped up onto the platform, "I'll go first." A light round of applause echoed through the room. April walked up to the podium and stuck out her hand; the man looked at her.

"I need your paper," she told him. The man searched his pockets, then quickly stepped down from the podium and retrieved the paper from a table at the side of the room. Upon returning, he held it out in front of him with a big grin. April shook her head as the room broke out in laughter.

"Are you ready now?" she asked him.

"Yes."

"So, your name is Murray?" she asked as she looked over the paper.

"Yes."

"What's your last name, Murray?"

"Didn't I write it down?"

"No, you didn't."

"Oh, sorry, it's Ackerman."

"Murray Ackerman?"

"Yes."

"And you are…" April paused, "I'm sorry, I can't really make this out, how old are you?"

"I'm 29," he said confidently. April stared at him. "Okay, I'm 30." April crossed her arms and sighed heavily. "All right, I'm 31," he finally conceded, "man, you're tough!" Once again, laughter filled the room.

"Have you ever studied dance Murray?"

"No."

"Have you ever taken a dance class?"

"Well, to be honest, my wife made me take a ballroom dancing class."

"How did you do?"

"I finished it."

"Would you ever take another class if she asked you to?"

"She won't ask me."

"Why not?" April asked.

"Because I almost broke her foot the first time," Murray admitted.

"Thank you, Murray." April smiled at him. Murray stepped down from the podium as more laughter and applause rose from the group.

"Okay, now it's your turn," he told them, "April and Sasha are going to start picking people at random to come up and be introduced. I want everyone to try and relax as much as you can and remember, there are no wrong answers. I just want to get to know you a little better."

"Thank you, Tessa," Murray said as the teenager quickly stepped down. He looked over at the next girl and smiled. She took a deep breath and stepped up onto the small square platform. April handed her paper to Murray. "Hello Cassandra."

"Hello," she answered.

"Did I get your name right?"

"Yes, most people call me Casey though."

"Oh, I see, would you rather I called you Casey?"

"Either one is fine."

"Thank you," he answered, "I see that you are 16 and that you have been studying dance since you were three years old?" Casey nodded. "Wow, that's a long time."

"I love to dance," she smiled shyly.

"So, what else do you like to do Cassandra," he asked, "besides dancing?"

"Um… I like to watch movies."

"What kind of movies do you like?"

"Love stories, ghost stories…"

"Do you like love stories about ghosts?" he jokingly interrupted; Casey nodded.

"Do you like the one with that Dirty Dancing guy?"

"You mean *Ghost*?"

"That's it."

"I love that movie."

"My wife likes it too," Murray told her, "she makes me watch it with her *all the time*." Casey laughed. "You have a beautiful smile Cassandra."

Casey felt her face grow warm. "Thank you."

"So, what else do you like to do?"

"I like to sing," Casey offered.

"Maybe I'll get to hear you later," he said, "Since you like to dance and you like to sing, would I be correct in assuming that you like listening to music?"

"Yes," Casey answered.

"Any favorites?" Casey paused. She wanted to say David was her favorite but wasn't sure if she should. After a few moments, Murray looked up from his clipboard and noticed that Casey was blushing. "I'm sorry Cassandra," he said, "I shouldn't have put you on the spot like that, you don't have to answer that one." Casey managed a smile through her nerves. "Thank you for talking with me, I really enjoyed our conversation."

"Thank you, Mr. Ackerman."

"Thank you, Miss McCallister," he said with a smile as she stepped down from the platform. Casey walked back over and joined her friend. "She remembered my name," Murray whispered as he handed Casey's paperwork back to April, "I'm impressed."

"She's the first one so far," April whispered back.

"How many more do we have?" he asked as he took the next name from Sasha. In unison the two women each held up a stack of papers. Murray sighed. "It's gonna be a long day ladies."

Casey sat quietly watching the others take their turns on the podium. She couldn't help thinking how much more mature most of the other girls seemed

"What's wrong, Casey?" Kelsey asked.

"I blew it."

"No, you didn't."

"Yes, I did, I sounded like such a baby." Kelsey wasn't sure how to console her friend. "Why didn't I answer him when he asked who my favorite singer was? I can't believe I just froze like that. He's not going to pick someone who freezes onstage." Casey crossed her arms over her bent knees and laid her forehead on them. "I was trying to sound professional, instead I just sounded stupid."

"You did not sound stupid Casey," Kelsey told her, "you sounded sweet and sincere and honest."

She looked up at Kelsey. "But did I sound *professional*?"

"You sounded like Casey."

"Yes," Casey agreed, "but was that enough?"

Kelsey smiled weakly and shrugged her shoulders. Casey laid her head on her arms again and waited with the others until the introductions were finished.

"Thank you very much ladies," Murray said to them after speaking to the last candidate, "It has been a pleasure meeting each of you. As Sasha calls your name, please come up and get a card from April, then you can go across the hall where a light lunch is being served. Remember to hold onto those cards and I will see you all back here in about an hour." Murray whispered a few quick instructions to his assistants and left them to the task at hand.

The four friends met each other in the lunch area and after getting their food, they found a corner table and made themselves comfortable.

"Well, what do you think so far?" Carrie asked.

"It's not too bad," Kelsey said.

"At least they were easy questions," Carrie added.

"Were you listening to some of the answers the other girls were giving?" Maggie whispered, "Talk about kissing up!" She glanced over at Casey. "Hey, what's wrong with you?" There was no reply.

"Are you feeling All right Casey?" Carrie asked her.

"She's worried," Kelsey told them, "she doesn't think she sounded professional enough."

"You've got to be kidding me!" Maggie said with a laugh, "Not professional enough? You're sixteen! How professional can you be at sixteen?"

"She's right Casey," Kelsey agreed. Casey sat silently moving the plastic spoon around in her cup of strawberry yogurt.

"It doesn't matter anyway," Carrie told her, "once they see you dance, they'll be convinced."

"I don't think I'll get a chance," Casey said without looking up.

"Why not?" Maggie asked. Casey held up her card and the other girls looked at theirs.

"Two red and two white," Carrie stated.

"That means two of us made it through and two of us didn't," Casey concluded.

"But how do you know your card means you didn't?" Kelsey asked her.

"Well, red usually means stop, doesn't it?" The friends glanced around at each other. "I should have answered that question."

"What question?" Carrie inquired.

"He asked me who my favorite singer was, and I froze."

"That wasn't a fair question," Maggie argued, "He already knew what you would say."

"But I should have said *something*."

"We both got red cards, so whatever happens, we'll be together," Carrie told her optimistically.

"Listen Casey," Maggie said, "there's no way you didn't make it through, you're the best dancer at our school."

"They haven't seen any of us dance yet Maggie," Carrie reminded her, "they don't know how good she is."

"But they will!"

"What if red really does mean stop?" Kelsey asked.

"If red means stop, then I'll switch cards with you," Maggie said.

"That wouldn't be fair to you Maggie."

"It doesn't matter, I only came here for fun. I never expected to get the job."

Casey felt a lump in her throat. "But…"

"Case, no one wants this more than you," Maggie paused, "heck, no one *deserves* it more than you." Carrie and Kelsey nodded in agreement.

"Thanks," Casey replied.

"Ladies, you have ten minutes," Sasha announced from the doorway of the lunchroom.

"Here we go!" Maggie smiled. The foursome emptied their trays and made their way back to the auditorium and once inside, they stood near the back wall. It wasn't long before Murray entered the room flanked by April and Sasha and walked up near the podium.

"Good afternoon everyone," he said into the microphone, "I trust you all had a nice lunch?" Several heads nodded in response. "All right then, let's get back to business." Maggie reached over and held tight to Casey's hand. "Everyone with red cards please hold them up so we can see them." The girls did as they were told. "April and Sasha will be handing out some forms. I need each of you to read them, fill them out and sign them. When everyone is finished, they'll come around again to collect them along with the musical selections you have chosen to use for the dance portion of your audition."

Casey's eyes widened.

"I told you!" Maggie whispered as she squeezed Casey's hand.

"Those of you with white cards, thank you for coming, that will be all for today. You may leave through the exit door here on my left."

Casey and Carrie hugged their friends as they said goodbye, then stood together with their red cards. Casey took a deep breath and blew it out slowly. Carrie put her arm around Casey's shoulder and smiled brightly at her.

The music thumped through the speakers and vibrated the floorboards of the auditorium as Carrie performed her routine. Murray watched every move as she danced, making notes and nodding throughout the song. As the song came to a close, Carrie moved toward the table at the front of the room where Murray sat. She did a quick spin and on the final beat, snapped around and flashed a smile at him.

"Excellent Carrie, very nice!" Murray said as the other dancers erupted in applause.

"Thank you!" Carrie replied through heavy breaths. She turned and went back to her place in the group. Casey gave her a congratulatory hug.

"That was amazing!" Casey told her.

"Thanks!"

"Miss McCallister, if you would please?" Murray asked.

"Yes sir."

"Break a leg!" Carrie said as Casey walked slowly to the center of the auditorium.

"Whenever you're ready Cassandra," Murray instructed.

Casey closed her eyes and took a few deep breaths, then she opened her eyes, looked straight ahead and gave a small nod for the music to start. She danced effortlessly across the floor, her movements becoming stronger and sharper as the intensity of the music grew. At the height of the song's passion, Casey suddenly leaped into the air and landed in a crouched position within a few feet of Murray's table. Gradually, she stood and turned as she moved smoothly through the last few measures of the music in the same way she had begun. The final notes played as Casey returned to her starting position, crossed her right arm over her chest, rested her cheek against her left shoulder and closed her eyes. As she waited, she could hear the others applauding and whistling.

"Brava!" Carrie yelled out. Casey opened her eyes to find everyone smiling while Sasha and April gave her a standing ovation. Murray sat between them, staring at her.

"Did you choreograph that piece yourself Cassandra?" he asked her as the applause died down.

"Yes sir," she answered nervously.

Murray stared at her again. "Thank you, Miss McCallister.". He turned his attention to the notes on his clipboard. "Miss Baxter, if you would please."

Casey went back to her seat next to Carrie, sat down and stared straight ahead.

"Casey, that was so beautiful!" Carrie said, trying to encourage her.

"He hated it," she said without looking at Carrie. Her eyes began to mist over.

"How could you think that?"

"He didn't even smile," Casey said, "he hated it." A tear trickled down her cheek. She wiped it away quickly and took a deep breath in. Carrie reached over and held Casey's hand as they watched the rest of the girls' audition.

"Thank you, ladies," Murray said after the last girl finished her audition, "I'm going to ask you all to step out of the room while we go over our notes. There are some refreshments in the room across the hall, please feel free to help yourselves." He began gathering his papers as the participants filed out into the hallway. Carrie tried hard to stay with Casey as she made her way through the crowd.

"Casey," Carrie said, "Casey, please talk to me." Casey sat on one of the chairs that lined the hallway and didn't say a word. Carrie sat down beside her and waited. "Well, if you don't go on to the next round, I won't go either."

"Carrie, you have to go on to the next round," Casey insisted.

"Not without you."

"You can't turn down a chance like this."

"Casey, I couldn't take this job knowing how much it means to you," she told her, "besides, they're not going to give it to me anyway."

"Sure they will, you're a great dancer."

"They want someone who can dance *and* sing."

"You can sing."

"They're looking for you Casey."

"No, they're not," Casey said sadly, "I'm not good enough to dance in a professional show."

"Stop it Casey!" Carrie scolded her, "We both know you're one of the best dancers here. When you were auditioning everyone in the room was watching you… everyone… and they all thought you were amazing!"

"Mr. Ackerman didn't," Casey countered, "and he's the only one who matters today."

"Listen, after the break we'll go back in there and whatever happens, happens. Then we'll go back to my house and stuff our faces with junk food, okay?"

Casey looked at the bright smile on her best friend's face and couldn't help but smile back. "Okay," she agreed.

The young women chatted amongst themselves as they came back into the auditorium and returned to their previous places along the outer edges of the room. Carrie and Casey found their spots and gathered their belongings.

"Good afternoon ladies," Murray greeted the group.

"Good afternoon," they replied in a spattering of voices. Murray smiled. He knew they were tired and nervous. "I know it's been a long day, please bear with us, it's almost over." He paused for a minute as he organized his papers. "Okay, after going over all of my notes and speaking with my very helpful assistants and after seeing all of you extremely talented young women perform, I believe I have finally been able to break the list down to a reasonable number. I have in my hand a list of the ten young ladies that I believe would best fill the position. I'm going to read the names in random order, if your name is called, please step to the center of the room." The room became silent as the girls waited.

Murray cleared his throat and then began slowly calling out the names on his list. After each name was called, a loud scream or round of applause was heard. "The next name on the list," Murray said, "is Carrie Wilmington."

"Oh my…" Carrie said as she looked at Casey in shock. Carrie walked tentatively to the center of the room and joined the first three girls. Murray continued calling names one by one as the girls waited anxiously. With each name, Casey grew more and more despondent. She had reserved herself to the fact that she wasn't good enough and even though she was thrilled for her best friend, she could almost feel her heart breaking.

"The next name on the list is Miss Maryann Saunders," Murray announced. Maryann screamed as her friends hugged her. She ran to the middle of the room and continued to jump up and down and squeal for a few minutes as the other girls laughed. "Are you All right Miss Saunders?" Murray asked cautiously. The girl squealed again and nodded that she was. "Okay, then let's get back to the list, I believe we have one more name." Once again, the room grew silent as Carrie glanced over at her friend. *Please let it be Casey,* she prayed silently.

"The last name on the list," Murray said as he looked around the room, "is Miss Cassandra McCallister." Carrie cheered happily as Casey looked up and stared unbelievingly at Murray for several seconds, then glanced around at the other candidates who were all smiling and applauding. "Miss McCallister, would you join the group in the center of the room please?" Casey looked back to Murray and then to Carrie who was motioning eagerly to her, then slowly moved over to where the others were standing. As she looked in Murray's direction again, he smiled warmly at her. "Congratulations ladies," Murray said, "you've made it to the final ten." Applause filled the room again as the finalists congratulated each other. Carrie and Casey hugged. "Now, if the ten of you will please go with April and Sasha into the hallway, I'll be with you shortly." The two assistants ushered the group out of the room, closed the door and returned to their places at the front of the room.

"To those of you who were not chosen, I would like to express my sincere gratitude to you for participating in this audition. You made it fun, you made it interesting, you made it entertaining and you made it very difficult for me to choose," he told them, "thank you so much for sharing your day with us and we wish you the best of luck in the future. If you would, please exit through the door on my left," he said as he politely motioned. He waited as the assistants said goodbye to the departing candidates and closed the door to seal off the room. "One more cut," he told April and Sasha. They nodded in response. "Might as well get to it."

"Well, how are you ladies doing out here?" Murray asked cheerily. He glanced around at all the nervous smiles. "I know it's stressful, just take some deep breaths and try to relax. I'd like to sit down and talk to you all for a minute if I may." He waited until all the girls had taken a seat. "I wanted to explain in a little more detail what we are looking for and what this job entails. Am I correct in assuming that you all know who David Steinman is?"

Smiles and nervous giggles filled the hallway. "I'll take that as a yes," Murray smiled back at them. "I have put together a small group of dancers to accompany David onstage, but I wanted to find someone to serve as a principal. I'm looking for someone who would be able to dance with the ensemble and as a soloist, as well as serve as David's partner for routines that are choreographed for a couple.

"In addition, the dancer we choose will also need to be able to sing as a background vocalist and occasionally as a soloist as well as sing duets with David." Murray paused for a few moments as he felt the excitement building among the group. "I know it's a lot to take in," he said as he looked around at them, "Maybe we should try a few of those deep breaths." He guided them as they all inhaled and exhaled together several times. "Okay, in the final step of our audition, I want to listen to each of you sing. I want you to pick a song. It doesn't have to be anything special; it can be anything from Ava Maria to Mary Had A Little Lamb. It makes no difference to me what song you sing, as long as you feel comfortable with it. I'm not concerned with your song choice; I'm only interested in the voice singing it.

"I also don't need to hear the entire song, a verse and a chorus would be plenty," he explained further. "April will let you know when to come in to audition and Sasha will be in the room assisting me with the paperwork. No one else will be there, so you don't have to worry about anyone else hearing you, just pick one of your favorite songs and have fun with it," he smiled at them. "We'll be ready to start in about ten minutes, so get those vocal cords warmed up!"

"What are you gonna sing?" Carrie asked Casey.

"I have no idea," Casey replied. She looked around at the other girls as they sang scales and cleared their throats.

"I think I'll do that one I sang in the recital last year," Carrie said.

"'Hey Big Spender'?"

"Yeah, that one." Casey smiled at her. "Well, he said to pick a song and have fun with it didn't he?"

"Yes."

"Okay then," Carrie concluded, "I might as well do a song I like."

"I agree."

"Have you thought of one yet?"

"There are a couple that come to mind," Casey told her, "but I'm just not sure about which one."

"Don't worry, you'll come up with something."

Casey couldn't stop herself from giggling as Carrie sang to herself, making little gestures reminiscent of her dance routine from their recital the year before. Casey thought hard about what song to choose, but none of the songs she and her friends listened to seemed appropriate. Maybe Carrie was right, she should sing a song she liked and just try to enjoy the experience.

The finalists mulled about in the corridor as one by one they were called in to audition. Each time the door would open, the activity in the hall would pause until the next name was called, then the girls would go back to their thoughts.

"Well Sasha," Murray said after the current singer had returned to the hallway, "so far we've heard three Christmas songs, two hymns, 'This Land Is Your Land', 'God Bless America' and the 'Star Spangled Banner', what could possibly be left?"

"You told them they could sing any song they wanted," Sasha reminded him with a laugh.

"I know," Murray sighed.

"There's only two more girls, I think you'll survive."

"Who's left?"

"Carrie Wilmington and Cassandra McCallister."

"Let's have Carrie first and save Miss McCallister for last." Sasha spoke the instructions into her radio transmitter to April and a few moments later, Carrie came through the door and walked eagerly over to them. "Hi Carrie," Murray said.

"Hi!"

"Have you decided on a song?"

"Yep!" Carrie said excitedly.

"You can start whenever you're ready."

Carrie took a few steps back, struck a dramatic pose and started to sing. Murray and Sasha watched as she went through all the movements just as she had done during her recital. Out in the hall, Casey moved closer to the door so she could hear better, smiling to herself each time Carrie hit a big note. Carrie sang the last line of her song and ended with a flourish and a bright smile. Sasha and Murray applauded for her.

"Thank you so much Carrie," Murray said, "great job!"

"Thank you!" Carrie beamed back at them.

"You can go back out now, please." Carrie walked quickly toward the door and left the auditorium. Casey was waiting for her when she reached the hallway.

"Carrie, that was great!"

"Thanks!" she replied as they hugged, "You're the only one left."

"Don't remind me," Casey said.

"Have you picked out a song?"

"No, not yet."

"Well, you've gotta choose *something*."

"Cassandra," April said, "they're ready for you." Casey nodded and looked anxiously at Carrie.

"You can do this," Carrie told her. Casey took a deep breath and blew it out slowly, then turned and entered the auditorium. Murray smiled warmly as she approached them.

"Hello Cassandra."

"Hello Mr. Ackerman."

"How are you?"

"Fine thanks," she replied softly.

"Not too nervous I hope." Casey shook her head. "Good. Do you have a song that you'd like to sing?" Casey paused for a second and then nodded. "All right then, whenever you're ready."

Casey looked at Murray and Sasha. She could feel her heart pounding and felt her mouth getting dry. She swallowed and cleared her throat as Murray and Sasha waited patiently. Casey tried desperately to calm herself.

"Cassandra," Murray said, "are you okay?" Casey looked at him nervously. Murray handed his clipboard to Sasha and walked over to where Casey was standing. "You don't have to be afraid, Cassandra."

"It's not that…"

"What then?"

"I don't know what to sing."

"I see."

"I'm sorry, I should have been ready."

"It's okay," he told her, "maybe I can help you." He thought for a moment. "Try this, if you knew you could only hear one more song for the rest of your life, what song would you choose?" Almost immediately a song came to Casey's mind. "Got one?" Casey nodded. "Ready to sing?" Casey nodded again and began to smile as she felt her nerves dissipate. Murray went back to his seat and waited. Casey took a deep breath, closed her eyes and started to sing.

Murray sat spellbound as Casey's voice drifted out into the openness of the auditorium. He watched intently as the shy girl who had walked into that room transformed into a seasoned young performer right before his eyes. As her clear strong voice echoed around him, he recognized the same confidence that he saw in David the first time he had heard him sing.

As the last note faded, Casey looked at Murray and breathed a sigh of relief. Murray and Sasha applauded her.

"That was… lovely Cassandra," he complimented, "just lovely." Casey moved her eyes away from them as she blushed. "Just out of curiosity, why did you choose that particular song?"

"Oh… um… my dad used to sing me to sleep with that song when I was little."

Murray smiled at her and then politely motioned toward the door. "Thank you, Cassandra." He sat back in his chair and watched as Casey left the room. He turned his head to find Sasha staring at him. "What?" he asked. Sasha looked back to her paperwork without saying a word. Murray glanced back at the door and smiled to himself.

Casey was met with applause as she reentered the hallway. She felt the sudden warmth of a blush return to her cheeks and quickly looked away from the group. "Thanks," she said. When she looked up again, Carrie was staring at her wide-eyed.

"Wow, Casey that was *beautiful.*"

"It's just a song my dad used to sing to me," Casey answered nonchalantly.

"I bet he never sang it like that!" Carrie replied.

"May I have your attention please?" They looked around to see Murray standing in the corridor. "I would like to congratulate you all on a job well done, you should be very proud of your performances during today's audition. You have conducted yourselves as true professionals and it has been a pleasure getting to know each of you on an individual level. Please believe me when I tell you that this is not an easy process. You are all extremely talented, but unfortunately, I can only choose one of you for this position." Murray looked around at them as the girls hung on his every word. "I'm going to take just a little longer to go through my notes and discuss it with my assistants before announcing my final decision. Once again, you may help yourselves to the refreshments in the lunch area while you wait. Thank you for your participation ladies, we'll be back with you in a little while." The group watched as Murray, April and Sasha proceeded down the long, carpeted hallway and disappeared into one of the many adjoining offices.

"Well, I guess there's nothing left to do but wait," Casey said.

"I guess not," Carrie agreed, "Wanna get something to eat?"

"Okay." The two friends headed in to join the others.

Murray followed the two women into the office and closed the door. He laid his clipboard onto the desk and heaved a heavy sigh.

"So how long are you going to make them wait?" April asked him.

Murray looked at her. "I beg your pardon?"

"Come on Murray, you've already made your decision," Sasha said, "Why drag it out?"

"It's cruel to keep them in suspense," April added.

Murray looked from one to the other. "Okay," he said shaking his head, "bring 'em in, but I want to talk to them one at a time."

"Do you want Cassandra to be first in line," April asked as she opened the door, "or last?" Murray shot them a surprised look as his assistants smiled.

"Let me talk to her first," Murray answered.

"Good," Sasha replied, "she's waited long enough."

Murray sat behind the desk in the office milling over in his head what he wanted to say to each of the dancers as he waited for April and Sasha to return. As he thought about each girl's audition, he tried to envision them dancing onstage with David.

Sasha stuck her head through the doorway. "They're ready!"

"Show her in," Murray stood and walked around the desk. Sasha held the door open as April escorted Casey into the room. Murray waited until the door was closed and the three young women were seated. "Hello again Cassandra."

"Hi."

"I wanted to bring you each in separately so that I could speak with you privately about your auditions," he explained as Casey listened, "but I wanted to speak to you first. You did very well today."

"Thank you," Casey said. Murray smiled at her.

"I did want to talk to you about it though, especially the dance portion. I believe the way I reacted may have given you the wrong impression and I wanted to apologize for that. You see, when I was watching you 1dance, I got lost…"

"It's okay if you hated it Mr. Ackerman," Casey quickly interrupted. Her statement caught him off guard.

"Wow, I really did give you the wrong impression, didn't I?" Murray moved over and sat in the chair across from Casey. "Cassandra, what I meant when I said that I got lost was that I was…" He paused as he tried to think of the right words. "I was completely captivated by your performance. It was impeccable. Every move was so precise, but at the same time you seemed so free and your interpretation of the song, the way you brought out all the emotions… you just seemed to flow with the music." Casey sat in stunned silence as he continued.

"I have conducted a lot of auditions and I've attended just as many others. I have seen performances by dancers of all ages and all levels of experience, but I have never seen anyone dance with as much passion as you did today. When you told me you chorcographed the routine yourself…" Murray paused and shook his head.

"So, you didn't hate it?" Casey asked cautiously.

"No," he answered with a smile and a light laugh, "I didn't hate it." Casey smiled back at him. "In fact, it was one of the most amazing performances I've seen in a long time, and I would consider it a privilege to work with you."

Casey felt her heart skip a beat. "What are you saying Mr. Ackerman?"

"What I'm saying, Cassandra… Casey… is that the job is yours."

"The… job… is… mine?"

"The job is yours."

"The job is mine?"

"Yes, the job is yours," he repeated a third time, "that is, if you want it. You do want it don't you?"

Casey sat for a few moments trying to absorb everything Murray had just said to her. "Yes," she finally answered, "yes, I want it."

"Good," Murray said, "I'm going to need to speak to your parents."

"I can call my dad," Casey suggested.

"That would be perfect. Why don't you go out and call him and while we're waiting, I'll talk to the other young ladies, okay?"

"Okay." She stood to leave.

"And Casey…"

"Yes?"

"Please don't mention any of this to the others yet, I'd like to speak to each of them privately first."

"I won't," she promised.

"Thanks."

As Casey stepped out of the office, April gently pushed the door closed. "Well, that's done," she stated.

"Yep," Sasha chimed in, "now all you gotta do is tell the rest of them that they *didn't* get the job."

"Right." He turned back to April. "Send the next one in."

As Casey left the office, she stopped momentarily and glanced up at the other girls that were waiting patiently to take their turn. Carrie's heart ached as she saw a tear trickle down Casey's cheek. Without a word, Casey headed down the long corridor, stopping only long enough to collect her belongings before leaving the building.

Once Casey was outside, she took her phone from the side pocket of her bag and dialed her father's number. After a short conversation, she put the phone back in its pocket and sat down on a nearby bench. She mulled over in her mind all the things Murray had told her. She was still having trouble believing that she had been chosen to be the principle dancer for David Steinman.

Casey searched through her bag and found her iPod. She placed the ear buds in her ears and switched on her favorite song. As David Steinman's voice swirled around her, she closed her eyes and tried to imagine being onstage with him, what it would be like for him to hold her in his arms as they danced. A shiver ran down her spine and she looked around quickly to see if anyone had noticed, but there was no one in sight. Satisfied that she was alone, she played the song again. As the last notes faded, she heard voices behind her and quickly put the iPod away, sitting silently as some of the other girls passed by her. Casey noticed that one of the girls was crying and she genuinely felt bad for her, but she couldn't ignore the happy feeling she had inside.

"Casey?"

She looked up to see Carrie standing by the bench. "Hi," she answered.

"Casey, are you okay?"

"Yeah."

Carrie sat down beside her. "I know you're disappointed, I can't believe he didn't pick you. He didn't pick me either." Casey tried her best to stay calm. "I think we both did pretty good though, considering this was our first real audition." Carrie paused as two more girls passed them in tears. "There'll be other auditions, we'll do better next time." Casey stayed silent; she knew Carrie was trying to make her feel better. "Why don't we call Maggie and Kelsey and we can all go to my house for a slumber party? I called my mom to let her know we're done here." Carrie reached into her bag and retrieved her phone.

"I already called my dad to come and pick me up," Casey told her without looking up.

"But I thought you were gonna stay over with me tonight."

"I think I need to be at home tonight."

"I know you really wanted this, Casey, but you did the best you could. Please don't feel so bad."

"Hello ladies," Murray said as he walked up to the bench.

"Hello," Carrie replied in a somber tone.

"Were you able to get in touch with your father?" he asked Casey.

"Yes sir, he's on his way."

"Casey, what's going on?" Carrie asked in a worried tone. Casey looked at her friend, then at Murray.

"Go ahead," Murray said, "I think she deserves to be the first to know." Casey turned back to face Carrie.

"I got it Carrie," she said calmly.

Carrie looked at her for a moment. "Got what?"

"The job, I got it."

"You got the job?" Casey nodded. "You got the job?" Carrie asked again as her excitement began to grow. Casey smiled and nodded again. "Casey McCallister, how could you?"

"How could I what?"

"How could you make me worry like that?"

"I'm sorry, I didn't mean to."

"Why didn't you tell me?"

"That was my fault," Murray interrupted, "I asked her not to say anything until I had a chance to talk to each of you."

"Oh, okay then," Carrie said, "I forgive you." The two girls smiled at each other. "Oh my God, Casey, you got the job!" They squealed and hugged each other as a car pulled up to the curb. "I gotta go," Carrie said as she hugged her friend again. She gathered her belongings and walked to the car, "Call me later, and remember, I want details!" Carrie slid into the passenger seat and shut the door as she immediately shared the news of Casey's good fortune with her mother. The two of them smiled through the windshield at Casey as Carrie's mother applauded to her. Casey laughed and waved as the car pulled away.

"That's some friend you have there," Murray observed.

"She's my best friend," Casey told him.

"May I?" Murray asked, gesturing toward the bench and Casey nodded. Murray walked around and sat down in the spot Carrie had vacated. "So, has it sunk in yet?"

"It's starting to," Casey replied, "Mr. Ackerman, may I ask you something?"

"Sure."

"What is he like?"

"Who?" Murray teased.

"You know," Casey said as she blushed.

"Oh, you mean David." Murray smiled at her.

"I was just curious. It's okay if it's private, I understand."

"No, it's all right. You're gonna find out soon enough anyway." Casey smiled at the thought of meeting David. "He's just like any other teenage boy." She gave him a doubting look. "You don't believe me?"

"He doesn't seem like any of the teenage boys I know." Murray laughed a little.

"Actually, David's a lot like you."

"Like me? How?"

"Well, you're both easy-going, polite, friendly, good sense of humor, talented. To be honest, I don't think either one of you realize just how talented you actually are." A car pulled up to the curb as they talked. "Is that your dad?"

"Uh-huh," Casey answered as a tall well-dressed man walked over to them. Murray stood to greet him.

"Mr. McCallister?"

"Yes," the man replied, "Adam McCallister."

Murray stuck out his hand. "Pleased to meet you, I'm Murray Ackerman."

"I'm pleased to meet you Mr. Ackerman," Adam said as they shook hands.

"If you could spare a little of your time, sir, I'd like to speak to you regarding your daughter's future as a professional dancer."

"Well, I think I could spare a few minutes for that," Adam said as he winked at Casey.

"Right this way," Murray led Adam and Casey into the building.

INTERLUDE

David had spent his summer rehearsing songs and working in the recording studio and even though he didn't really take it too seriously, he did the best he could and tried to make the most of the experience. Murray was there every day, as promised, giving him as much advice and guidance as he could. Over the months, a close friendship had formed between them and as the summer vacation drew to a close, David felt a bit discouraged.

"What's on your mind kiddo?" Murray asked as he sat down next to David at the lunch table.

"Nothing."

"Dave…"

The boy looked at him and sighed. "School starts next week," he said glumly.

"So?"

"I hate school."

"What do you mean you hate school?"

"Well, I don't really *hate* it," David explained, "it's just that I don't fit in anywhere." He picked some green grapes from the bunch that lay on the platter in the middle of the table and popped them into his mouth. "And what about this?"

"What about it?"

"How can we do this if I have to be in school every day?"

"The same way we did it last year, remember?"

"Yeah, I remember, but…"

"Listen, I made a promise to your mother and I'm not about to break it. We'll just work around it until you graduate, like we planned." David took the remaining grapes from the platter and slumped back in his chair. "Besides, I think things might be different this year."

"Why?"

"I don't know," Murray smiled, "I just have a good feeling about it." David gave him an inquisitive look. Murray took a paper plate from the stack and began filling it with items from the lunch platter in front of them. "I've got some paperwork to take care of," he said, "I'll be in my office if you need me."

David watched him as he headed out of the room, then pulled a few more grapes from the bunch. "I hate school," he grumbled under his breath before shoving them into his mouth.

CHAPTER 1

The silence in the room made every minute seem like an eternity and David tried hard to keep his mind focused on the page in front of him, but he was just too restless. After one last futile attempt to read a few more lines from his text book, David glanced up to see Mr. Beck talking to the vice-principle, Mr. Connelly. Murray was there as well, along with a very pretty young girl with the most beautiful eyes David had ever seen.

"Can I have your attention, class?" Mr. Beck said, "We have a new student. This is Cassandra McCallister..."

"Casey," she said, correcting him.

"Casey McCallister," he paused, smiling at her. "Miss McCallister comes to us from the state of Michigan, please make her feel welcome." Scattered hellos were heard around the room. "Casey, you can take that empty seat there," Mr. Beck continued, pointing to a seat in the fourth row directly across from David's third row seat. As Casey settled in, Murray knelt down between the two students.

"David, this is Casey. Casey, this is David."

"Hi," she said softly.

"Hi."

"By the way, Casey's also your new dance partner." David looked at the man in surprise. "I'll see you at the studio Dave," Murray said, patting him on the shoulder.

"Yeah," answered David. Murray shook Mr. Beck's hand before he and Mr. Connelly left the room. David sat there in shock at what Murray had just told him. He could hear everyone in the room, especially the guys, whispering to him.

"All right David!" they were saying, "Way to go Dave!"

David turned his head slowly toward Casey. She smiled at him timidly and he quickly moved his eyes back to his desk.

"That's enough whispering, people, back to the books." Mr. Beck's strong voice brought David's attention back to the classroom. As he stared at his open book, two thoughts filled his head—first, he couldn't get over how beautiful she was... and second, *What happens when she finds out I can't dance?*

"Are you coming?" David didn't answer. "David?" she said, touching his shoulder gently.

"What?" he questioned, a little startled.

"Are you coming?" Casey asked again.

David looked around the emptying room. "I have to go to my locker; you go on ahead."

"I can't," she said bluntly.

"Why not?"

"Because I don't know where to go."

"Didn't they give you a schedule?"

"They told me I'd have the same classes you have, they said you would show me." Casey looked at him, "They didn't tell you about me, did they?"

"No, they didn't."

Casey stood quietly while David gathered his books. Sensing that he was a little upset about her surprise arrival, she was afraid to say anything else. David stood up and started to walk toward the door when all at once he stopped.

"Oh, great!" he moaned.

"What's wrong?"

"Look." Casey glanced over at the door of the classroom, which was full of people, mostly girls.

"So?"

"So? So their blocking the door."

"You make it sound as if we're trapped for life!" she laughed. "They're just people David. Now c'mon, or we'll be late for class!" Casey grabbed David's hand and pulled him through the crowd at the doorway. Once they were out in the hall, she stopped. "Where do we go from here?" she asked, still holding his hand.

"American History."

"Lead the way!" Casey was trying to stay upbeat but was finding it difficult. *I hope he isn't always this moody*, she thought. David led her to the second floor and into a classroom, where they were mct by whistles, catcalls, and applause.

"Do you always get this kind of reception when you walk into a classroom?" she whispered.

"No… Casey..."

"Yes?"

"Would you please let go of my hand?"

"What?"

"My hand."

"What about it?"

"Let go of it!" he whispered firmly.

"Oh... sorry," she said, trying to apologize for embarrassing him. David went to his seat at one of the front tables and sunk into his chair.

"Can I help you, young lady?" the teacher asked.

"Excuse me?"

"I said, can I help you?" She handed the teacher one of the papers from the admissions office and in return he handed Casey a book from the shelf behind his desk. "Welcome, Miss McCallister. You may take a seat anywhere you wish."

"Thank you," she said. She walked over to David's table, but hesitated a moment. David looked up at her, then sighed and pulled the chair out for her. She gave him half a smile as she sat down next to him.

"As per the class itinerary, today we will begin the recitation of the reports you were all working on so diligently last week," the teacher stated as he positioned himself in a desk at the back of the classroom.

"Oh no!" David panicked quietly.

"What?"

"I forgot to stop at my locker and get my report."

"As I said during yesterday's class, we will be starting at the bottom of the list and alphabetically working our way up. Mr. Wayman, will you please start us off?" John Wayman walked to the front of the room and proceeded to give his report. "A good report, Mr. Wayman," the instructor said as the boy returned to his seat, "however, in the future please keep your note cards in order. I would like to know of a man's birth before I learn of his death." There was a small amount of laughter from the class. "Next we have Mr. Tanner."

As one of the best students in the class, Brent Tanner's reports were always incredibly detailed and precise, and he was always very proud of himself. When he concluded his report, he asked for questions, thanked the class for their attention and then returned to his seat.

"Thank you very much, Mr. Tanner, as always an excellent report."

"Thank you, sir," Brent replied smugly.

"Continuing up the list, we now come to Mr. Steinman..."

"Oh God..." Casey looked at him, wishing there was something she could do for him. She couldn't help feeling she had caused David to forget his report, since she hurried him through the crowd of girls so fast and so suddenly...

"If you would please Mr. Steinman." David sat still, wondering what he should do.

"Mr. Steinman, you did write a report?"

"Yes sir."

"Well then..." David remained seated. "We are waiting Mr. Steinman." David slowly made his way to the front of the room and looked out at the other students, but he didn't know what to say, no words would come to his mind. "Is there a problem Mr. Steinman?"

"No sir... uh, yes sir, I mean..."

"What exactly do you mean, Mr. Steinman?"

"My report..."

"Yes?" the teacher asked, obviously irritated.

David breathed a deep sigh, "My report is in my locker sir."

"Your report is in your locker."

"Yes sir."

"Well now, am I correct in assuming then, that you will *not* be giving your report today?"

"Yes sir."

"You do realize you lose one letter grade for every day your report is late?"

"Yes sir."

"Will you be better prepared tomorrow?"

"Yes sir."

"Take your seat Mr. Steinman. Let that be a lesson to the rest of you. Miss Simmons, if you would please." David slid into his scat and spent the rest of the class period staring at a blank page in his notebook.

When the bell rang, David got up from his seat and left the room and it was all Casey could do to keep up with him. If she lost him in the crowded hallway, she knew she'd never find him again.

"David... David, wait," she called, but he didn't stop. "David, *please*." He stopped and waited for Casey to catch up.

"Where are we going?" she asked as they started walking again. "David, where are we..."

"Lunch."

Casey followed David through the lunch line and then to an empty table in the far corner of the room. They sat for a short while without saying a word until Casey couldn't bare it any longer.

"I'm sorry about your report, David."

"It wasn't your fault," he said without looking up.

"I know, but I can't help thinking..."

"Look, Casey, I screwed up, it had nothing to do with you."

Casey watched him as he moved a fork through the food on his tray. "I can't believe they didn't tell you about me."

"Yeah, well, they didn't tell me I had to dance either." David took a bite of his lunch. "Yuck, how can anyone eat this crap?"

Casey looked at the food in front of her. "It does kinda look like toxic waste, doesn't it?" she said, scrunching up her nose. David couldn't help but laugh at the face she was making and at last, the tension had broken. They salvaged the only part of their lunches they deemed edible—the milk—and as they sat, David made a list of all his classes, teachers and room numbers and gave the list to Casey.

"Here."

"What's this?"

"The names of all my classes and where they meet, just in case we should happen to get separated."

"You mean just in case I get lost," she smiled, slipping the paper inside her folder.

"That's another way to say it," David smiled back at her.

"Where to?" Casey asked as the bell rang.

"Photojournalism."

"Sounds interesting."

"That depends, how do you feel about cameras?"

"Film is my life!" she joked, striking a pose. They both laughed as they headed down the hall.

The last bell signaled the end of the school day and David and Casey made their way through the crowd of students to the rows of brightly colored lockers near David's homeroom.

"Did they give you a locker?" David asked her.

"They gave me the one..."

"Next to mine?" he asked. Casey nodded. "Basically, they just told you to follow me around."

"You got it!"

"Are you riding my bus too?" he asked.

"I'm supposed to."

"Okay, follow me!" The whispering and staring started as soon as they boarded the bus and sat down together. Casey leaned over to David.

"Do they always stare at you like that?"

"Some do, but they're staring more now than usual," he teased.

"David!" she whispered, scolding him as he smiled devilishly. David reached into his backpack, pulled out a blue folder and sighed. Casey glanced over at him. "Your report?"

"Yeah." Casey looked away, attempting to avoid the subject. "Casey, I told you it wasn't your fault."

"Really? I mean, are you sure you don't hate me?"

"I'm sure Casey," he said, taking her hand, "I don't blame you for anything."

"Go for it Steinman!" one of the guys yelled as the other boys around them hooted and whistled. David blushed, let go of Casey's hand and turned toward the window.

"What a goof!" Casey commented. "I swear, some people have no manners whatsoever. Who does he think he is anyway?"

"I believe he's the captain of the football team," David said.

"Seems more like Captain Crunch to me," Casey retorted. They looked at each other as they tried to subdue their laughter. Casey opened one of her books and proceeded to study. David watched her for a moment and then turned to stare out the window as the bus pulled away from the curb.

CHAPTER 2

The school bus stopped at a corner in an uptown part of the city and David departed with Casey in tow. She followed him down the path toward a modern two-story brick building.

"What a beautiful place, is this where you live?" Casey asked.

"Not hardly!" David laughed, "This is Murray's studio. I come here every day after school to rehearse. Murray rides me home afterwards."

"Do you live far from here?"

"Casey, compared to this, I live on a whole different planet!"

"I don't understand."

"You will."

At the front door, Casey stooped down to admire the rows of flowers growing on both sides of the walkway and blooming along the entire front of the building.

"Oh, how pretty, I love flowers!" She leaned over and inhaled their sweet scent.

As Casey fawned over the various blossoms, David stood wondering about the young woman before him. Casey was unlike any girl he had ever known. There was a certain maturity about her and by just watching her, no one would have ever guessed that she was only 16, even David had trouble believing it. He kept going over the day's events in his head—Murray's introduction, how she pulled him through the crowd of girls at the door, forgetting his report, lunch, the bus ride....

"Well, I see you both made it here All right." David was jerked from his thoughts as Murray greeted them. "Beautiful, aren't they?" Murray commented to Casey.

"They're wonderful," she smiled back, "did you grow them yourself?"

"Sure did. I tend to spend a lot of time here and the gardening helps me to relax. I grow some of my own vegetables in a little garden out back, too, I'll take you out and show you some time."

"Great! I'd love to see it."

"Right now, we better get to work," Murray said. The three went into the building and Murray led them into a moderately-sized meeting room. There were four people seated at the table—two men and two women—that David had never seen before. Murray put his arms around David's and Casey's shoulders. "David, Casey, I'd like you to meet some friends of mine. This is Debbie, JoAnn, Mark and Jerry," he said, introducing everyone at the table. "Folks, this is Casey McCallister and the one and only David Steinman."

"Murray, do you have to introduce me like that?" David blushed as everyone laughed.

"Sorry," Murray replied with a smile. They took their seats as Murray began to go over the agenda for the afternoon, but before he could get started there was a knock at the door, after which a twenty-something brunette popped her head into the room.

"Is anyone here?"

"Claire! Come on in!" Murray went to the door and hugged the woman. "I was wondering when you'd get here."

"Sorry I'm late, I've had a very busy day," she replied as she hugged Murray.

Claire? David thought, *who's Claire?*

"Let me introduce you to everyone," Murray said as they turned to the group, "You already know Casey."

"Yes," Claire replied, ""Hi Sweetie!"

"Hi," Casey smiled back.

"This is Debbie, JoAnn, Mark and Jerry and this," he continued as he walked over and stood behind David's chair, "is David."

She walked over to David and sat against the table beside him. "So, you're David."

"Yes ma'am."

"You're the little wonder that Murray has been raving to me about," Claire smiled at him. "Stand up."

"I beg your pardon?" he said, surprised by her directness.

"Stand up, let me look at you." David slowly did as she asked, wondering what she was looking for. "Turn around." David looked at Murray, who gave him the 'go ahead' sign. David made a gradual 360° turn. "Uh-huh…" Claire walked in a circle around the boy. "Oh yes, I can see what you mean."

"Wait till you hear him sing!" Murray said excitedly.

"Well, let's get started! Where can we change?"

"Dressing rooms are across the hall. We'll meet you in the room next door to that." The group followed Claire and Casey out of the meeting room. Several minutes later, they rejoined Murray and David in the rehearsal hall, all of them dressed in leotards, tights, leg warmers and ballet shoes and they immediately began stretching and bending in order to warm up their muscles. David stood by the door of the room with Murray watching the group's activities.

"Excuse me, Mr. Ackerman," Claire interrupted jokingly, "could we possibly have some musical accompaniment?"

"Oh, of course." Murray walked over to a control console in the wall by the door, pushed a few buttons, turned a few knobs and within seconds, David's music began to spew from speakers embedded in the ceiling. The two watched as one by one, the dancers took turns creating their own routines to the songs. When the music changed to the slower, softer strains of a love song, most of the group stopped to take a break and to catch their breath, but there was one who didn't.

She was alone on the dance floor and as the music began, she could feel the warmth, the tenderness and the strength of the love that the lyric was expressing; its passion overwhelmed her, the heartache came next, diving deep into her soul and bringing out the tears and misery of a forsaken love and then finally, the hope that love will come again. As the song faded, the fair ballerina bowed down gracefully, and the group began to applaud and congratulate her on a job well done. David stood in amazement, wondering if this lovely princess could be the same young girl who seemed so shy in a new school, the same girl who felt so guilty about a forgotten report.

Murray walked over to the control panel to change the music; David followed.

"Are you sure she's only 16?"

"What?"

"Is she really only 16?"

"Yes, she's 16, why?"

"I don't know," David said, "she just seems a lot older."

Murray turned to look at Casey. "She's good, isn't she?"

"*Good*? She's amazing!"

"Well, she's been studying dance for most of her life, she's very dedicated to it, that's one of the reasons I chose her." He turned back to the console as David continued watching Casey and Claire go over some new steps with the group.

"She really does love to dance, doesn't she?" David commented. Murray stopped for a moment, looked at him and smiled.

"You like her, don't you?" he teased.

"No, I just think she's a great dancer."

"Admit it Dave, you're falling for her."

"No, I'm not."

"Yes you are."

"I am not falling for her, okay?"

"Okay," Murray said, putting his hands up in surrender and David walked away in a huff. Murray watched him a minute, then went back to working with the console as he smiled to himself. "Oh yes you are."

"All right friends, let's take a half hour break," Murray said, "David, could you stay for a minute please?" David separated himself from the pack and waited. After everyone had left the room, Claire and Murray stood looking at David.

"What?" David asked, wondering what kind of trouble he had managed to get himself into this time.

"Come here honey," Claire said, motioning to him with her finger. "I want you to stand right here." Murray and Claire went over to stand by the wall at the front of the room, leaving David in the middle of the room by himself. "Okay," Claire said as the music began to play, "dance."

"Say what?"

"Dance," she repeated.

"Dance?"

"Yes, move around to the music, dance, you know what dancing is, don't you?" Claire questioned him.

"Yes, I know what dancing is," he answered sarcastically.

"Well then, dance."

"I don't dance."

"You don't dance?"

"No, I don't dance."

"Why not?"

David hesitated, a little embarrassed to answer. "Because I don't know how."

"Oh, well, I guess we'll have to teach you then."

"Yeah, right, and I bet you could teach a goldfish to sing, too."

"Probably, if the goldfish was willing to try," she replied, smiling back at him. David looked at Murray who was standing behind Claire trying to hide his laughter. "Don't look at him, he can't save you. As a matter of fact, this was all his idea."

He looked back at Murray, giving him the 'evil eye'. "I should've known."

"Oh come on, David," Claire urged him, "it's not *that* bad." She walked over and stood directly in front of him. "You're a teenager, aren't you?"

"Yeah."

"Well, you go to school dances, don't you?"

"No, I don't."

Claire was astonished at David's response. She hesitated a moment, looking at him curiously.

"You don't go to school dances?" David shook his head. "Have you *ever* been to a school dance?" Again, David shook his head. "Surely, you're joking." Once more, David shook his head no. "Then what do you do on Friday nights?"

"Stay home, watch TV, read, do homework, listen to music," he answered, shrugging his shoulders.

"I don't believe it," she declared, folding her arms across her chest, "a teenager with no social life."

"I have a social life," David said in an irritated voice.

"Oh, really?"

"Yeah, really," he growled back at her, "I just prefer to stay home, is there anything wrong with that?"

"No, nothing at all!" The two stared at each other for a few seconds, then Claire turned and started walking toward the door.

"Please don't give up so fast," Murray begged quietly as she drew up to him.

Claire paused beside him. "Give up? I'm just getting started!" She glanced over her shoulder at the young man in the center of the room. "When I get back, David and I are going to start from square one." She looked back at Murray. "This is going to take longer than half an hour, Ackerman." Murray gave David an exasperated look, then followed Claire out into the hallway.

David sat cross-legged on the floor and rested his chin on his fists. How could he compete with the abilities of professionals who have been studying dance all their lives? He thought of how beautiful and graceful Casey was when she danced. Casey had come here for the sole purpose of being David's dance partner. "I'm going to make a fool of myself," he thought aloud.

It wasn't long before Murray and Claire returned and without a word, Murray went immediately to the control console. Claire walked over to David, stopping about five feet in front of him and motioned for him to stand. As he did, he heard the click of the door latch and looked over to find that Murray had left him alone with this obstinate woman. "Okay, David," she said nicely as the music started again, "let's see what you can do."

"I told you," he said quietly, "I don't *do* anything."

"All you have to do is move to the beat."

"I don't know how!" he said, raising his voice.

"Just pick your feet up!" she said, raising her voice above his.

"I can't!" he insisted loudly.

"Damn it, David, you can! All you have to do is try!"

Claire was yelling at him now, clearly frustrated at David's unwillingness to even attempt any dance steps at all. David stared at the floor; his arms folded tightly across his chest. They stood without speaking as the music continued to fill the air around them. David wanted to run, he wanted to get away from this place and away from Claire. He was beginning to wish he hadn't gotten involved in any of this. The music stopped and David looked up to see that Claire had moved over to the control console.

"David, why won't you even try?" she asked without turning around.

"Because I can't do it."

"Can't do it" she asked as she turned to face him, "or won't do it?" He looked back at the floor. "David?" Once again, he glanced up at her.

"Both, I guess." Claire sighed. "I'm sorry, I'm not a dancer. I guess I'm not the 'little wonder' you thought I was."

"Oh, but you are," she said with a caring smile. "Look at you, you're only sixteen years old and you have a hit record."

"So?" David said, unimpressed.

"So, you've accomplished something that most adult performers only dream of! You have every right to be proud of yourself." She walked over to him and took his face gently in her soft hands. "David, you have something special, you have a natural talent. You can deny it every day of your life, but it won't go away. You were born with it, it's part of you, it's in your blood."

"But I'm not a dancer." He was becoming upset, and he could feel the tears welling up in his eyes, and he hoped to God they didn't show.

"I'm not asking you to *be a dancer*, that's a title you have to earn, and it takes years of training and experience."

"Good," he said with a sigh of relief.

"But I am asking you to dance." Claire went over to the console and switched the music on again. "Listen to it David," she said as she rejoined him in the middle of the room. "Listen to the rhythm." David stared into Claire's eyes. "Do you hear it?" After a moment, he nodded. "That's the music's pulse, the beat of its heart, and everything we'll do, we'll do to this beat, in counts of eight."

"Counts of eight?" he asked curiously.

"Counts of eight. What that means, is that on each number or count, you'll do a certain move, like this...step one, step two, step three, turn four, step five, step six, step seven, bow eight," she counted as she demonstrated. "Understand?"

"Yeah, I think so."

"Okay, since you don't have a lot of experience at this, we'll start with the most basic move you can do."

"Which is?"

"Well, can you bend your knees?"

"Yeah."

"Great! Then we'll start with that." Claire knelt on the floor in front of him and placed her hands firmly across the top of each of his feet. "Now all I want you to do is listen to the beat and count like this...one and two and three and four and five and six and seven and eight and. On 'one', you bend your left knee slightly. On 'and' you straighten it. On 'two' you bend your right knee slightly.

On 'and' you straighten it. When you get to eight, start all over again. The count will be seven and eight and one and two'...got it?" David nodded. "I'm going to count with the beat, but you start when you're ready."

As a new song started, Claire began counting out loud. David tried counting with her to himself, and whispering a small prayer, he looked down at his knees and attempted to do as Claire had explained.

"Don't lift your feet, just bend your knees." She glanced up at him. "And don't look down, look at the wall in front of you." David looked up. "Good. One and two and three and four and...you're doing great!" David looked down immediately to confirm to himself that he was doing as well as she claimed. "Don't look down! If you watch yourself, you'll screw up, close your eyes if you have to, but don't look down." David closed his eyes and tried to concentrate on the beat. The bass coming through the speakers seemed to make the room shake, and he could feel the vibrations through the soles of his feet.

"That's it, you've got it!" Claire said to him happily. As his knees continued their rhythmic cadence, he felt Claire's hands ease their hold on his feet. "Now, each time you bend your knee, lift your heel." David followed her instructions almost involuntarily. "Good, good...wonderful David, keep going," Claire encouraged, but David didn't hear her, his mind was lost in the music…

CHAPTER 3

David loved music and that love was instilled in him by his father, Daniel Joseph, a musician. He taught David that there were many kinds of music and that he should listen with an open mind. David learned to respect performers and musicians because, as his father always told him, "their work came not only from their minds, but from their souls".

While growing up, David spent as much time as he could with his father, following him everywhere and asking 'why's' and 'what's' as all small children do. He could always be found by Daniel's side, watching and listening as Daniel worked on his music or rehearsed at one of the many clubs where he played. Daniel was thrilled by his son's eagerness to learn and he took great pleasure in showing David 'the ropes', breaking everything down to the most basic of explanations.

A few months after David's 10th birthday, Daniel passed away suddenly. David was crushed, unable to believe that his father would ever leave him. At the funeral home, David sat silently at his mother's side as relatives and friends filed by to pay their respects. One by one they offered their condolences, the ladies touching his face lovingly and the men laying their hands on his shoulder as they passed by him, but David sat stoic through the entire event and never uttered a word to anyone. He stared at the casket where his father's body lay in state. He knew what was happening, but he felt detached from the whole scene. During the funeral service at the cemetery David could hear the preacher giving the eulogy. He could hear his sisters crying and could feel his mother's hand on his, but none of it seemed real. *It couldn't be*, he thought, *Papa said he would be waiting for me...*

The sound of the door latch pulled David back from his memories and he opened his eyes. He had been so engrossed in his thoughts that he hadn't heard the song end. Claire was sitting on the floor at the front of the room, her back against the wall, one leg stretched out in front of her and her hands around the bent knee of the other with her fingers laced together. She had an inquisitive look on her face and Murray was standing beside her.

"What were you thinking about?" Claire asked David. He looked away from her, his eyes following the cracks in the floor where the boards came together. "David, are you okay?" she asked with some concern.

"Can I take a break now?"

"What's wrong, Dave?" Murray asked.

David didn't look up. "Can I take a break now?" he asked again in a loud, anxious voice.

"Yeah, sure," Murray answered, "take as long as you need." Murray and Claire watched as David quickly left the room. Claire was astonished by David's behavior.

"Wow, what was that all about?"

"I wish I knew," Murray replied, still staring at the door, "He's really a great kid, but every now and then he sort of hides inside himself and won't let anyone else in."

"But it was such a sudden change," Claire commented, "one minute he was fine, the next...." She paused for a moment. "You know what it sounds like…"

"What?"

"It sounds to me like our little friend is having trouble adjusting to his new lifestyle."

"No, I don't think so, if that was the problem, he would have talked to me about it."

"Don't be so sure. We've both seen it happen before Murray. An unknown kid like David suddenly hits it big and they end up with a lot of problems because they don't know how to deal with it. If you're going to do something about it Ackerman, now's the time."

David walked quickly down the long hallway, through the front door and out onto the lawn. He sat down in the shade of a spacious oak tree and stared at the grass, slowly moving it around with his fingers. Casey saw David leave the building and decided to follow him, keeping her distance while she watched him so as not to be discovered. There seemed to be something curious about him. He was sitting on the verge of superstardom, yet he seemed so introverted, so alone...almost as if he didn't want any part of it and actually acted as if he were bothered by all the attention. She walked closer to where he sat, wondering if she should speak or just stay hidden, but her curiosity finally got the better of her.

"What are you thinking about?"

"Why does everyone keep asking me that?"

"I'm sorry, I didn't mean to intrude."

"You're not intruding."

"Are you sure? I can leave if you'd rather be alone."

"No, it's all right.

"What's bothering you, David?" she asked as she sat down beside him on the grass. David shook his head. He reached over and snapped a dandelion off at the base of its stem and began twirling the little flower back and forth between his finger and thumb.

"I just don't understand it," David said, staring at the dandelion. "What do they want, what do they see? How can they be so sure that everything is going to work out the way they say it will? How do they know this isn't all just dumb luck? I'm just not sure I can live up to their expectations."

"They're professionals David, they know what they're doing," Casey said, trying to cheer him up, "You just have to trust them and have faith."

"Faith in their expectations?"

"Faith in yourself."

David turned and looked at her and she gave him a soft smile. He returned half a smile and looked back at the flower he still held in his fingers. He reached over, handed the flower to Casey, and gave her a peck on the cheek.

"Thanks." He stood up and started walking back to the building.

"Anytime," she replied softly. She smiled to herself and sniffed the flower.

Murray opened his office door and almost ran into David as he was passing through the hallway.

"I was just coming to find you," he said, trying to sound positive, "Is everything okay?"

"Everything's fine."

"Everything's fine?"

"Yep, just peachy, why?"

"No reason, I just like to ask once in a while, just to be sure." He paused. "You know, if you ever do have a problem, you can come to me with it. I mean, whatever the problem is, we can talk it out."

"Yeah, I know." He sat down in one of the chairs in front of Murray's desk and munched on some cashews from the bowl that was sitting on the table next to him. "Is there something I should know about, Murray?"

"No, I just wanted to make sure you knew you could come to me with any problems you may have."

"You mean problems with the music?"

"Not necessarily, you can talk to me about other problems, too. I'm your friend, Dave, I'm here for you if you need me."

"Can I ask you a question?"

"Anything."

"What brought all this on?"

"What do you mean?"

"Come on, Murray," David urged, "you said you were my friend."

"I am your friend."

"Then why do you sound like a psychiatrist? Talk to me like a friend, be straight with me."

Murray looked at David and sighed, then walked over and sat next to him. "You're right," he agreed. He reached over and took a few cashews from the bowl. "The truth is, Claire is worried about what happened with you in the studio earlier, she thinks that you might be having some trouble coping."

"Coping with what?"

"With your new life."

"My new life?"

"Yeah, you know, being recognized, chased after, stared at, asked for autographs... that sort of thing."

"Oh, that," David replied with a grin, "it is a bit strange, but so far there haven't been any issues, nothing I haven't been able to handle."

"You'd tell me if there were any issues, right?"

"There's no one else I could tell, no one else would understand," David said reassuringly as he popped a few more cashews into his mouth. "I'm starving."

Murray glanced at his watch. "I told your mother you'd be home in time for dinner tonight and when I told her about Casey, she insisted that we bring her along. Where is Casey anyway?" He walked over to the doorway and looked up and down the hall.

"The last time I saw her, she was out front on the lawn," David answered.

"When was that?"

"Right before I came in."

"I'll go see if she's still out there," Murray said, moving toward the front door. He yelled back to David. "Get your stuff together and I'll meet you at the car."

David got up from the chair, grabbed a few more nuts from the bowl and went down the hall to the meeting room to retrieve his backpack and jacket. While he was in the meeting room, he noticed music coming from the studio. He went over and opened the door just enough to stick his head in. What he saw was more breathtaking than anything he had ever seen before.

David was captivated by her loveliness. He just couldn't turn away. She wore a pink leotard with a matching wrap skirt, leg warmers and ballet slippers. The color reminded David of cotton candy. Her thick braid stretched to her waist and her skirt fluttered around her as she twirled. David watched silently as she moved lightly across the dance floor. The gentle music that filled the room seemed to wrap around her like a warm blanket, protecting her from any harm that may threaten her. She belongs there, David thought. Murray came back from looking for Casey and noticed David staring through the studio door.

"What are you looking at?"

"I found her," David whispered back. Murray stuck his head through the opening above David's.

"I should have known to look here. I better tell her were leaving."

"No, let her finish." Murray smiled to himself as he thought back to the audition held to find a dance partner for David. So many young ladies tried out and they were all talented, but none of them seemed quite right. Then Casey auditioned. Immediately, Murray knew he had found the perfect dancer for the job. Watching her now reminded Murray of the way she danced at that audition, every step, every turn was perfect, every move followed the pattern of the music so effortlessly. Her performance was so uninhibited, which seemed to Murray to be exactly what was needed to bring David out of his shell.

"I can't believe you want me to dance with her."

"What?"

David pulled his head out of the doorway. "I said, I can't believe you want me to dance with her."

"Why is that so hard to believe?"

"Murray, have you ever seen me dance?"

"No, not that I recall."

"Did you ever think that maybe there's a *reason* why you've never seen me dance?"

"Actually, I never really thought about it."

"Well, rest assured, there are *definite* reasons."

"Such as?"

"Such as I'm clumsy, I'm uncoordinated, I have two left feet, I'm short, I have no rhythm..."

"David, David," Murray interrupted with a chuckle, "you know none of that's true."

David looked astonished. "Are you saying I'm not short?"

"All right," Murray agreed, "that much may be true, but none of that other stuff is."

"How do you know? You've never seen me dance."

"I saw you working with Claire earlier and you were doing great," Murray said, trying to sound encouraging.

"You saw me bending my knees, that's not exactly dancing."

"Not exactly, but it's a start." David laughed and shook his head. "You really don't believe you can do this, do you?"

"I believe I can do the singing, but dancing? No, I don't think so."

"But you're at least willing to try, right?"

"I didn't know I had a choice." He looked at Murray, who didn't answer. "Besides, now that we've started, I don't think she would let me quit."

"You mean Claire? Probably not," Murray smiled at him. "We'd better go, your mom will have my head on a platter if we miss dinner."

"I'll get Casey," David said.

"I'll get Claire," Murray told him as they headed in opposite directions.

David opened the studio door and stepped inside. Casey was sitting on the floor in the middle of the room doing stretching exercises. He watched her for a few moments.

"Hungry?" he inquired.

Casey glanced up from her stretches. "That depends, is it take out?"

"My mother has invited you, Murray and Claire over for dinner, if you'd like to come."

"I'd love to," Casey said in a relieved voice, "I haven't eaten a home-cooked meal for two days."

David walked over, bent down slightly and offered his hand to her. "Shall we then?"

"Yes, we shall." She took his hand as he helped her up. Casey started for the door but after a few steps, she felt a tug on her arm that stopped her. She turned to find David standing there holding onto her hand and staring at her. She stared back for a moment and then with a wicked grin, she pulled with all her might. "Come on, I'm hungry!"

CHAPTER 4

"Is it very far to your house, David?" Casey asked as Murray pulled the car onto the highway.

"No."

"It's only about ten minutes away," Murray added, "You'll love it, there are girls everywhere."

"The fans come to your house?"

"He means my sisters," David clarified.

"Oh, do they all still live at home?"

"Only five of them. The others have moved out or gotten married."

"I've never met a family with twenty children before," Casey said with a touch of excitement in her voice, "It must be a fun place to live." Claire smiled at her.

"Not if you're the only guy in the house," David countered.

"Well, at least you have your own room," Murray pointed out.

"Yeah, too bad it doesn't come with a private bathroom." The others laughed out loud, which made David smile. He was nervous about Casey going to his house. He was sure that Casey would be expecting a big fancy home with beautiful furniture in a well-to-do neighborhood. The truth was nothing like that at all.

As Murray drove, Casey watched the long driveways, large porches, balconies, and manicured lawns change to smaller, older houses that were weather-worn and tired-looking, a few of which were empty and deserted. They drove through a small business district and then headed south. Casey also noticed a change in David as they got closer to the neighborhood where he grew up. He seemed more relaxed, more at ease than he had been earlier in the day. It was a subtle change, but noticeable just the same.

Murray pulled up in front of a two-story chocolate-brown brick house and parked. David opened the door as soon as the car was stopped. He walked around the back of the car and stepped up on the curb where Casey joined him. She stood and looked up at the house.

"So this is where you live," she stated.

"Not what you expected, right?"

"I expected a house, should I have expected more?"

David looked at her for a few moments, then looked back at the house. He had lived here most of his life and he loved this house. It had been his haven, the one place on Earth where he knew he was always welcome and where he knew he was accepted and loved. It was the one place where David could be David. He knew to others it was just another old pile of bricks, but to him it was the world.

"I can't wait to meet your mother," Casey said.

"You'll love her, she's great with kids."

Casey smiled. "Really?"

"Yeah, she's got tons of experience," he said as he started to laugh, "come on." He led the way through the gate which took them into the yard that ran down the entire length of the left side of the house. At the back end of the yard was a small patio area and beside that, an old shed which was painted the same chocolate brown. A sidewalk ran between the yard and the house from front to back and on the side of the house was a concrete porch whose cinder block banisters were beginning to crumble. Behind the house stood a one-car garage made of the same type of gray cinder blocks with a slanted shingled roof.

David quickly went up the two steps onto the porch and entered through a door that led into the dining room. The group followed him into the kitchen where his mother and two of his sisters were putting the finishing touches on the evening's dinner. David went over and stood by the table, eyeing the goods.

"Hey David," his sister, Peggy, greeted him.

"Hey," David replied. David's mother turned from the sink when she heard them come in.

"Well, it's about time you all got here, we could've used a few more hands in the kitchen," she smiled at Murray.

"We are at your service, madam," Murray offered with a small bow.

"That's okay, we're just about done anyway. Come on in the living room and relax, the girls can finish up in here and let us know when dinner's ready." She wiped her hands on the towel and hung it back on the towel ring, then escorted her guests into the living room.

"David, don't you want to help?" Jeannie asked him as he turned to walk away.

"No."

"Why not?"

"Ma said 'the girls' can finish it."

"So?"

"So, I'm not a girl," he explained. The two sisters made faces at him and he returned the gesture as they laughed. David went to the living room and sat down on a little footstool near his mother's chair.

Rose Steinman was a cheerful woman with a friendly disposition. She was well-liked by everyone who knew her and had many friends in the neighborhood. She spoke softly, but directly and was quick with a laugh and a smile. Her features were soft, but anyone who looked into her large brown eyes could see there was inner strength that lay just below the surface.

"So, somebody introduce me to these lovely ladies," Rose requested.

"Rose Steinman, this is Claire Evans," Murray began.

"It's nice to meet you, Ms. Evans."

"Likewise, Mrs. Steinman, and please, call me Claire."

"Only if you call me Rose," she smiled.

"It's a deal."

"And who is this beautiful young lady?"

"Casey, nice to meet you."

"It's nice to meet you, too. Is Casey short for anything?"

"Cassandra."

"Oh, what a pretty name. I don't think I used that one. Maybe one more sister, huh, David?" she teased.

"No, thanks," David answered; Rose laughed.

"So what do the two of you do?"

"Claire is a dance instructor and choreographer and Casey is a dancer," Murray offered.

"Casey is your student, Claire?" Rose asked.

"Not exactly, Casey is already an accomplished dancer. I'm here to teach David to dance with her."

"You're going to teach *David* to *dance*?" They turned to see David's sister, Sandy, in the doorway.

"That's right."

"Good luck!" Sandy teased as David rolled his eyes.

"Sandy, did you interrupt us for a reason?" Rose asked. Sandy's smile left quickly.

"Jeannie said to tell you that dinner will be ready in five minutes."

"Thank you. Why don't you go make sure the table is set?" Rose gave her youngest daughter a stern look.

"Yes ma'am," Sandy replied as she turned and headed into the dining room.

Rose glanced over at David who was staring at the carpet, his chin resting on one hand with his elbow on his knee. Rose stretched her foot out just enough to gently push on David's leg. When she did, his knee shifted, and his elbow fell toward the floor. The sudden jerk made him look up at her.

"So, you're gonna be a dancer, too?" David scowled slightly and looked back at the floor; Rose could tell that he wasn't too crazy about the idea. "Well, I guess we'll just have to wait and see, won't we?" She leaned over until her face was looking directly into David's. "Won't we?" she asked again softly with a little bit of a smile.

"I guess," he finally answered, "Can we eat now?"

"Yes, we can eat now. Why don't you and Casey go ahead in and we'll be there in a minute." She gave him a gentle squeeze and a little peck on the top of his head, and the two teenagers got up and went to the dining room while Murray and Claire stayed behind to talk to Rose.

"You're sure he can handle this, Murray? I know he can sing, he gets that from his father, but he's not a dancer, at least not that I've seen."

"Rose, you know how I feel about David's talent," Murray said, "I believe that, with the proper instruction and guidance, David could take this as far as he desires."

"I know, Murray, you've always said that, and I believe he could, too. What about you, Claire, do you think he can do it?"

"Well, I've only worked with him one on one for about an hour, but I could tell he has a good feel for the music, and I do see the potential that Murray sees. I think there's a lot of work to be done, and I mean a *lot* of work, but I feel the same way Murray does. He can take this all the way if he's willing to do the work."

"So, he agreed to all this then, or did you surprise him with it?"

"Blind-sided him," Murray smiled at her, Rose returned the smile.

"It's probably just as well, if you would have asked him straight out, he would have fought you tooth and nail."

"Oh, he fought," Claire confirmed.

"That's my boy," Rose conceded with a nod of her head. "Let's go have some dinner." She got up from the chair and led them to the dining room where the rest of the family was waiting. David and Casey were talking to Sandy as Peggy and Jeanie were bringing in the rest of the food from the kitchen. Rose went to the table and started seating her guests.

"Murray, you sit here," she said, pulling out a chair at the end of the table, "and Claire can sit next to you. David, you and Casey can sit on the other side next to Murray."

They all happily did as they were instructed. Rose sat at the head of the table as Peggy, Jeanie and Sandy filled the remaining seats.

"Are Lisa and Erin coming?" Peggy asked her mother.

"Lisa is working, and Erin has a late class tonight, so this is it."

"Lisa and Erin are your sisters, too?" Casey asked David.

"Yeah, I have ten."

"And he has nine brothers, too," Sandy added, "Poor David's the baby of the family." David elbowed her lightly and she gladly returned the gesture.

"That's enough you two," Rose corrected them, "that's not how we act with guests in the house, you know better." The two siblings quickly settled themselves.

Sandy was only three years older than David and they had spent more time together growing up than he had with his older siblings. They lovingly picked on each other as brothers and sisters do but were the best of friends as well.

"Murray, would you like to say grace?" Rose offered.

Everyone at the table joined hands and bowed their heads as Murray blessed the meal. When they were finished, a collective "Amen" was heard and then the clinking sound of plates and silverware began.

As Casey looked up from her prayer, she noticed that David's head was still bowed. A couple moments later, he looked up and joined in the meal. She wondered what it was he was silently praying for, but she dared not ask as prayers are private and she refused to intrude on that, but she still couldn't help wondering...was he saying an extra prayer for help and guidance, or was he asking God to make everyone leave him alone and let him go back to his normal life? Even though David's mood had seemed to lighten up a little since they had first been introduced, she still wasn't sure that he was happy about why she and Claire were there, and wondered if he secretly wanted them to leave.

"What are we having tonight, Rose?" Murray asked from the opposite end of the table.

"Why, my famous meatloaf, of course," she smiled as she passed the plates around. "There's plenty here for everyone, so help yourselves."

"So where are you from, Casey?" Peggy asked.

"Michigan."

"Really? How long are you staying?"

"We're moving here, I'm staying with Claire for a couple of days while my mom and dad finish packing up and sell our house."

"You're moving here?" David asked in an astonished voice.

"Uh huh," Casey nodded.

"What's wrong, Dave, don't you want her to?" Sandy asked sarcastically.

"I didn't say that."

"They don't need your permission," Jeanie added.

"I know."

"Then what's the big deal?"

"Ma," David pleaded for her to intervene.

"Girls, that's enough."

"I'm sorry, Dave," Murray interjected, "I should have told you earlier."

"It's okay, really, I was just surprised that your whole family is moving here. What about their jobs or your brothers and sisters?"

"Well, my dad is a lawyer with an independent practice, so he can work anywhere, and I don't have any brothers or sisters."

"None?" Sandy asked.

"Nope."

"Lucky you," David said as the others laughed.

Rose smiled at her son. She knew it was difficult being the youngest child in a large family, since she was the youngest of nine, but she also felt the youngest should not be babied. She believed they should be held to the same standards as the older children in the family and not be given special treatment just because they were the youngest. Still, she had a special place in her heart for her baby boy; he just seemed to need her more than his brothers and sisters had. He had such a loving heart and she was always afraid that he would be easily hurt by others who weren't as kind. There were times when she had to resist the urge to wrap her arms around him and protect him. She knew she had to teach him to deal with the outside world on his own, after all, there would come a day when she wouldn't be there for him to turn to and he would have to depend on himself.

After dinner, Murray, Claire, and Rose sat in the living room and talked over coffee while the girls went about the business of cleaning up. Normally David would be helping as well, but Rose excused him because he had company. Since it was a clear, warm night, David and Casey decided to go outside to the porch where they sat looking at the stars.

"Aren't they beautiful?" Casey commented. David stared into the night sky. She looked over at him when he didn't answer. "Aren't they?" He was sitting on a small banister of the porch, lost among the stars he was admiring. "David?" she said again from her place on the opposite end of the porch. She walked over and lightly touched his arm. "Hey… David…" He turned to see her concerned look.

"What?"

"Are you okay?" she repeated, "You seemed a little lost for a moment."

"Oh," he replied, "I'm fine, just tired."

"I know the feeling, my world has been spinning ever since Murray told me I got the job."

"The job?"

"Being your dance partner."

"Oh, that."

"Well, don't sound too happy about it," she said, a little hurt by his tone of voice. "I might get the feeling that you don't want me here."

"I'm sorry, it's not that, it's just nobody told me about it."

"About me?"

"About you, about Claire, about dancing..."

Casey was a little confused about what the problem was. She could understand that he was upset because he wasn't included in the decision process, but she didn't understand why he was so bothered by having to dance since he was a performer.

"You don't like to dance?"

"I don't dance."

"You don't dance?"

"That's what Claire said."

"I'm sorry, I don't understand."

"Why?"

"Why what?"

"Why don't you all understand?" Casey stood quiet for a moment, unsure of what to say to him. "Why doesn't anyone understand that I don't dance? I don't dance at home; I don't dance at school...I don't dance!"

"Okay, you don't dance," Casey conceded.

"Thank you!"

"You're welcome."

David looked out into the darkness of the yard. He felt like screaming and crying, but he did the best he could to hold his emotions in check. Casey walked back over to the opposite end of the porch, all the while trying to choke back her own tears as well. The silence was broken by Murray and Claire coming out of the house, followed by Rose.

"Thank you again for dinner, Rose, it was delicious!" Murray leaned over and kissed her on the cheek.

"Yes, it was," Claire agreed.

"You can join us anytime you like, you're always welcome," Rose said, extending an open invitation.

"Be careful," Murray laughed, "you may end up with a few 'adopted' children."

"I'll take 'em!"

"Casey, are you ready?" Claire inquired.

"Yes," Casey answered without turning around. She was thankful for the darkness so they couldn't see her face clearly. She took a deep breath, turned, and smiled at them. "Thank you for having us," she said to Rose.

Rose leaned over and hugged her. "You're welcome, sweetie. You make sure you come back and see me again, okay?"

"I will." They smiled at each other.

They all said goodnight to David telling him they would see him tomorrow and then got in the car and headed back to the studio. Before going back into the house, Rose told David not too stay up too late, reminding him that he had to get up for school in the morning. He assured her that he wouldn't and she kissed him, said goodnight and disappeared into the house.

David had always had trouble sleeping, and now, with all of this singing and dancing business going on in his head, he knew he wasn't going to get to sleep anytime soon. He sat and stared at the stars for a while, contemplating what his life was and what it was becoming. He was beginning to think that he had gotten in way over his head and it scared the hell out of him. Still, he didn't dare admit that to anyone. They all seemed to believe he could do no wrong, that he had so much talent. They had all done so much for him and worked so hard; how could he tell them that he wanted out? How could he tell them that he was too afraid to go on? Maybe after they realized what a terrible dancer he really is, they'd all agree that this was a crazy idea from the start, and he can go back to being unknown and inconspicuous. That, he felt, was his only hope. As he sat thinking about it, he felt his emotions begin to take over. He decided to stay there on the porch a little longer, in the dark, where no one could see his tears.

CHAPTER 5

The next day in school Casey didn't say much, she was friendly, but didn't offer much else. David assumed she was probably just tired, so he didn't question her about it. The bus ride to the studio wasn't any different, she studied the entire way while David stared out the window. When they reached the bus stop, she was off the bus and almost into the building before he hit the sidewalk where he stood looking after her as she disappeared through the door.

David walked into the studio and set his backpack on a chair, then went into the kitchen and got a soda from the refrigerator. As he took the first drink, Claire came into the room and glared at him.

"What?" he questioned after the first swallow.

"I want to talk to you."

"About what?"

Claire looked around the table at the others. "Privately." She turned and headed out of the room.

"Okay," David said, setting his drink down and following her. Claire went to Murray's office and waited as David came in and shut the door behind him.

"What did you say to her?" she asked angrily.

"I beg your pardon?"

"I want to know what you said to her."

"To who?"

"To Casey! I want to know what you said to her last night while you were out on the porch."

"We talked about the stars, why?"

"That's it? The stars?"

"Yeah. Why?"

"Why? I'll tell you why."

"Please do."

"Because she cried herself to sleep last night, that's why. She doesn't know that I know, so keep your mouth shut."

"I won't say a word."

"You had to have talked about more than just the stars," Claire said, pushing the issue.

"Well, we talked about dancing."

"I knew it, what did you say?"

"I said I don't dance."

"And?"

"And I told her I don't see why no one seems to understand that."

"Are you sure that's all you said?"

"Yeah."

"There's got to be more to it than that, that wouldn't make her want to quit."

"*She wants to leave*?"

"I overheard her talking to her parents on the phone this morning. She told them she's having second thoughts about taking this job." Claire looked at David.

"I don't know." He thought for a moment. "I may have raised my voice a little."

"*You yelled at her*?"

"Well, not at her, at the situation..."

"Go find her and apologize!"

"What do I say?"

"David, this job means the *world* to her, you have to fix this."

David sighed heavily as he turned and left the office to look for Casey. He hadn't realized he had hurt her feelings the night before. He was so wrapped up in his own fears he hadn't even thought about anyone else. He had no idea what to say to 'fix' the problem, but he did know he didn't want Casey to leave.

After looking in the places he thought Casey might go, David decided to try looking in some of the smaller studio rooms toward the back of the building. He looked through the long thin window on each door and finally found her in one of the last rooms. She was sitting in a corner in the back of the room, her legs folded with her arms around them and her head resting against the wall. He stepped back from the door and thought for a few moments about what he could say to make her want to stay, but nothing he came up with sounded right. He decided to just go in and if she didn't throw him out then he would go on from there.

David took a deep breath, gathered what little courage he could find, opened the door and quietly stepped into the room. He heard the click of the door latch behind him, then silence. He waited, still wondering what he should say, or if he should say anything at all. Casey didn't acknowledge him. David noticed the sadness in her expression and realized how much he had upset her. He decided then that whether she stayed or not, he would make sure she knew he was sorry. All he had to do was figure out a way of telling her without becoming an even bigger jackass than he had already made himself into. David slowly walked over to where Casey was sitting. He stopped a couple of feet from her and waited; finally, she looked up at him.

"Hey."

"Hey," Casey answered softly. She looked away again and David stood there with his hands in his pockets.

"I was looking for you." Casey didn't answer. "This place has so many rooms I wasn't sure where to start."

David stood there for a few uncomfortable moments, then went over and sat on the floor beside Casey. Even with the tension between them, he felt relaxed around her. He decided he would just say what he needed to say. If she still wanted to leave, then there wouldn't be anything he could do to change her mind.

"Casey, I'm sorry, about last night, I mean. When we were out on the porch, I snapped at you and I shouldn't have. I'm responsible for putting myself in this situation, not you. It's just that I signed on for something that I'm not so sure I can handle and sometimes I get scared. I mean, I know I can sing, but I've never been very good at dancing and the thought of getting up in front of a bunch of strangers and... anyway, I'm sorry. I'm glad you're here and I hope you can forgive me." David got up and walked for the door, when he reached the front of the room he turned around and looked back to Casey. "I'll be with the others if you wanna talk, or if you just wanna smack me or throw something at me or whatever."

As he turned to leave he heard a tiny laugh from Casey. He looked back to see her wipe a tear away and suddenly he felt a lump in his throat. He looked back tour the door so she wouldn't see.

"David?"

David cleared his throat. "Yeah?"

"Are you really glad I came here?"

He turned to face her. "Yes, I am."

"But you don't want to dance, you don't like to dance...you obviously don't need a dance partner." Casey quickly wiped away the tears that she couldn't hide. David walked back over to where Casey was and sat down beside her again.

"Now wait a minute. I never said I don't *like* to dance, I said I don't know *how* to dance, there's a difference, you know."

"I know," Casey said with a sniffle.

"I mean, maybe with the right teacher and lots of practice, I could learn."

"Claire's a fantastic dancer, I'm sure she could teach you in no time."

"I'm sure she could," David agreed. They sat for a moment before David got up and walked to the front of the room.

"Are you leaving?" Casey asked.

"I want to show you something." He went over to the control console by the door. "When Murray built this place he made each studio room special and one day he showed me how they work. This room is one of my favorites." David typed in some commands and pushed a couple buttons, then he turned around to face Casey. "Watch."

David pushed one final button and the room began to change. A tile in the ceiling slid open and a mirror ball lowered. Gradually the lights dimmed and one single spotlight shone on the mirror ball causing little spots of light to dance slowly around the room. Casey's eyes lit up as the room transformed around her.

"Oh, wow." She stood and walked out toward the middle of the room. David pushed a few more buttons, then walked over to Casey.

"Maybe you could teach me how to slow dance." He held out his hand to her as beautiful music began to play. She smiled as she placed her hand in his, guided David's other arm around her waist and put her arm around his shoulder. As she began to lead him in the steps, David glanced toward his feet.

"Don't look down," she whispered.

"Sorry," They both smiled. About halfway through the song, Casey let go of David's hand and put both of her arms around his neck, laying her head on his chest. David was a little surprised, but didn't say anything. He wrapped his free arm around her small waist, then closed his eyes and somehow knew he was forgiven.

Claire paced back and forth in the main studio worriedly until Murray couldn't stand it any longer.

"Claire, will you please sit down somewhere?"

"How can you be so calm?" she asked him.

"There's no reason to get so worked up."

"No reason? What if she decides to go home? Do you realize how much work we are going to have to do? We'll be back at square one, we'll have to hold new auditions and interview hundreds of new girls...it'll set us back months!" Claire said as she continued to pace.

Murray laughed. "Relax, Claire, that's not going to happen."

Claire stopped pacing and looked at him. "How do you know?"

"Because I know David, he's a good kid, he'll make it right."

Claire walked over and sat on a chair by the wall, and breathed a heavy sigh. "It's just that this is a big opportunity for Casey and I don't want to see her give that up."

"Casey is a mature, intelligent young lady, she'll make the right decision." Murray looked through some papers on a clipboard and scratched a few notes in the margins, his calmness making Claire even more anxious.

"Damn it! What is taking them so long?" she exclaimed as she popped up out of the chair and starting pacing again. Murray saw that Claire was about to burst, so he tossed the clipboard onto a table and took Claire by the hand.

"Come on, we'll go check on them." He stopped by the door and looked at her, "but you have to be quiet and not say a word."

"I won't."

"No matter what happens?"

"No matter what," she agreed reluctantly. They continued out the door and toward the back studios. As they got closer to the rear of the building, they could hear music playing in one of the rooms.

"Over here," Murray whispered. He led Claire to the studio at the end of the hallway. They leaned over and peered through the long narrow window in the door and saw David and Casey together on the dance floor as the tiny circles of light from the mirror ball sparkled around them.

"Look at them! They look absolutely wonderful together!" Claire whispered.

"I know," Murray whispered back.

"They're perfect for each other!"

"I know."

"And he's *dancing*!"

"I know," Murray whispered with a huge smile. Claire straightened up and looked at him.

"Is there anything that you *don't* know?"

Murray placed his finger across his lips. "Shhh..." They watched for a few more moments, before heading back to the main studio where the other dancers were warming up.

"Okay folks, let's get down to business, we've got a lot of work to do," Claire said. The group spread out around the studio dance floor as Murray picked up his clipboard and headed for his office.

CHAPTER 6

As the car pulled up in front of his house, David grabbed his backpack and unhooked his seatbelt.

"Thanks, Murray," he said as he jumped out, "I'll see you tomorrow."

"Hey, Dave."

"Yeah?"

"You did good today."

David rolled his eyes and laughed a little. "Thanks." The pair smiled at each other.

"See you tomorrow."

David waved as Murray pulled the car away from the curb and rounded the corner at the end of the block. He heard his mother call from the kitchen as he entered the house.

"Davey, is that you?"

"Yeah."

"How was your day?"

"It was okay," he said, "I'm hungry, is dinner ready?"

"Just about," Rose smiled at him, "I'll call you when it's done."

David turned and quickly climbed the back stairs to his bedroom. He dropped his backpack on the floor, went over to the CD player and picked out some music, then laid down on the bed and stared at the ceiling of his room. He couldn't get the events of the afternoon out of his mind. He thought about when he and Casey had met the day before—how she appeared so strong-willed and outgoing—but today at the studio she seemed so delicate and fragile. She had gone from speaking her mind to not speaking at all, from tough to tender.

David closed his eyes and tried to relax, but the sadness he had seen in Casey is eyes haunted him. Knowing he had caused pain of any kind to another human being genuinely upset him; knowing it was Casey made him feel worse. Tears began to well up in his eyes and he sat up on the side of his bed and dried the moisture from his cheeks just as his mother came to the door.

"Dinner will be ready in a few minutes."

"Okay, thanks," David said as he tried to hide a sniffle.

"David, are you all right?"

"Uh huh." Rose walked over to the bed and sat beside him.

"What is it, Davey?" David looked down at the floor without answering. "David, I know there's something wrong, tell me what it is."

"I made her cry, Ma."

"Who, baby?"

"Casey."

"How?"

"I yelled at her."

Rose was shocked at what she was hearing, it just wasn't in his character to be mean or confrontational. "Are you sure it was you? Maybe it was something at school..."

"No, it was me."

"When did this happen?"

"Last night after dinner, when we were out on the porch."

"David, we were just inside the door, we didn't hear any yelling."

"I didn't exactly yell, but I did snap at her. I didn't even realize I hurt her feelings until today at the studio."

"Did she say something to you about it?"

"No, she didn't really talk to me all day, but Claire told me Casey cried herself to sleep last night and told her parents on the phone that maybe she shouldn't have come here."

"Oh, David…"

"I didn't mean to hurt her, Ma," David said as a few tears dripped down his face.

"I know you didn't, Davey," she reassured him, "but it's Casey you should tell that to."

"I did, I apologized to her and told her I was glad she's here."

"Did she accept your apology?"

"I think so." He wiped his face on his shirt sleeve.

"Everything is good then?"

"I guess," David shrugged. Rose could tell that it wasn't.

"Something is still bothering you, isn't it?"

"When I went to apologize, she was crying, and I can't get her face out of my mind."

"I see," Rose said, "well, I hate to tell you this, but that image may stay with you for some time, maybe for the rest of your life." David looked at her. "That's a good thing, though."

"How can that be a good thing?"

"Because you'll never forget the circumstances that led up to it. All of our actions have consequences, Davey."

"I know."

"Well, sometimes remembering the consequences keeps us from repeating those actions. Understand?"

"Yeah."

Rose put her arm around her youngest son. "I have to go finish dinner, want to help?"

"No, I think I'll just stay up here for a while."

Rose stood up and walked to the door, then looked back to David. "Are you gonna be all right?"

"I will be, I just hope Casey's okay."

"I'm sure she is. I'll be down in the kitchen if you need me." Rose turned and headed down the stairs. David lay back down on the bed and closed his eyes as the expression on Casey's face flashed through his mind again. Seeing tears in her beautiful brown eyes broke his heart, but knowing he put them there devastated him. He swore to himself that he would never let it happen again.

Casey heard a light tap on the door and looked up from her textbook to see Claire standing in the doorway.

"Can I come in?"

"Sure," Casey invited. Claire walked over to the bed and sat next to Casey.

"How are you doing?"

"I'm okay," Casey replied.

"Everything going good at school?"

"So far."

"Rehearsal went rather well today, don't you think?"

"Yes, it did."

"I think David's starting to come out of his shell a little bit, but he's going to need a lot more work."

"I agree." They sat for a minute or so without talking as Casey continued reading.

"Casey, you're not leaving, are you?"

"What makes you think I'm leaving?"

"I heard you crying last night," Claire admitted, "then this morning, I overheard you on the phone."

"Oh…"

"I'm sorry, I really wasn't trying to eavesdrop. I know David upset you, but I'm sure he didn't mean to. He seems to be a great kid and his family is so nice, I think he's just a little overwhelmed with all of this attention, he's not used to it. I think it's all just freaking him out and he's not sure how to handle it, but he'll come around and it'll all work out, you'll see." Claire stood and began to pace.

"Well...."

"I mean, I can understand how he feels, it's a lot to take in. One minute, you're just another kid on the school bus and the next, you've got strangers wanting your autograph."

"Claire, it's okay..."

"Heck that would freak out any well-grounded adult, David's only 16!"

"Claire, please..." Casey said raising her voice a little. Claire stopped talking, looked to Casey and sighed.

"Just tell me you're not going to quit and move back to Michigan."

Casey smiled at her. "I'm not going to quit and move back to Michigan."

"You're not?"

"I'm not."

"Promise?"

"Claire..."

"Okay, I believe you." She sat down on the bed. "So, what happened with you two this afternoon?"

"What happened?"

"We were waiting for a long time…" she paused. "I'm sorry, it's really none of my business."

"It's all right," Casey assured her, "he apologized."

"That's it?"

"Yes, why?"

"Oh, no reason," Claire replied, trying to sound convincing.

"You're looking for details, are you?" Casey asked, laughing.

"Who, me?"

"He was very polite and genuine. He told me he was sorry he upset me and he's glad I'm here."

"Go on..." Claire urged with a grin; Casey smiled playfully.

"Well, then he dimmed the lights, turned on some soft music and asked me to teach him how to slow dance." Casey looked at Claire with a twinkle in her eye.

"That little devil!"

"It was *so* romantic," Casey swooned, "I just had to forgive him."

"Sounds to me like someone's got a crush."

"I do not!"

"Is that so?"

"Okay, maybe a little," Casey admitted, "but he's my dance partner."

"So?"

"So, I don't date guys I work with."

"Right," Claire said, obviously not convinced.

"I don't."

"Fine. He is kinda cute, though." Claire grinned as Casey smiled back at her.

"I know, and he's so sweet."

"He so quiet, though."

"I like quite guys," Casey said, "They're much more interesting than the loud obnoxious ones."

"Really?" Clair asked; Casey nodded. "I never would have guessed that, I mean, I knew you would never date a big macho jock type, but I thought you might be attracted to someone a little more outgoing than David."

"I think there's more to David than we can see," Casey said, "oh, and he's a *great* slow dancer, too." She smiled again as Claire perked up.

"So he really does have some moves, then?"

"Oh, yeah," Casey said, giggling, "When he put his arms around me, it just felt like we fit together, you know what I mean?"

"Yeah, I know."

"Claire, you won't tell any of this to anyone, will you?" she asked nervously.

"My lips are sealed."

"I'm serious, I really like everyone here, especially David, and I don't want to make things more difficult for him than they already are. Besides, it would be too embarrassing for both of us right now."

"Casey, I would never do anything to ruin this for you or David or anyone else involved. I mean, come on! I'd be out of a job if you two quit!" They laughed together. "I think the two of you make a great team." Claire gave Casey a small hug, then got up and walked to the door. "It's getting late, you better get some sleep."

"As soon as I finish this chapter."

"Okay, dear."

"Claire?"

"Hmm?"

"Thanks."

"You're welcome, goodnight."

"Night, Claire," she said as Claire closed the door.

Casey began reading her textbook again, but she couldn't keep her mind on her studies. Every time she tried to concentrate, the events of the day would distract her. She couldn't stop thinking about how beautiful David's apology was, or how gentle he was with her or even how she could hear the sound of his heartbeat as he held her close when they danced.

Claire was right, Casey did like David…she liked him a lot. She became a fan of his music from the first song she heard and now that she had met him and his family, she realized her feelings were growing deeper than just being a fan, but she could never admit that to him, he had enough to deal with right now. What he needed was a good friend—someone he could confide in, someone he knew he could trust and for now, she would have to be content in just being there for him. Casey put down her book and turned off the light, then slid under the covers, laid her head on the pillow and closed her eyes. She was still thinking of David as she began to dose off.

"Goodnight, David," she said to the darkness, "sweet dreams."

CHAPTER 7

David stood in front of the bathroom mirror combing and re-combing his hair. Unbeknownst to him, his brother, Michael, stood watching him from the doorway. David turned suddenly when he heard a muffled laugh behind him.

"How long have you been there?" he snapped.

"Calm down, Dave."

"Well, you shouldn't sneak up on people like that." David turned back to the mirror and resumed the battle with his hair. After a few futile attempts, he pounded his fists on the sink counter.

"Dammit!"

"Whoa," Michael laughed, "you better not let Ma hear you."

David sighed heavily as he stared at himself with a frustrated look. Michael closed the door and walked over to his brother. "Look at me," he said as he took the comb from David's hand, "what's with you tonight, anyway?"

"Casey's coming over for dinner."

"She's been here before, hasn't she?"

"Yeah."

"So, what's so different about tonight?" Michael asked as he straightened David's mane.

"Her parents are coming with her."

"And?" David and Michael looked at each other for a few long seconds, until Michael realized what was really bothering David. "Oh, I get it," he said as a smile began to take over his face, "you like Casey so you're trying to impress her parents." David took the comb out of Michael's hand and turned back toward the mirror with a bothered expression. Before Michael could say anything else, there was a knock on the door. "Come in," Michael answered. The door moved a bit and Scott stuck his head through the opening.

"Everybody decent?"

"Yeah," Michael answered. After closing the door, Scott joined his brothers at the bathroom counter.

"What's the occasion?" he asked as he looked David up and down.

"Dinner guests," David answered without looking at him.
"Oh?"

"Casey's coming over," Michael volunteered.

"So?" Scott shrugged.

"*With her parents*," Michael added with a grin.

"Ah," Scott replied, "now I understand."

David was becoming aggravated by the two of them. He turned to face them again. "And what's wrong with trying to make a good impression?"

"Nothing," Scott answered. Suddenly the two brothers broke out in laughter. David looked at each of them with disgust in his eyes as another knock caught their attention.

"Hey, are you guys having a party in there or what?" called a female voice. Scott reached over and opened the door to let Lisa and Erin in.

"Nah," he answered, "we're just trying to help Dave make a good first impression."

"Can we help?" they asked sarcastically, as they tried to muss his hair.

David flinched in defense. "Knock it off!"

"Didn't you girls have plans for this evening?" a familiar voice asked from the doorway. The siblings turned to find their mother looking at them with raised eyebrows.

"Yes ma'am," they replied, "night, boys!" They made kissy faces at David as they laughed, and he sneered back at them as their giggles faded down the hallway. Rose moved her eyes to her older sons, and without a word, the men straightened up and cleared their throats.

"I better head home," Scott said, "night Dave, night Ma."

"Goodnight, sweetie," she replied, hugging him.

"You know, now that you mention it, Ma, I gotta be gettin' home, too." Michael kissed his mother as he slipped passed her, then leaned back in the door. "Don't worry, D, they'll love you. Night all!"

"Goodnight, Michael," Rose said as he headed down the stairs.

"I swear, sometimes there are just too many people in this house," David huffed, Rose smiled. She watched as he tried once again to fix his coif and she could see his frustration growing.

"Would you like some help?" she asked him. He sighed, reluctantly handing the comb to her, and she stepped up behind David and began styling his hair for him. "You know, you really don't have to try so hard."

"What do you mean?"

"I mean just what I said, you really don't have to try so hard to impress Casey's parents. They'll like you just as much as Casey does." She smoothed a few stray hairs. "There, all finished." She handed the comb back to him and David stared at himself in the mirror as Rose watched him.

"Do you really think so?"

"Of course I do, why wouldn't they like you?" David shrugged. She put her hands on his shoulders and looked in the mirror at him "You look more like your father every day." David smiled at the memory of his father as Rose moved toward the door. "By the way, Claire called a little while ago, she and Murray and the McCallisters will be here in about half an hour."

"*Half an hour*?" David echoed worriedly.

"David, relax."

"It is just us tonight, right, Ma?" he questioned, "There isn't going to be a whole houseful of people?"

"Yes, dear," she answered, "we will be alone with our guests for the entire evening."

"Are you sure there won't be any surprise visits?"

"Yes, I'm sure."

"But what if...."

"David Anthony, stop worrying and trust me!"

"Sorry, I can't help it."

Rose smiled at him. "Get finished and come downstairs before they get here." David nodded and his mother left him alone. Looking back at his reflection, he thought about the last few months of his life. Things had happened so quickly since Casey had come to work with him. He felt that something inside of him had changed and he knew it was for the better. He examined himself in the mirror one more time just to check every detail. "David?" Rose called to him, "David, Casey's here."

"Dammit!" he cursed quietly as he ran out of the bathroom. Without thinking, he bounded down the stairs as fast as he could, his feet landing with a sudden thud at the bottom. He looked up to see the surprised faces of his guests. Even Casey looked startled, though she smiled when he looked at her.

"This must be David," Casey's mother said.

"Yes," Rose replied as she put her arm around her youngest son's shoulders and pulled him toward her, "this is David." She gave him a look that let him know he should have been down sooner. He looked at her apologetically. "Casey, would you like to introduce David to your parents?" Rose asked.

"Sure, um, David, this is my father, Adam McCallister," Casey began. David looked up at Casey's father as the man's six-foot-one frame towered over him. Adam offered his hand and David reached out to shake it.

"Hello, young man," Adams deep baritone voice greeted him.

"Hello, sir."

"And this is my mother, Cadence McCallister," Casey continued. Cadence shook David's hand as well.

"It's nice to finally meet you, David," she said.

"It's nice to meet you, too, ma'am," David answered, returning her warm smile.

"Well, now that we all know each other, is anyone hungry?" Rose asked.

"I'm starving!" Murray replied. The group laughed as they followed Rose into the dining room.

As the ladies stepped up to the table, the men began pulling their chairs out for them. David watched as Murray helped Rose, then turned to help Claire and Adam helped his wife. Rose gave a quick look in Casey's direction and David reached over and pulled the chair out for her, then sat down in the chair beside her. Rose stood to begin serving, but Murray stopped her. "Please, Rose, let me do that for you."

"Thank you, Murray."

"It's only fair. After cooking for us all day, you should get to sit and relax a little."

"It smells wonderful, Rose," Cadence complimented.

"Yes, it does," Adam agreed.

"Thank you. I made one of David's favorite dishes."

"I hope you didn't go to too much trouble, Rose," Cadence told her.

"It was no trouble at all, I'm used to cooking for a much larger group than this, so it was actually very easy to handle."

"Well, I must admit, I have been looking forward to this all day," Adam told her, "Casey has told us so much about your cooking that I've been anxious to try some of it."

"Bless you, Casey, dear!" Casey smiled brightly at Rose.

They all passed their plates around the table one at a time to Murray as he dished out the food and passed them back. Once everyone had been served Murray took his seat and waited for Rose. "If everyone would please join hands," Rose requested, "I'll say grace." As everyone bowed their heads, Casey slowly reached over and took David's hand in hers. David smiled to himself and closed his hand gently around Casey's. As the prayer ended, Adam looked over at them.

"You two can stop holding hands now, it's time to eat," he grinned. Casey looked to David as he quickly let go of her hand and picked up his fork.

"Daddy, stop it!" she scolded, "You're embarrassing me!"

"Adam McCallister, you are shameful!" Cadence smiled at him as the others laughed.

Adam held his hands up in surrender. "I was just teasing!" David took a bite of his pot roast and stared at his plate as he chewed. Adam glanced over at him, then to Casey. Casey gave him a stern look that told him he needed to do a fast recovery or he would be in trouble when they got home. "So, David, Casey tells us you have nine brothers."

David looked at him tentatively. "Yes, sir."

"And he has ten sisters," Casey chimed in quickly.

Adams eyes widened. "Ten sisters?"

"Yes, sir."

"So, you know what it's like to have the women of the house gang up on you then?" he asked as he gestured in the direction of his wife and daughter. Casey and Cadence looked at him in astonishment as he gave David a quick wink. David began to relax a little as he realized that Casey's father was attempting to apologize in a roundabout way. A smile spread across David's face.

"Yes, sir, I do." David looked to Rose who was giggling at them.

"Well then, we'd better stick together or they'll eat us alive!"

"Hey," Murray interjected, "don't forget about me!"

The entire table erupted in laughter as the tension broke. Casey reached under the table and gave David's leg a little squeeze. He looked over at her as they shared a smile. *God, she's beautiful,* David thought.

After the meal was finished, the adults retired to the living room to have coffee and get to know each other better. David and Casey decided to go outside to get some air.

"He likes you," Casey told him.

"Who?"

"My father."

"How do you know?"

"What do you mean how do I know? He's my father."

"Did he tell you he likes me?"

"No."

"Then how do you know?" Casey stopped walking and looked at him. "What?" he asked.

"Why is this so important to you?"

"I don't know," David answered with a shrug, "it just is."

"Well, I can tell if my father likes someone or not, and he likes you." They continued walking in silence until they reached David's front door. "It's really starting to get cold," Casey said.

"Do you want to go in?" Casey hesitated to answer. She was enjoying her time alone with David, but she didn't want to tell him that. "Come on," he urged, "I'll get Ma to make us some hot chocolate."

"Oh, no, I don't want to bother her."

"Casey, she won't mind."

"No, David...."

David gave her his best puppy-dog eyes and Casey couldn't resist. The two headed inside to get warm.

CHAPTER 8

"All right, folks. Let's go through it one more time so I can see it from the audience," Claire instructed as she walked down the stage steps and out among the rows of seats. "Everyone ready?" The music director raised his hand in the air and waited for Claire to count them off. "One, two, ready and..." As her voice trailed off, the music began playing from the towering speakers at the sides of the stage. She kept a sharp eye as the group did each move with perfect precision. David stood in the wings and watched them rehearse.

Even though he had seen them perform this routine at least a hundred times, he was still amazed at how well the dancers were able to execute each step. They made it all looks so easy, but David knew differently. He had lost count of how many times he had stumbled while attempting a dance step. It took him hours, or even days to learn things that Casey and the others had picked up in minutes. He had been practicing for months on end, trying his best to remember everything he had been taught. Claire assured him he was doing fine and that it would get easier for him as time went on, but despite all his efforts, he still felt unsteady and unconvinced of his abilities. He knew no matter how hard he worked, his dancing would pale greatly in comparison to everyone else on the stage. He was more than willing to get out there and do his best, he just wasn't sure his best would be enough to please a crowd of thousands.

"Fabulous!" Claire exclaimed as the music stopped abruptly. "Okay everyone, take a break and catch your breath. In a few minutes, we'll try it again with everyone." David moved aside as they passed. Casey stopped and smiled when she saw him.

"Hey!"

"Hey."

"What's the matter?"

"Nothing."

Casey paused for a moment. "Aren't you excited?" she asked, trying to change the subject.

"About what?"

"About tonight, silly," she laughed.

"Oh, that. I don't think excited is the word I would use."

"What word would you use then?" David walked out and stood in the middle of the stage, shoved his hands in the front pockets of his jeans and looked out at the massive open space before him. Casey walked out and stood beside him.

"How about petrified?" he offered. Casey wanted desperately to give him some words of encouragement, but she knew nothing she said would comfort him. She could see the fear in his eyes and knew the only way for David to conquer that fear was through experience. Still, she wished there was a way she could assure him that everything would work out.

Casey went to the front of the stage and sat down, letting her feet dangle over the edge as she began adjusting her leg warmers, David joined her. He stared out at the empty chairs in front of him. He could see that the front row had been labeled with the names of his and Casey's immediate family members.

"You're thinking about your father, are you?" David looked over at her and was about to speak when Claire came down the aisle toward them.

"Just the two people I've been looking for. Let's do a few last minute tweaks." Casey stood up and walked to the back of the stage and joined the others as David reluctantly followed. As the band played David's songs, he did the steps he was taught as the ensemble followed suit. After going over several routines, Claire excused them all for a dinner break before they were to get ready for the show. She ran to catch up with David as he passed through the exit door.

"So, do you think you're ready for tonight?" she asked as she came up beside him. David continued without answering; Claire stopped and waited a few moments. "David," she called after him. He stopped in the middle of the hallway. "Do you think you're ready for tonight?"

David turned around and looked at her. "Do you?"

"Truthfully?" David nodded. "Yes, I do."

"Really?"

"Yes, really."

"I wish I was as sure as you are." David walked over and looked through the window on the cafeteria door. He could see everyone eating dinner and talking and laughing seemingly without a care in the world. "They're ready," he said of his colleagues.

Claire joined him at the small window. "Yes, they are," she agreed, "but they've all done this before. Most of them have worked with other performers, they know what to expect."

David turned away from the window and started slowly down the hallway. Claire had been working with David for several months, teaching him everything she could about dance. She watched him as he worked day after day to get every step down. Claire saw David's attitude change during that time from a scared naive kid to a determined young man; instead of being afraid and hiding, he was in the studio before everyone else practicing each move over and over. Most days, Casey was right there by his side helping him to perfect each routine. Claire knew he was ready for this show; Murray knew he was ready; Casey knew he was ready. The only person who doubted that David was ready was David himself. Claire wasn't sure how to convince him otherwise.

"Do you want to get something to eat?" Clair asked, trying to take his mind off the show for a little while.

"No," David answered as he stopped again, "I'm too nervous to eat."

Claire thought for a few moments. "Come on," she said to David as she started down the hallway.

"Where?"

"Just come." David followed behind Claire as she made her way through the back passageways toward the dressing rooms. She continued until she reached a set of double doors with a lighted 'EXIT' sign above them, then she stopped and turned to face him. "Out," she instructed as she motioned toward the door.

"Out?"

"Out," she repeated. David gave Claire a puzzled look and she sighed heavily. "Will you just open the door?" David pushed down on the bar latch and stepped through. He looked out across the parking lot of the arena and saw a large group of people, mostly girls, who looked to be about his own age, some even younger. Barriers kept them back away from the stage door and several security guards did their best to keep the peace. When the group spotted David, they began screaming his name and jumping around, and a few even held up signs that said things like 'I Love You' and 'Marry Me David!'

David stood and stared. "Who are they?"

"Groupies," Claire answered with a smile.

"*For me*?"

"Yep, they're here because you're here."

David watched the crowd for a few moments, then began walking toward them. The closer he got, the louder they screamed. Claire stood back at the door and watched as David stopped about halfway between her and his fans; he raised his hand and waved at them. To his amazement, they all waved back as they screamed, ""Hi David!" and "We love you, David!" He felt his cheeks get warm as the blood rushed to his face and he quickly turned and headed back to where Claire stood.

"How long have they been there?" he asked, looking back in the direction of the crowd.

"Security said they started showing up around ten last night," Claire told him.

"They've been out here *all night*?" David couldn't believe what he was hearing.

"That's what groupies do, David."

"But they haven't left, not even to eat?"

"I'm sure they've eaten," Claire answered, trying to sound convincing. She looked toward the grouping of girls.

"There's plenty of food in the cafeteria, maybe we should send something out to them."

Claire smiled at him. "Maybe we should," she agreed, "I'll talk to the arena manager and see what we can arrange."

"Thanks." He glanced at the group again.

"Kinda cool, huh?"

"Yeah," he agreed, "and kinda creepy." He turned and went back inside the building. Claire laughed to herself as she followed him. When they reached the cafeteria, David joined the others while Murray stopped Claire at the door.

"Where were you two?"

"I took David out to meet some of his fans."

"You mean those kids in the parking lot?" Claire nodded. "So, what happened?"

"He felt sorry for them," she said.

"He felt *sorry* for them?"

Claire nodded again. "He wants us to send out some food."

"Really… and?"

"And I told him I would arrange something with the manager."

"Well, then, let's arrange something with the manager." Claire smiled and ventured out to find the person in charge of food.

David sat alone in the dressing room staring at his reflection in the mirror. He was supposed to be getting dressed, he was supposed to be excited, and he was supposed to be ready for this. Instead, the only thing he was ready to do was sneak out the back door and disappear forever and as much as he wanted to, he knew he couldn't. Too many people knew him now and too many people depended on him, not to mention the fact that Murray had put everything he had into David's career – time, energy, money, even his reputation – if David walked away from this now, Murray would lose everything. There was no way David could live with himself if he let that happen. No, he would stay.

"It's only two hours," he said to the young man in the mirror. Lost in his thoughts, he didn't hear the knock or the sound of the door opening behind him.

"Davey?" said the familiar voice. There was no answer. "Davey?" the voice said again, startling him back to the moment. David turned to see his mother standing beside him. She looked worried. "Davey, are you feeling all right?"

"Yes."

"Are you sure, you look a little pale." Rose felt David's forehead and face as mothers do. "You don't feel warm," she said as she cradled his face in her hands. For a few moments she looked at him and thought how young he was and how in less than an hour he would take the biggest step of his life. "You're okay, then?" she asked as she lowered her hands.

"Yes, ma'am, I'm fine." Rose could tell he was trying to be brave. David leaned his elbow on the table in front of him and rested his chin on the heel of his hand.

"You're scared to death to walk out onto that stage, aren't you?"

David looked over at his mother. "Does it show that much?"

"David, any normal human being would be afraid to go out there."

"Papa was never afraid."

"There are a lot of things you don't know about your father. There were many times when he would have rather not had to go out and face those crowds."

"Papa?"

"Yes, your papa, but he knew if he even once let that fear get the best of him, he would never walk out on a stage again." David was astonished, he couldn't remember ever seeing fear in his father's eyes.

"But, how...why did he keep doing it?"

"He did it because he loved it, Davey, it's what was in his heart. You love it, too, don't you?" David looked at her with a cockeyed smile. "I could tell, you are your father's son." Her eyes sparkled as she spoke about her late husband. "I know you miss him, Davey, I miss him, too." Feeling as if he might cry, David stood up and walked over to the other side of the room.

"It's not fair, Mama. Papa worked for this his whole life and never got it. I *never* wanted it and they're practically dropping it at my feet. You know, I've always thought that Papa could have done so much more with his music if he didn't have all of us to worry about."

"Well, you see, that's something else you didn't know about your father," Rose answered, "It was no secret that Daniel loved music and he worked very hard for many, many years to earn the respect of his peers, but he loved you kids even more than his music, and gaining *your* respect was much more important to him. Music was his passion, but his children… his children are his legacy."

"I wish he was here right now, Mama."

"Me, too." She walked over to him and taking him by the hand, led him to the small sofa that lined the far wall of the room. "Come and sit with me for a minute Davey, I want to talk to you." Once they were settled on the sofa, Rose continued. "When your brother, Danny, was born, your father and I were so excited to be parents that we could hardly contain ourselves. Daniel was at the hospital every day just watching your brother through the nursery window. There wasn't a prouder papa in the entire hospital." Rose laughed at the memory; David smiled with her. "One day while I was sleeping, the nurse brought Danny in and let your father feed him. When I woke up, Daniel was just talking and talking to that baby, he said he had so much love and joy in his heart and he wanted to express it all to his new son." Rose stopped for a moment and blinked back the tears in her eyes.

"Mama…"

"Don't interrupt, Davey." David waited for her to compose herself. "He said he wanted Danny to know how happy we were that he was born and how much we had looked forward to his birth. I suggested that he write your brother a letter that he could read when he was older, so that's exactly what he did. As a matter of fact, he wrote letters to each of you on the days that you were born." David listened intently. He never knew of the letters his father had written to him and his siblings, none of his brothers and sisters had ever mentioned them before.

"But Papa never gave me a letter."

"Your father decided that he would give the letters to each of you at a time in your life when you really needed to hear what the words of the letter said," Rose explained.

"But Mama, Papa never gave me a letter." Rose gave him a bothered look, and he apologized for interrupting again.

"That's because he was waiting for the right time. He made me promise to give it to you when you needed it the most, it was almost as if he knew..." Her lip quivered as her voice trailed off and David tried hard to grasp on to what she was saying. Rose reached into the pocket of her sweater and pulled out an envelope. When she handed it to him, he could see handwriting on the front of it that he recognized as his father's. He read the words on the envelope to himself – 'To My Son, David Anthony'.

"What does it say?"

"I don't know," she answered, "I never read any of them. Daniel sealed them in the envelopes right after they were written and put them away, then one by one he gave them to each of you. Yours is the only one left."

"But why didn't anyone tell me about it?"

"Your father asked each of you not to mention it to the others."

David looked at the envelope. He wanted to read the letter his father had written to him, but he couldn't bring himself to do it. He held the letter out to his mother.

"Open it."

"No."

"Mama, *please…*"

Rose gently pushed his hand away. "Whatever is in that letter is between you and your father, Davey. You have to read it yourself and I think now would be the perfect time." Rose leaned over and kissed him on the cheek, then got up from the sofa and walked to the door. "I'll be with the family if you need me." David nodded his acknowledgment. Rose waited a moment and then quietly left the room.

David sat staring at the envelope. It was all too much for him. First the show, then the 'groupies' in the parking lot, now this. It had been six years since his father's passing and David still had a hard time dealing with it. Now, here he sat holding a letter his father had written to him on the day he was born. He felt more afraid of reading that letter than he did about going out on that stage.

David walked back to the dressing table and sat down in front of the mirror. He looked at the writing on the envelope again, then looked at the reflection in front of him. Taking a deep breath, he turned the envelope over and slid his finger under the corner of the flap. He pulled the letter out and unfolded the pages, his hands shaking as he started to read the words his father had written.

> *"Hello David,*
>
> *My name is Daniel and I am your father. I am writing this letter to you, David, because there are some important things about life that I want to tell you and I am so excited about your arrival that I'm afraid I'll forget and leave something out.*
>
> *Your mother, Rose, and I have waited quite a while for you to join our family. After your brothers were born, we assumed that you would be the next to come along. We were so sure you were coming that we had already picked out your name, but you, being a true gentleman, allowed your sisters to come to us first. Then, in your own sweet time, you blessed us by becoming our son.*
>
> *As your parents, we can make some promises to you that will always be kept. We promise to do everything in*

our power to keep you healthy and safe. We promise to be there when things are going great for you, to share your joy and we promise to be there for you to lean on when things aren't so good, to share your tears. Your mother and I have many hopes and aspirations for your future, but we also know that you will have dreams of your own. We promise to be there to support you no matter which road you decide to travel in life, even if we do not agree with your decision. We promise to always be there whenever you need us with open arms and open hearts.

At first sight, I knew you were a very special little boy and I immediately fell in love with you. When I held you for the first time and sang to you, you looked right at me and I am sure I saw you smile. I knew then that you would be musical, and it was at that moment that I made the decision to share everything I know about music with you. I know as you grow up, we will be spending many hours together and I am truly looking forward to it.

Many people will tell you what it takes to be a man but let me share with you what I have learned. The true measure of a man is not his physical strength. To be a man, you must be able to accept others as they are and do your best not to judge them. You must be willing to help when all others turn away. You must be willing to give when all others are taking. You must be able to smile when all others are crying, but not be afraid to shed a tear now and then. You must be willing to accept the blame when you are at fault and the credit when it is due to you.

There will be times in your life when you feel confused, when you're not sure which way to turn or if the decisions you have made are the right ones. It is during those times, David, when you should ask God for His guidance and follow Him. He has helped me many times and I know He will help you as well. Do your best to recognize and appreciate God's blessings and remember to thank Him for each and every day, for they are gifts He has given us, and we should use them wisely.

There are going to be challenges in your life that make you doubt your abilities. You'll be worried that you *don't have what it takes to face what lies ahead of you. Don't be ashamed to admit that you are afraid, but don't let that fear stop you. Always believe in yourself, David. There will be times when you are the only one who does.*

Now, I'm going to tell you four little words that could change your life – always follow your heart. No matter what anyone says or does, always follow your heart. No matter how much they criticize you, or how much they laugh at you, always follow your heart. No matter how wrong they tell you that you are, or how many times they tell you that you can't do it, always follow your heart. It will never steer you wrong.

Even though every physical life has an end, never forget that I am with you. If I can't be there in body, I will be there in spirit and I will be standing beside you in everything you do, cheering you on. You are going to accomplish great things David, and I'll be there to share them all with you. As long as you keep me in your heart, we'll always be together.

Above all else, please remember this. None of us know for sure how long we will be on this beautiful Earth, so always remember to let people know you love them. You may never get another chance.

Thank you for choosing me to be your father. It is an honor I will cherish forever.

I love you, David Anthony.

> *With all my heart,*
> *Your father, Daniel"*

As David finished reading the letter, he began sobbing softly. What his mother said was true—it was almost as if his father knew he wouldn't be alive when David read the letter. David spread the pages out across the table and looked deeply at them. Slowly, he moved his fingertips across the words on each line, feeling the indentations made by the pen his father used to write them. He could hear his father's voice repeating the words of the letter – "Always believe in yourself, David. Never forget that I am with you. I love you, David Anthony" – it was as if he was there in the room. When David glanced again at the reflection of himself in the mirror, he saw something he hadn't noticed before. In the eyes of the child he knew he was, he saw a young man staring back at him.

David took a couple of tissues from the box on the dressing table, dried his eyes and blew his nose. He carefully put the yellowing pages of the letter back in order, folded them and placed them back into the envelope. He laid the envelope face up in front of him on the table so the writing could be seen. David knew now what he had to do, and he finally felt ready to do it.

CHAPTER 9

David ran the brush through his hair one last time then laid it on the table. There was a light knock on the door.

"Come in."

"How's it going in here?" He looked in the mirror and saw Murray standing behind him.

"Okay."

"Just okay?"

"Well, my stomach is doing cartwheels, but I'm not sure if it's from excitement or fear."

"I see," Murray walked over to David's chair and stood behind him. "This is the night we've all been working for." David sat quietly looking at the mirror. sat down beside his friend. "Dave, you don't have to do this. I can go out there and make an announcement that the show's been canceled. We can refund the ticket money and I'll take care of any other issues that may come up. All you have to do is say the word and you can go back to being just David."

He looked at Murray. "Is that possible," he asked, "to go back to being just David?"

"Probably not," Murray admitted, "I mean, everyone knows you now. I can't change that. I guess the difference would be..."

"What I'm known for."

Murray nodded. "It's your decision, Dave."

"Murray?"

"Yeah?"

"Do I look okay?" David asked as he stood from the chair and straightened his clothes. Murray walked back and brushed David's shoulders a little.

"You look great."

"Really?"

"Would I let you go out there if you didn't look your best?"

"No."

"Then take my word for it, you look great."

"We'd better go then," David told him, "we've got a show to do." He looked at Murray's reflection in the mirror and smiled.

Murray looked back at him. "We do?"

"We do."

"Right, we do," Murray agreed. He walked over to the door and opened it, then moved so David could pass. David turned and took a step toward the door, but then paused and turned back to the dressing table. He reached over and lovingly touched the words on the envelope with his fingertips, then closed his eyes and smiled to himself. A moment later he felt a hand on his arm. He looked over at Murray's concerned face. "Ready, kiddo?"

"Ready," David answered. He turned and walked out of the dressing room. Murray followed, closing the door behind them.

As the two men walked along the passageway that would lead them to the stage, David tried hard to stay calm and kept telling himself to relax. Every so often he would hear someone backstage call out to him.

"Good luck!" one yelled.

"Break a leg!" another told him.

He followed Murray up a small flight of metal steps into a darkened area where Brian, the stage manager met them.

"Have a great show, David!" Brian said.

"Thanks."

Murray stood behind David and placed his hands on the boy's shoulders. As David waited, he could hear the band and the singers warming up. He could hear the people milling around in the audience. Every now and then he would hear a few squeals of excitement. *The groupies,* he thought with a little smile. As a member of the crew passed by them, the curtain at the side of the stage brushed against David's hand. His eyes followed it up toward the ceiling. He could see the rigging that held the lights in place, and the steel scaffolding that went across and down to the stage wings on the opposite side. He tried to focus on something sparkling in the darkness, soon realizing it was Casey.

When Casey saw David waiting in the wings, she gave him a small wave; he waved back. She stepped out into the light and turned around slowly so David could see what she was wearing, then gave him an expression as if to ask, "How do I look?" David mouthed back to her, "Wow." Casey nodded a thank you, then twirled her finger at him; David turned around for her. Casey waved her hand in front of her as if the room was hot and David looked away. When he looked back, she smiled at him and gave him a 'thumbs up' sign, to which he mouthed a silent "Thanks".

Suddenly, the house lights dimmed and came back on a few times; the groupies screamed in response.

"What's happening?" he asked.

"Relax," Murray said, "that's just to let the audience know that we're getting ready to start the show."

"Oh." He looked around as the band readied their instruments. He could hear the stage manager doing some final checks and talking to people through his headset.

"Okay, David, this is it. If you're gonna back out, now's the time." David turned and looked at the band, then at Casey waiting with the other dancers on the opposite side. *I can't quit now, Casey has worked too hard for this, she deserves this chance…they all do.* "I gotta know now, Dave."

"Let's do it," David answered without looking away from Casey; he turned to face Murray.

Murray saw a look of confidence in David's face that he hadn't seen before and he nodded in agreement. Murray gave a signal to Brian. "Let's do it," he repeated.

"It's a go!" Brian said into his headset. A few seconds later, the house lights went down and stayed dark and once again, the groupies screamed enthusiastically.

David felt his heart begin to beat faster. "Breath," he told himself, "just breath." He heard the band playing the intro music.

"Here," Murray said, handing him his microphone, "Remember the words to the first song?" David nodded that he did. "Good."

"Place's everyone!" Brian instructed. He leaned toward David and covered the microphone on his headset. "Don't worry, boss, you're gonna be fantastic!" He smiled and winked at David, then went back to his work. When David looked back at the stage, he could see Casey and the other dancers standing on their marks. Cascy looked over at him and waved her hand, trying to hurry him along.

"Still scared?" Murray asked.

"Yes."

"Still wanna do this?"

"Yes."

"The stage is yours," Murray said, motioning to him.

David walked to center stage and took his mark. As he stood in the dark and waited, he heard his father speak to him again—"You are going to accomplish great things David and I'll be there to share them all with you.' David tightened his grip on the microphone as he heard the first notes of the overture start. "Breath," he whispered to himself, then took a deep breath and blew it out slowly, his heart pounding. Just beyond the faint glow of the footlights, he could see his family seated in the front row. He saw Casey's parents seated next to his mother. On Rose's opposite side was an empty chair. David looked a little closer at the vacant seat and saw a picture of his father there. As he closed his eyes, he heard his father's voice once more—"Believe in yourself David." He raised the microphone to his lips, took another deep breath and began to slowly sing the first line of the opening song.

"You've waited so long for someone to love you..."

David paused. As the band finished the chord, a universal scream came back at him from the audience that caught him off guard. He did his best to compose himself and sang the next line.

"To kiss your lips and hold you tight..."

He paused again; this time the screams were twice as loud. As he stood in the shadows, he could see girls in the crowd jumping up and down and clapping wildly. David smiled to himself. Again, the band waited. David felt his fear begin to dissipate as he sang the third line.

"But now I'm here and I'm gonna show you..."

The screams and applause came like a huge wave. David looked to his left and saw Casey standing there. She smiled and winked at him. David straightened up, looked out toward the crowd, and sang the last line of the song's introduction.

"Come over here, girl..."

He paused for the last time as the drums pounded behind him. With each beat of the rhythm, a spotlight appeared on each member of the ensemble. On the final downbeat a bright white spotlight hit David. The crowd went crazy as he sang the remainder of the introduction. "And let me love you right!"

All at once, the stage lit up with a rainbow of colors that pulsated to the beat of the music. The dancers began their routine as David stepped forward and continued the verses, mirroring the dance steps that Casey and the others did as he got caught up in the performance. On the final beat, they snapped into the end position of their routine and the stage went dark. The dancers stood motionless for several seconds as the arena erupted into a frenzy of cheering fans. David stood motionless and out of breath, sweat running down the sides of his face as he looked out at the crowd of screaming girls, some of them in tears. Murray and Claire applauded along with the stage crew.

"Yes! Yes! Yes!" Murray yelled with excitement.

"Perfect!" Claire exclaimed. She and Murray hugged each other. "Did you see that, Murray?? Did you see that??"

"I saw it! I saw it!" Murray answered.

In the audience, David's mother and Casey's parents sat in amazement, as David's brothers and sisters cheered loudly. Cay McCallister reached over and touched Rose's hand.

"Are those really *our* children?" Cay asked Rose.

"Yes, they are!" Rose answered happily.

As the spotlights came up, David stood center stage. The cheers from the crowd became more enthusiastic when they saw him. He stood staring at his fans for a few moments as a smile formed on his face, his eyes surveying every nook and cranny of the arena. There seemed to be a person in every seat for as far as he could see. *So many faces*, he thought. He raised his hand and waved to the massive crowd; they waved back at him, the groupies screaming with excitement, and he laughed out loud at the sight of them.

David stood in awe of the people applauding him. His fear gone, he raised the microphone and spoke to them. "Wow," he said, "this is amazing, you're amazing," He paused as the herd of admirers cheered in response. "Would you like to hear a love song?" The fans screamed their approval and David smiled brightly as he walked back and took his place on a stool that had been put there for him. Casey and the others had already seated themselves on stools to David's left and right with microphones in hand, ready to provide the necessary background vocals of the song. The band began to play as a single spotlight shone on David and the crowd grew silent as he sang a sweet romantic verse.

As Rose listened to her youngest son, she could hear the teenage girls around her swooning. Daniel leaned over to her at the end of the song.

"He's back, Mama," Daniel whispered; Rose smiled.

"Yes," Rose confirmed, "he's been hiding from the world for so long, I thought we'd never reach him again." Daniel took her hand, aware that she was referring to the way David shut down his emotions after their father had died, not seeming to care about anything and now here he was, performing for this enormous crowd.

"What happened to bring him back?" Daniel asked.

"Your father spoke to him," Rose said as her eyes twinkled. Daniel wasn't sure what she meant at first, but a few moments later it came to him.

"Papa's letter?" Rose nodded as she watched David on the stage. "Leave it to Papa, he always knew just what to say." The two of them sat back and watched the remainder of the show.

David thanked the throngs of fans and bid them a good night as the curtain lowered. He followed his fellow performers into the wings where Murray and Claire were waiting.

"Well, how did I do?" David inquired. Murray and Claire looked at each other in astonishment.

"*How did you do*??" Murray asked back as his eyes widened, "*Are you kidding*??"

David looked at them both, unsure of their opinion of his performance. "Was it that bad?" he worried. Murray threw his head back and laughed. "Ackerman, tell me!"

Murray looked him straight in the eyes. "You were *incredible*!!!" He took David's head in his hands and planted a kiss on his forehead.

David looked to his teacher. "Claire?"

"You hit every step," Claire told him with tears in her eyes. She reached over and hugged him.

Murray touched him on the arm. "Listen." As they all stood in the wings, they could hear the crowd chanting 'WE WANT DAVID! WE WANT DAVID!' Murray looked at David. "They want an encore."

"What do I do?"

"Get out there!!" Claire and Murray answered in unison as they pushed him toward the stage. Casey and the other dancers followed as the band members resumed their places. The music director turned to David.

"Ready?" David nodded. The music director gave a nod to Brian who gave the okay to raise the curtain and the music director counted off the song. "One, two, one, two, three, four!" The crowd cheered as David and Casey danced together, then David turned to the crowd and started to sing. As before, the girls in the audience screamed and shouted, they clapped and sang along as they danced in their seats and David watched them as he sang. The more excited they got, the more confident he became, putting all his energy into the final refrain. When the song ended and the stage went dark, David stood trying to catch his breath as the spotlights came up, then he thanked the crowd and bid them goodnight once more, waving as he exited into the wings. Again the spectators continued to cheer, and again the chanting began.

"DAVID! DAVID! DAVID!"

"They want more??" David asked. Murray shrugged his shoulders and smiled. As the curtain rose again, David walked out alone and stopped center stage. As he looked out at the massive crowd of cheering fans, he smiled and shook his head. Slowly, the noise died down to silence; Claire took Murray's hand as they waited to see what David would do.

David looked down at the first row of seats and saw the picture his mother had placed there, his father's loving eyes looking back at him. He saw the smile and the tears on his mother's face. He closed his eyes for a moment to compose himself, then raising a hand to his lips, he blew her a kiss. Rose returned the gesture.

As he looked down the row to his left, David saw his brothers and sisters beaming with pride. *They're all here.* He gave them a quick wave. In return, each sibling held up a little square sign that read '10.5' as if they were judges giving scores and David's smile widened as he laughed out loud. Murray put his arm around Claire as she began to cry.

David glanced over into the wings and motioned for Casey and the others to join him. When she reached center stage, Casey looked down at her parents and waved excitedly. They waved back and blew kisses as David's mother had done. Casey took David's hand and leaned over to him.

"My father's crying," she whispered in amazement; David smiled.

As the clapping died down, David walked back to the music director and whispered something to which the man nodded in agreement. David returned to his place center stage as the dancers all seated themselves on stools to either side of him. The music director spoke quickly to the band, who in turn, rested their instruments and sat silently. As he watched from the wings, Brian spoke through his headset and told the lighting technician to lower the house lights. Sitting alone in the spotlight, David raised the microphone to his lips.

"This one's for you, Papa," he said softly as he glanced toward the heavens. He took a deep breath and began singing a cappella. "Amazing grace...how sweet the sound..." He inhaled again. "That saved a wretch like me..." David fought back his tears. "I once was lost, but now I am found..." He could feel his emotions taking over. "I was blind, but now I see..." His hand began to tremble and his eyes welled as he finished the song. "I was blind, oh, but now I see..." He closed his eyes and felt the tears stream down his cheeks. As he looked out at the audience for the last time, he could see they were giving him a standing ovation. He smiled out at them and blew a kiss into the air as the curtain descended.

Murray rushed out and took David in his arms. The boy sobbed quietly as the two friends stood behind the curtain in the dark while the crowd cheered and applauded wildly on the other side.

CHAPTER 10

Cay and Rose sat in shock of what had just transpired. In just a few short hours, it seemed their children had changed completely. Cay looked at her husband as the house lights came on and saw his tear-stained cheeks.

"My little girl," he said as he stared in wonder at the now quiet stage, "my sweet little girl..."

Cay wrapped her arms around him. "I know, honey," she said, trying to comfort him, "I know."

"Mama!" David's sister Janet exclaimed, "Mama, can you believe it?" Rose smiled brightly at her.

"Little Brother is back!" Patrick said happily to his family. He hugged his mother tightly as the rest of David's siblings gathered around them.

"Excuse me, folks," a security guard said to them, "I was asked to escort you all backstage. Would you follow me please?" The guard headed toward the far side of the stage as Rose, Casey's parents and David's brothers and sisters followed close behind. He led them through the gate and down a back hallway until they came to a group of doors, one of which had David's name posted on it.

"Oh, how cool!" Sandy exclaimed. The guard knocked lightly on the door and within a few seconds, the door opened a crack; Claire peeked out.

"Yes?" When she saw Cay and Rose, she threw the door open and ran out to meet them before the guard could answer. "Come in! Come in!" Claire said as she ushered them through the door. Inside, everyone was chatting away about how the show went. Through the small crowd, Rose managed to find David and he grabbed her and squeezed her tightly.

"Mama!"

"Davey, you were wonderful!" She looked down at his smiling face as her other children crowded around them.

"Cassandra, I had no idea you could...I'm so proud of you," Adam told his daughter as he lovingly touched her cheek.

"Thank you, Daddy!" Casey turned and hugged her mother.

"You looked beautiful, sweetheart."

"Thank you so much for letting me do this! You're the best parents!"

"Well, yeah, we know," Adam joked. Casey and Cay laughed out loud.

The families followed the long hallway that led them through the backstage area. David walked toward the back of the bunch as he talked with Danny.

"I'm really impressed, D."

"Thanks," David replied, "I still can't believe I was able to get through it. I was so nervous; my whole body was shaking. I've never been so scared in my life!"

"You hid your fear well."

"Seriously? You really couldn't tell?"

"Seriously," Danny confirmed.

The group reached the stage door and began filing out into the parking lot behind the arena. They stopped short when they saw the two long black limousines waiting there; Rose looked at Murray in disbelief.

"Murray, these can't be for us," she half insisted. Murray grinned mischievously and raised his eyebrows. A few moments later, Danny and David exited through the stage door and joined them. From the darkness of the distant parking lot came a collective scream that immediately caught their attention.

"*They're still here?*" David asked as he looked in the direction of the sound. Murray walked over to him, his eyes following David's gaze.

"Groupies can be hard to shake sometimes," Murray replied.

Casey's parents gave Claire a curious look. "Fans," Claire explained, "They've probably been out here since the show ended."

"Why?" Adam asked.

"They're waiting for David," Murray told them.

"You're kidding," David's brother Scott said. Murray shook his head and the two families became quiet as they tried to grasp the gravity of the situation.

"What should I do?" David asked him.

"What do you want to do?"

David thought for a moment. "I want to talk to them."

Rose became worried. "I'm not sure if that's a good idea, Davey."

"But they've waited out here all this time, Ma."

"Still, David, it sounds like there are a lot of people over there."

"He'll be fine, Rose," Murray assured her, "the security guards are there, and I'll go with him."

"Are you sure it's safe, Murray?" David sighed heavily and looked at Danny, almost silently begging him to come to the rescue.

"I'll go, too," Danny chimed in.

"Daniel…"

"Ma, the least I can do is say hello to them," David insisted. Rose looked at David as they waited quietly for her response; she touched David's cheek lovingly and sighed.

"Go," she answered. The three of them began walking toward the crowd of admirers, when David suddenly stopped.

"Can Casey come with us?" he asked Murray.

"If she wants to." David looked back at Casey, who looked to her parents.

"You'll make sure she's safe?" Adam asked David with a stern look.

"Daddy!" Casey quietly scolded.

"Yes, sir, I'll take care of her." Casey smiled at David, then looked back at her father. Adam gave his daughter half a smile and nodded toward Murray and the others. Casey ran over to join them and the four continued toward the gathering of fans.

"You'll take care of me?"

"Did I say something wrong?"

"No." As they continued across the parking lot, the screaming grew louder. Back at the cars, Rose's concern increased. Her late husband had dealt with fans and 'groupies', but this felt different, these were screaming teenage girls…lots of them. Her husband had never dealt with this magnitude of admiration in his career and in turn, Rose wasn't sure what to make of it all.

"I'm not sure I like this," she said out loud.

"They'll be okay, Ma," Lisa said as she put her arm around her mother's shoulder.

"I don't know, Lisa." Lisa could see the worry in Rose's face. They had all become concerned about David since their father's death. He had become very introverted, and seemed afraid of so many things – a completely different person than he had been before. Earlier, as she had watched him perform, Rose finally saw the old David emerge again, and she was so relieved to see him come out of the protective shell he had built around himself, but she was still afraid that he wasn't fully prepared to face the world again.

"This is so cool!" Sandy said as her excitement finally bubbled over. They all looked at her. "What? Don't you think it's cool??" Sandy went over to her mother, "Come on Ma, his own concert, backstage passes, David's name on the dressing room door, and now *limos* and *groupies*?" Sandy's eyes widened. "You gotta admit, that's pretty cool!!" Rose grabbed her daughter and hugged her tightly.

"Yes, dear," she agreed, "it's pretty cool!" The others laughed and Rose relaxed a little as she felt the mood lighten.

As the foursome got close to the group of fans, David could finally see the faces that belonged to all the screams; he stopped a few feet away and looked them over. They stood staring back at him, eyes wide and mouths hanging open.

"Hi," David said to the group.

"Hi, David!" they chimed back happily; David smiled.

"Does everyone know Casey?" he asked as he turned toward her. Casey blushed as the fans said their hellos.

"Can I have your autograph?" a pretty girl in the front asked.

"Sure," David said. She handed him a notepad and a pen. David scribbled his name quickly and handed the items back to her. Suddenly it seemed everyone had pens out ready for him to sign.

"Can I have your autograph, too, Casey?" the first girl asked. Casey blushed again as she nodded and took the pen and notepad from the girl.

"So, did you enjoy the show?" David asked them. They all began answering at the same time and he tried hard to follow what they were saying.

"You are *so* cute, David!" one of the girls yelled out and

David felt the blood rush to his face as he thanked the fan for the compliment.

"Will you marry me, David?" another asked.

"Marry you? I'm only sixteen!" As Casey and David continued signing autographs, Murray and Danny stood quietly in the background. When they heard the fan's proposal, Danny laughed.

"Unbelievable," he said softly.

"It's amazing, isn't it?" Murray asked him.

"Unbelievable," Danny repeated.

David and Casey said goodbye to their fans and headed back to the cars with Danny and Murray. As they reached their families, they could tell that everyone was waiting to hear every little detail of their meeting with the 'groupies'.

"What?" he asked innocently. They all stared at him impatiently and David shrugged his shoulders.

"So what happened?" Peggy finally asked him. David looked from one face to the next.

"Well," he began slowly, "they kept screaming and grabbing at me and trying to tear my clothes off; Danny and Murray had to pull them off of me and throw themselves in front of us." He paused and looked at them with the straightest face he could muster. "One of them even asked me to marry her." Rose looked over at Murray and Danny who were trying hard to stifle their laughter.

"David Anthony," she began to scold him. David and Casey looked at each other and started to giggle.

"Okay, so they didn't try to tear my clothes off, but they were screaming for a little while and one of them did propose to me." Rose gave him an exasperated look. "Don't worry, Ma, I turned her down." They all laughed and began to pile into the waiting limousines.

CHAPTER 11

David lay on his bed watching the colorful images move about on the silent television screen. He looked up when he heard the floorboards creak near his bedroom door.

"Whatcha watchin'?" Danny asked.

"Nothin' really."

"Want some company?" Without answering, David moved over to make room for his brother to sit next to him on the bed. The two sat watching as the pictures changed and the reporter's lips moved quickly. "Don't you want to know what they're saying?" Danny asked him after a few minutes. David didn't respond and again, they sat in silence. Several more minutes went by and Danny began to get curious. "D, why don't you turn the sound up?"

"Shhhhh!"

"Dave, what are you…"

"I'm waiting for something," David told him without taking his eyes off the T.V. Danny looked back at the screen and waited. After a few more stagnant minutes, he began to get restless.

"What exactly is it…"

"Hang on," David interrupted, his eyes still glued to the screen.

"Just tell me what…"

"Shhhh! This is it!" He quickly turned up the volume. The two brothers listened intently as the entertainment reporter for the local news talked in detail about David's concert the night before, showed video clips and interviewed fans. After the report ended, David reduced the volume.

"Wow."

"I know," David said, "they've been talking about it all day."

"Really?"

"Uh huh." Daniel glanced over at his baby brother. David had a new sense of maturity about him; the change in his brother made Daniel smile. The two sat in the quiet room and watched as the scenes flickered in front of them.

"Danny, do you ever remember Papa being afraid to go out

on stage?" David asked. Daniel thought about the question.

"Yeah, there were a couple of times I can remember."

"Really? Why can't I remember them?"

"Probably because you hadn't been born yet," Daniel concluded with a laugh.

"That's probably it," David smiled back, "so what happened?"

"What happened?"

"Yeah, what happened? I mean, he still did his show, right?"

"Yeah."

"So why was he so afraid?"

"Well, there were different reasons at different shows," Danny answered, "Why do you want to know?"

"Just wondered," David shrugged, "so how did he handle it?"

"There was only one way to handle it, you go out on the stage and do your show. Papa always said that his job was no different than anyone else's."

"Everyone has a stage," David added.

"Right, and it doesn't matter where your stage is, you gotta go out there and give your best performance every time."

"And it doesn't matter if they like you or not, either way, they'll respect you," David said, finishing his brother's thought.

"Exactly."

"I remember Papa telling me that."

"He was right, ya know." David nodded in agreement and their conversation dropped off as memories of their father flooded their minds. "Look," Daniel said, pointing at the television, "it's on again." David aimed the remote at the set to turn up the volume and they watched as news clips flashed with pieces of his show and more interviews.

"Hey!" David said suddenly, "There's Murray!" They listened as Murray was interviewed by a local news crew.

"David, you're on T.V.!" David's sister shouted as she ran in the room.

"We've been watching it, Sandy," Daniel told her. Sandy sat on the opposite side of David's bed and fixed her eyes on the screen.

"And, as the curtain rose and the footlights glowed, we got our first glimpse of the amazing young phenomenon that is David Steinman." As she finished speaking, the station showed a few moments of David and the others performing their routine during the opening song of the previous night's concert; David and Sandy looked at each other, wide-eyed.

"*Phenomenon*??"

"Daniel," Rose called from downstairs, "can you help me, please?"

"Coming, Ma," Daniel called back as he stood up from the bed. He paused for a few moments as more images of the night before streaked across the set in front of them.

"Daniel?" Rose called again.

"Coming!" he repeated as he hurried down the stairs. A large group of girls appeared on the screen and when the reporter asked them what message they would like to send to David, they all screamed together, "We love you, David!!" Their declaration was followed by shouts of excitement and applause.

"Can you believe that?" Sandy asked.

"Hey," David said, squinting at the screen, "I think she's in my math class."

"What did you need, Ma?" Danny asked as he reached the bottom step.

"Can you put this box on the top shelf of the hall closet for me, please?" Daniel picked up the weighty box and headed for the hallway in the front of the house as Rose followed. He stopped when he reached the closet and waited for his mother to open the doors. "Was David still watching the news reports?" she asked as he slid the box onto the closet shelf.

"Yeah, he said they've been talking about it all day."

"They have."

"Why do I get the feeling you're not too happy about all of this?"

"I'm just not sure this is a good thing for David."

"Why?"

"He's only sixteen, Danny, I'm not sure he's ready for this." She turned and walked back to the kitchen as Danny followed; he sat down at the table as Rose poured him a cup of coffee.

"He seems to be doing all right to me, Ma." Rose looked worriedly into her coffee cup. "Well, has he said or done anything that would give you cause for concern?"

"No, not really," she admitted.

"Then what is it?"

Rose sat next to him at the table. "Your brother has more or less kept to himself since your father passed. He hasn't let anyone outside this family into his life, he doesn't have any close friends, he hasn't tried to be involved in anything at school," she paused, "he hasn't even been on his first date yet, Danny. Now, out of the blue, he's singing in front of thousands of people, they're talking about him on T.V. and teenage girls are screaming that they love him."

Danny smiled. "Ya know, Ma, to a 16-year-old boy, teenage girls screaming that they love you isn't necessarily a bad thing."

Rose looked up from her coffee and smiled back at him. "I know," she replied, "but what happens if they don't love him?"

"I'm not sure I follow you."

"You know how the music business is, Danny. One week they love you and the next, you're old news. I don't think David can handle that kind of rejection." Rose stood and took her cup to the sink as Daniel sat quietly. "I'm his mother, Danny, I'm supposed to protect him." She looked out through the small window above the sink. "I'm just not sure I can protect him from the entire world." As Daniel watched his mother, he could tell that even she was feeling a bit overwhelmed by all that was happening around them.

"I understand how you feel, Mama, but I really think David's gonna be okay with all this."

"But Danny," Rose began as she turned to face him.

"Ma, relax," he said, trying to soothe her nerves. Rose sighed heavily as she leaned back against the counter and folded her arms across her chest; Daniel walked over to her. "You're right, David is young and inexperienced and naïve, and yes, he is only sixteen, but he's a smart kid, Ma, he's got a good head on his shoulders. He may not know everything there is to know about how the world works, but he knows right from wrong, you and

Papa taught him that." As he spoke, a tear escaped down his mother's cheek and Rose quickly wiped it away. "I know you're afraid for him, Ma, we all are – even Murray and Claire are – but we're more excited for him than afraid. Come on, you saw him on that stage, he's *really good*."

"I just don't know, Danny…"

"Well, what would Papa say if he were here?" Daniel posed.

Rose's face softened at the thought. "If your papa were here, he would have taken David down to the club and showed him off to anyone who would listen." They laughed together.

"Think about it," Danny continued, "this is the first time in six years that David has shown any interest in *anything*; this could turn out to be the best thing that's ever happen to him." Rose refilled her cup and walked back to the table; Daniel turned to face her. "David can't hide behind these walls forever Ma, he's got to go out and face the world eventually, and you're gonna have to let him."

Rose sipped her coffee. She knew what Daniel was saying was true, but she just couldn't shake her fears. She wanted David to go out into the world and find his place in it, but this all seemed to be happening so suddenly…

Daniel walked over and kissed his mother. "Try not to worry too much, Mama, David's gonna be fine." Rose looked at her eldest son and sighed. "I gotta run, call me if you need anything."

"I will," she called after him.

Rose sat quietly contemplating her youngest child's future. She wondered how long the excitement would last, and how it would affect him if it ever faded. She was shaken from her thoughts by the sound of pounding feet on the stairs behind her and a few seconds later, David plopped down in the chair that had formerly been occupied by his brother. He sat silent as he rested his head on his palm; Rose watched him for a moment.

"Are they still talking about your show on T.V.?" she asked.

"Yeah."

"Don't you want to watch it?"

"No," he replied, "I'm getting tired of hearing how

wonderful I am… I mean, geez, you'd think they never heard anyone sing a song before." Rose smiled. "I'm gettin' hungry."

"How 'bout we order a pizza?" his mother suggested. David's face brightened.

"Can we get extra cheese?"

"Sure," she answered, "whatever you want."

"Cool!"

"Go ask your sister what kind of pizza she wants." David quickly headed up the stairs, yelling at the top of his lungs.

"Hey, Sandy! Ma wants to know what kind of pizza you want!"

Rose rolled her eyes and shook her head as she laughed. *The outside world may see him differently*, she thought, *but he's still my Davey*.

CHAPTER 12

"Davey!" Rose called up the stairs, "Davey, are you up?"

"Yes!" David called back to her as he started down the steps, Rose turned as he reached the bottom.

"You better hurry or you'll miss your bus," she told him. David dropped down in a chair at the end of the table and poured himself a bowl of cereal, drowned the flakes with milk and shoveled a spoonful into his mouth.

"Very attractive," Sandy said, watching him eat. David shot her a look as milk dribbled down his chin; Sandy tossed a napkin at him.

"All right you two," Rose scolded them, "Sandy, leave your brother alone. David…"

"I'm going, I'm going," he interrupted. He gulped down the last few bites of cereal from the bowl and wiped his mouth, grabbed his backpack and headed quickly toward the door.

"David," Rose said as she followed him, "David!"

He spun around to face her. "What?"

Rose cradled his face in her hands. "I love you," she smiled at him.

"I love you, too, Ma."

Rose kissed him and watched as he headed out for the bus stop. When he was out of sight, she went back to the kitchen and started clearing the breakfast dishes from the table. Sandy sat quietly munching on cinnamon toast and hovering over one of her college textbooks. Rose poured a cup of coffee and joined her at the table. About halfway through her coffee the door opened and Rose looked up from the paper she was reading to see her youngest son standing in the kitchen doorway.

"You missed the bus?" David nodded. "Davey…" she sighed, "Well, I guess Sandy will have to give you a ride then."

Sandy looked over her shoulder at them. "But I'll be late for my class," she argued.

"Not if you go now."

"All right, c'mon," Sandy gathered her books. She picked up her purse and keys from the table by the door and headed out to her car with her brother in tow.

"Thanks for the ride, Sandy," David said after they had driven a while.

"No problem," she answered, "just don't get used to it." David smiled. "So will you and Casey have the same schedule again this year?"

"No," he said, "we got to pick our own electives. We might be in a couple classes together, though."

"Well, have fun!" Sandy joked as she pulled up to the curb.

"Yeah, right!" David laughed. He got out of the car and waved to his sister as she drove away.

David turned around and looked at the massive school building. He thought back to the first day of his sophomore year and remembered stepping off the bus and feeling very small compared to the other students. He remembered how afraid he was to talk to anyone and how alone he felt in this strange new place... he also remembered all the curious looks he'd received from people he'd never met and noticed he was getting those same looks now from some of the new sophomores. *Some things never change,* he thought. As he glanced around, David noticed small groups starting to form near him. He decided it might be a good idea not to stay in one place for too long and started walking toward the main entrance of the building.

David could feel many eyes following him as he walked across the plaza in front of the school. He could hear girls whisper to each other as he passed. Memories from the prior school year filled his mind again. The whispers and stares caught him by surprise last year and he didn't know what to make of it all, but today, he felt differently about it. As he passed by one small group of girls, he heard them giggle. David turned and gave them a smile.

"Hi," he said as they became quiet and their eyes widened, "I'm David." He took a couple steps toward them. "Is this your first year here?" The girls nodded their heads slowly as they continued to stare. "Well, if you need help finding your classes, just ask." He waited a few seconds as they stood frozen in shock. "See you later," he said giving them another friendly smile. He turned and began walking toward the school again. His smile grew as he heard them trying to suppress their squeals of excitement.

David opened the door and entered the main lobby of the school where many students had gathered. They were all chatting and getting reacquainted after their summer vacations and paid him no mind. David looked around for someone familiar and went over to join the conversation.

"Hey," he said to the girl in front of him; she turned around quickly.

"David!" Casey said excitedly, "I've been looking for you!"

"Here I am," he smiled.

"I didn't see you get off the bus."

"Um, I missed the bus."

"On the first day?" she asked in amazement.

David laughed a little. "Yeah, Sandy gave me a ride."

Casey shook her head. "What am I gonna do with you?" David shrugged. Casey turned back to the group. "Look who I found," she said.

"Hi, David," they greeted him.

"Hi, guys." The morning bell rang to signal the start of the day. The groups began to disperse as the students headed for their respective classrooms.

"Well, are you ready?" Casey asked him as they walked together.

"I think so."

"I'll see you later. Have a good day!"

"You, too." David waited until she had vanished up the stairs, then turned and headed toward one of the hallways in the back half of the building where his homeroom class was located. He walked casually into the room, found a vacant seat and tried to settle in for what he assumed would be a long and uneventful day.

David decided to pass the time by making a list of his classes for Casey when the teacher gave out their schedules. He took a notebook and pen from his backpack and opened the notebook to the first blank page, but before he could make a mark he felt a light tap on his right shoulder. He turned his head and saw a pretty blond sitting beside him.

"Hi, David," she smiled.

"Hi."

"You remember me, Tara, from homeroom last year?" David looked at her skeptically. "You *do* remember me, don't you?"

"Yeah, I remember you."

"I knew you would," she replied with feigned sweetness, "I'm having a party at my house this weekend. It's a pool party—kind of a last-fling-of-the-summer type of thing—and I'm inviting you."

"Well, my weekends are kinda busy these days," he told her.

"Why don't I give you my number anyway, you know, just in case," she said, winking at him. She pulled a small heart-shaped post-it notepad from her purse. "May I use your pen?" she asked as she batted her mascara-enhanced eyelashes at him. David handed it to her and she used it to jot down her information. When she was finished she stood from the chair, stepped closer to David and leaned over so her face was next to his. "Here," she said quietly. She gently pressed her lips to the paper to leave an impression before sticking it onto the open page of his notebook. "Call me if you happen to find some free time," she whispered. David stared at the note. "You won't forget, will you?"

"No, I won't forget." Tara ran her finger through the hair at the nape of his neck. David watched her as she walked back to her desk and sat down. It was then that he realized the entire homeroom had watched as the scene between he and Tara played out.

"David," Mr. Peyton said as he entered the room.

"Yes, sir?"

"The principal would like to see you in the gym."

"In the gym?"

"In the gym," Mr. Peyton repeated. David shoved his notebook and pen into his backpack and walked up to the teacher's desk. "Here's your locker number and combination and your class schedule."

"Thanks," David replied as he took the papers. He exited his homeroom and turned left down the hallway toward the north end of the school. "In the gym?" he said to himself as he walked. When he reached the hall that ran between the gym and the music department, he saw several teachers there. He knew from his experience the year before, that these were the teachers who would be getting classes of new sophomore students. Mr. Blake, the assistant principal for the junior class, met him at the gymnasium door.

"There he is!" Mr. Blake said cheerfully.

"Did you want to see me, Mr. Blake?"

"Yes, David, come with me," he said as he led the young man through the double doors. David was amazed to see the entire sophomore class looking down at him from the bleachers. He stopped for a few moments, unable to move. Mr. Blake quickly came back and guided him to the podium where the school's principal was standing.

Mr. Connelly smiled at David when he saw him. "Hello, David."

"Hi," David said anxiously, "what's going on? Did I fail tenth grade?"

"No, no, David," Mr. Connelly chuckled, "it's nothing like that. We thought it would be a good idea for the new sophomores to meet you now so they won't be so surprised when they see you during the school day."

"Meet me?" David asked, "All of them?" He looked at all the young expectant faces. "*Individually?*"

"No, David," Mr. Blake assured him as he slowly ushered him toward the podium, "we'd just like you to say a few words to the class as a group."

"But do you really think this is a good idea?" he asked as the last half of his question echoed through the microphone. David stood unnerved at the podium and looked out at the expectant faces of his new classmates with an uneasy smile. "Hi," he said, "I'm David Steinman." His introduction was met by loud applause and several screams, David felt his cheeks warm as he waited for the crowd to quiet down. "Um…welcome to Park High," he stuttered.

He paused as he desperately searched his mind for something witty to say, but nothing came to him and he began to think it might be easier if he broke out in song. He looked to his right and then to his left as Mr. Blake and Mr. Connelly looked on happily from both sides. "You'll like going to school here, the teachers are really nice and everyone is very helpful." He paused again, having no idea what they expected him to say. His palms began to sweat and his mouth became very dry. "If you need help finding your classes, don't be afraid to ask someone," he forced out. He gave Mr. Connelly a panicked looked and the principal stepped over and put his arm around the boy's shoulders.

"That's very good advice, David," he agreed, "Folks, if there's anything you need help with or any questions you might have, please don't hesitate to ask. We're all happy to help you." He smiled down at David. "Why don't we give David a round of applause for visiting with us?" The students began to cheer again. "Thank you, David, you can go back to your homeroom."

"Yes, sir." David waved to the sophomores and tried hard to look appreciative as he headed for the hallway, doing his best to keep as normal a pace as possible. Once he was out of their line of sight, he made a beeline for the boy's restroom, knowing it was one of the few places in the building where he would be left alone. He locked himself in the farthest stall and leaned back against the wall of the room.

David closed his eyes and tried to wrap his mind around what had just taken place. He could feel his heart pounding in his chest, and he breathed as deeply as he could to slow it. After a few minutes he began to relax and decided to make his way back to class before the mass of students from the gym invaded the halls.

The final bell of the day pealed loudly, and students poured from the many doorways that speckled the long halls of the high school. David swung his backpack over one shoulder and snaked his way through the crowds toward the front doors. When he reached the main lobby, he met up with Casey just as he had that morning.

"Hi, stranger!" Casey greeted him.

"Hi," he returned as they walked toward the doors, "I haven't seen you all day!"

"I know," she said, "what classes did you get?" They exchanged schedules as they continued to follow the swell of people that flowed through the doorway and spilled out onto the front plaza.

David squinted to see as the hot afternoon sun shone in his face. "We don't have any classes together at all," he said, "not even lunch." Casey looked back and forth from one schedule to the other.

"Well, at least we'll have something to talk about later," Casey said as they continued toward the row of buses. David smiled and shook his head.

"What?"

"Nothing," he laughed. They joined the other students who were waiting to board the bus.

"You're gonna ride the bus?" a boy behind David asked.

"Yeah," David answered.

"Then do you mind if we use the limo?" another boy asked, smiling eagerly.

David looked at him strangely. "Limo?"

"Yeah," the boy said pointing to the curb in front of the school bus, "the limo!"

David looked to his right and saw Murray leaning with his back against the vehicle and the car's driver standing beside him; he and Casey walked over to them.

"Murray, what are you doing here?" he asked.

"I came to pick you up."

"Why, is there something wrong?"

"No."

"Everybody's okay?"

"Everyone's fine," Murray assured him.

"Then why are you here?"

"We managed to squeeze in a last-minute interview at one of the local radio stations, I thought it would be faster if I just picked you up."

"In a limo?"

"Yeah."

"*Here?*"

"Yeah, why?"

"Why??" David looked around at the groups of onlookers that had started to gather.

"Dave, it's just a car."

"Murray, it's a *limousine.*"

"Well, I thought you might need some extra room to do your homework."

"Who does their homework in a limousine?"

"Um, we do," Casey told him. The driver opened the back door for them as Casey led him by the elbow toward the car. David looked around at the many eyes that were watching them, then looked back to Murray, who just shrugged. He let out a sigh as he slid onto the seat beside Casey. Murray glanced back at the gawking teenagers and gave them a quick smile and a friendly wave as he disappeared into the classy black automobile.

CHAPTER 13

Casey stood quietly in the doorway of her parent's bedroom and watched as her mother styled her hair in front of the vanity mirror. After adjusting a few last strands, Cadence looked over at her.

"Well, how do I look?"

"Beautiful," Casey answered.

"Thank you," she smiled.

"Can I ask you a personal question, Mom?"

"Sure," Cay said, turning away from the mirror to give Casey her full attention, "what's on your mind?"

"How did you know you were in love with Daddy?"

"Why do you want to know that?" Cay asked with surprise.

Casey shrugged. "I was just curious."

Cay stood up and walked over to the closet. "Well," she began, "I'm not really sure." She stopped and thought for a couple of moments. "We were just friends for quite a while." She pulled a dress from the closet as Casey came into the room and sat down on the bed. "But I do remember one particular day when we were out socializing with some other close friends. We had gone to a dance and there were some girls there that didn't have dates, wallflowers, we used to call them," she paused as the pictures of that night filled her mind. Cay sat on the bed next to her daughter.

"All during the time we were there, there was one little girl that no one had asked to dance. She looked so sad and lonely and it just broke my heart, your father asked me what was wrong, so I told him. Just at that point, they announced that it was the last dance of the evening, so we all paired up with our dates, but that poor little girl just sat there all alone, I just couldn't take my eyes off of her."

"How awful," Casey sympathized.

"I thought so, too, but then Adam asked if I minded if he danced with her. I told him I didn't mind at all, so he excused himself and went over to her. The way her face brightened when he asked her to dance made my night." Cay smiled at her. "On the way home, the other boys teased him about dancing with her and my friends said I shouldn't have let him do it, but I understood why he danced with her, so it didn't bother me."

"That's when you fell in love with him?"

"I don't know if that's when I fell in love with him, but I did see him in a different light after that," she concluded. "He just seemed more mature to me, more grown up than most of the boys I knew. I really didn't mind giving up that one dance with him," she recalled, "somehow I just knew there would be many more dances in our future to make up for it." Casey smiled at her. "So, tell me young lady, why all these questions about being in love?"

Casey looked away from her and shrugged again. "I don't know."

"Do you think you might be in love with someone?" Casey sat silent. "Is it David?" Again there was silence. "Cassandra, look at me." Casey turned to her mother. "Is it David?" The girl still didn't answer, but Cay could tell from the look in her eyes that she was right. She wrapped her arms around her daughter and held her for a few moments, then looked at Casey again and wiped the tears from her face. "Does he know?" Casey shook her head. "Then you have to tell him."

"No, Mom," she answered as fear filled her eyes.

"Casey..."

"I can't tell him I'm in love with him, he'll just think..."

"What? What will he think?" Casey wiped more tears away. "That you're stupid or silly?"

"That I'm just a crazy fan, like all those other girls who are always screaming that they love him and want to marry him. He'll think I took this job just to get close to him."

"Oh, sweetie, he would never think that about you, David knows how serious you are about your dancing career."

"What if he doesn't love me?" Casey asked, "What if we have to stop working together? I couldn't take that, Mom."

"Casey, that won't happen."

"But what if it does?"

"It won't."

"How can you be so sure?" Casey stood up from the bed and walked to the mirror. Cay walked over and stood behind her.

"Cassandra, nothing bad ever came from telling someone that they're loved."

"I just don't want to lose him, Mom," Casey admitted.

"You won't lose him," Cay told her confidently. Casey

looked up at their reflections in the mirror.

"Do you really think he could be in love with me?"

Cay leaned forward, wrapped her arms around Casey's shoulders and laid her cheek against her daughter's. "How could he not love you?"

CHAPTER 14

David lay on the bed listening to music from his CD player and trying to unwind after a busy day of rehearsals. It seemed the more popular he became the harder he had to work at it. He thought it was rather ironic, since he had never really wanted to be one of the 'popular' people, but this career he had inadvertently stumbled into apparently wasn't going away anytime soon, so he figured he might as well make the best of it. He closed his eyes in an attempt to drift off into some much-needed sleep, but just as he was getting lost in the melody of the song that was playing, there was a knock at his bedroom door.

"Who is it?" he called, hoping the annoyed tone of his voice didn't show.

"It's Casey," replied the voice behind the door, "I'm sorry if I woke you but…" David opened the door before she could finish.

"It's okay, I wasn't sleeping, I was just listening to some music."

"I couldn't sleep. I didn't want to wake your sister and I really didn't want to sit there alone in the dark… I thought you might be having trouble sleeping, too."

"I always have trouble sleeping."

"I know," Casey smiled at him, "I thought maybe I could sit with you for a while. Do you mind?"

"No," he replied, "come on in." He stepped back and opened the door so she could pass through. "You wanna watch TV?" he asked nervously.

"I'd rather listen to the music, it's very relaxing. Is it okay if I sit down?"

"Yeah, sure, sit anywhere you like." Casey sat down on the side of David's bed and waited as David stood at the door.

"Is this okay?" Casey asked, a little unsure of herself.

"It's fine."

"Do you want to talk for a while?" David nodded and closed the door; he sat down next to Casey.

"What do you want to talk about?" he asked, trying to breathe as normally as possible.

"I don't know," she shrugged, "anything you want." David

hesitated. When they were onstage together, he knew exactly what to say and do, but offstage he still felt awkward around her.

"David, I have a confession to make."

"A confession?"

"Yes."

"What is it?"

"I…" she stopped abruptly and sat looking at him for a few seconds before turning away, "never mind."

"What's wrong, Case?"

"Nothing, I'm just a little embarrassed, that's all."

"Embarrassed? About what?"

"It's nothing, just forget I even mentioned it."

"You don't have to feel embarrassed, Casey," he said, turning his body to face her, "you can tell me anything."

"Really?"

"Of course, we're friends, right?"

"Yeah… friends."

"But if you don't want to tell me, that's okay, too. I mean, if you'd rather not…"

"No, I want to tell you. I've wanted to tell you for a while now."

"Okay, what do you want to tell me?"

"I… I wanted to tell you…" she paused as she tried to gather her courage.

"What?"

"I wanted to tell you… that I love you, David."

David felt the air go out of his chest; Casey looked away. David reached over and touched her hand and when she raised her face to meet his, she noticed a tear on his cheek.

"What did you say?" he asked her in almost a whisper.

"I said… I love you, David," Casey repeated quietly. "I'm sorry, I shouldn't have said anything."

Completely amazed at what he was hearing, David closed his eyes and lowered his head, unable to stop his tears… she loved him… Casey *loved* him. He wanted to wrap his arms around her and never let go, he wanted to climb up on the rooftop and tell the world "She loves me!!" For the first time in his entire life, he actually *wanted* to dance.

"David, I'm sorry, I didn't mean to…" she paused for a

moment, trying to hold back her own tears, "I just wanted you to know how I felt."

"Case…"

"It's okay if you don't feel the same," she said, stopping him.

"Casey…"

"Really David, you don't have to…"

"I love you Casey, I have since the day we met," he finally admitted.

"But… why didn't you say something?"

"I was so afraid you might not love me." He lowered his head again.

"Kiss me, David."

He looked up at her slowly. "What?"

"Kiss me… please?"

A wave of excitement flowed through him, immediately followed by a wave of anxiety. He had dreamed about kissing Casey more times than he could remember, but now that the moment was here, he wasn't sure if he could get through it.

Casey leaned toward him and as her lips got closer to his, he felt the blood rush to his feet. His heart raced as the waves of excitement and anxiety came back over him again and he began to feel faint as her lips pressed gently against his. David closed his eyes as all his emotions welled up inside him and when their tongues met, Casey could taste his tears; she caressed his cheek with her fingertips. As the kiss ended and Casey moved away, David's eyes met hers and he knew his naivety was showing.

"You've never kissed a girl before, have you?"

"I was praying you would be my first."

"Me too." She gave him a smile, then leaned over and gently kissed him again, laying her forehead against his as she closed her eyes. "I love you David."

"I love you too, Casey."

CHAPTER 15

Rose straightened the knot on David's tie and smoothed his collar. She looked at his face and smiled softly as her eyes began to mist over and David knew she was about to cry.

"Ma, don't," he pleaded.

"I'm sorry," Rose said as she attempted to stifle her tears, "it's just so hard to believe you're graduating already."

"It's hard to believe I'm graduating at all," David joked.

"I'm very proud of you, David."

"Thanks Ma," he answered, "So, where is everyone?"

"They're all out in their seats. Murray and I thought it would be better if everyone waited until we were back at the house before they tried to see you. We didn't want to cause any problems with security."

"Can you believe all of that?" David asked, rolling his eyes, "It's just a high school graduation, for Pete's sake!"

"Calm down," Rose said, "they're just being cautious."

David huffed slightly as he rolled his eyes again. "They could have just mailed my diploma to me and avoided all this mess."

"David Steinman, I will not let you deprive me of the privilege of seeing my youngest child graduate from high school," she told him, "Now fix your robe." Murray entered the room as David zipped the front of his robe closed.

"Just about ready kiddo?"

"Yeah," David answered. Just as he started toward the door, Rose quickly reached up to straighten her son's hair. David and Murray stopped and waited as she paused for a moment to look him over.

"Satisfied?" Murray asked. Rose nodded and took a step back. "Don't forget to smile for the cameras!" Murray grinned at David as he handed him his mortarboard.

David sighed heavily. "This is so embarrassing." He took the hat from Murray and followed him out into the corridor where two security guards were waiting.

"This way, please," one of the guards said. He led them into a large room where half the senior class had already gathered.

"We'll see you later, sweetheart," Rose told him, kissing

him on the cheek.

"Okay Ma," he said as they left him at the door. As he continued into the room, the student's chatter quieted some and David felt his face getting warm. A teacher at the front of the room motioned for him to follow her. She stopped near the middle of one of the rows and began checking her chart to find David's alphabetical spot.

"Let's see," she said, "Sorenson, Speakman, Squire, Stackhouse, Stammons, Stark, Steinman, Summers…" The teacher paused and looked up at the students. "What's your last name?" she asked one boy.

"Stark," the boy answered.

"And you are?" she asked the petite girl behind him.

"Summers."

"Okay," the teacher said, "you go here." She took David by the elbow and moved him to a spot between the two students. The classmates went back to talking amongst themselves as they waited for the festivities to begin. "All right, folks," the teacher announced from the front of the room, "let's quiet down. We'll be starting in about five minutes, so please zip up your robes and put on your caps." David opened his cap and looked it over, trying to discern the front from the back and after spinning it back and forth in his hands a few times, he stood staring at it in defeat.

"Do you need some help?" said a tiny voice from behind him. David turned to his classmate, nodded and handed her his cap. He stooped down as she placed the hat on his head and positioned it correctly. After she adjusted his hair and smoothed the tassel for him, David stood up straight. "There," she said, "perfect!"

"Thanks," David replied as he blushed.

"How do I look?" she asked him with an excited smile.

"Perfect," David smiled back at her.

The girl extended her hand to him. "Sheila Summers."

"David Steinman." Sheila giggled at his introduction. "What's so funny?"

"I already know your name," she reminded him.

"Right," David smiled, "I forgot." He stood lost in his embarrassment.

"Ladies and gentlemen, may I have your attention, please?" The students turned to face the front of the room where their school principle stood to address them. "I wanted to speak to you before the ceremonies begin. As you all know, there are a lot of reporters and a lot of photographers in the audience tonight, and we all know why they're here." David felt his face heat up again as heads turned in his direction. "I am expecting all of you to be on your best behavior. I want you to remember that anything you say or do will not only reflect on you, but also on our school and on your family members who are here tonight. I ask that you treat each other with dignity and respect and try to make this a night that you can all look back on with pride." Mr. Connelly paused a moment. "On a more personal note, I'd like to say that it has been a privilege serving as your principle during the past three years. I am extremely proud of every one of you and I wish you all good luck and prosperity in the years ahead. Congratulations to you all. Now, let's all just try to relax and enjoy the evening."

The students gave Mr. Connelly a round of applause as he left the room, then went back to their personal conversations. David stood quietly, listening to the voices around him. Every so often, he would hear his name whispered quickly; he closed his eyes and thought about Casey. How he wished she was there beside him, but unfortunately, Casey had to meet with the other half of the senior class in a room on the opposite side of the arena. He wouldn't be able to see her until sometime during the ceremony. *I hope she's doing better than I am*, he thought.

"Okay, folks, get ready!" The teacher stood by the door of the room and prepared to start the procession of students.

David looked toward the front as everyone took their places in line. He could hear the band playing "Pomp and Circumstance". As the students began leaving the room in single file lines, David felt his heart flutter. He inhaled deeply, trying to calm himself and after rubbing his hands together in a futile effort to dry the sweat from his palms, he lowered them to his sides and shook them to get his nerves out.

"David," a lowered voice spoke to him, "hey, David!" David looked at the boy in the line next to him. "Relax man, relax," the boy smiled at him sarcastically, the other graduates in the lines around them smiled and giggled. David tried to smile back, then turned back toward the front of the room. As the line beside them began to leave, David felt a small hand touch his elbow. He turned to see Sheila smiling at him and her excited expression made him laugh, relieving some of the anxiety he was feeling.

The students left the confines of the meeting room, passing through a group of photographers that had gathered near the door. David tried to ignore the annoying flashes from the cameras as they began taking pictures of him. He wanted today to be as normal as possible, though he knew it was fruitless.

The students lined up in front of the rows of chairs that had been set up on the arena floor. As they waited for their signal to be seated, David scanned the crowd of blue and white robes trying to locate Casey. He stood on tip toes to see over the heads in front of him and finally, off to his far right and about three rows ahead, he recognized her long flow of silky brown hair that hung down her back. Seeing her there made him feel less alone in the sea of people that surrounded them.

As the band played the National Anthem, David glanced over at Casey again. This time she had turned and was staring in his direction. Casey made a silly face at him and David looked away to stop himself from laughing.

Before long, the ceremony was underway. The students listened as speeches were given and applauded when it was required, until finally Mr. Connelly spoke the words they had been waiting for.

"Ladies and Gentlemen, it is with great pride that we now present to you the Park High School graduating class of 2015!" Ushers guided the students up the ramp one by one so they could cross the stage when their names were announced. Various teachers and education board members took turns handing out the diplomas. Casey reached the top of the ramp and waited for her name to be called.

"Miss Cassandra Lee McCallister!" the announcer's voice said over the loudspeaker. As her family and friends cheered for her from the stands, Casey walked to the center of the stage where one of her teachers was waiting with her diploma. The photographer's cameras clicked as flashes went off all around them.

"Congratulations, Casey!" Mrs. Wilson said to her as they hugged, "Good Luck!"

"Thank you!"

"You take care of that young man of yours, now, he needs you."

"I will!" Casey assured her. Casey glanced out at David and smiled brightly. As she exited the stage on the opposite side, she looked up in the stands and waved to her parents, then returned to her seat.

After several minutes and what seemed like a thousand more names, it was David's turn. As he stood at the top of the ramp waiting for Mr. Stark to receive his diploma and leave the stage, he could feel all the eyes in the crowd beginning to focus on him. Mr. Connelly reached over and took a diploma from the stack on the small table to his right, then looked at David and smiled. David smiled weakly back at him as the photographers got into position to get their best shot. Looking off to one side, he saw a TV crew getting ready to film his graduation for the evening news. *Oh God*, he thought, *please just say my name!* As if in response to his silent wish, the announcer spoke.

"Mr. David Anthony Steinman!" David crossed the stage and reached out to shake Mr. Connelly's hand. As the two stood posed for the cameras, David's family and friends cheered and whistled for him. Here and there a fan who was lucky enough to have a family member in the same graduating class could be heard screaming in the distance.

"The whole family's here, huh?" Mr. Connelly teased.

"Yes sir."

"Well, they have a right to be proud, keep up the good work son!"

"I will Mr. Connelly."

"Good luck and congratulations, David!"

"Thank you, sir," David smiled as the handshake ended. He continued across the stage and down the exit ramp, looking up at his family as he passed. Bright flashes exploded around him as he walked back to his seat among the rest of the students.

Everyone waited patiently as the rest of the diplomas were handed out and the benediction was given. After the ceremony ended, the graduates were escorted out of the main arena in the same fashion as they had entered and gathered back in their original meeting rooms. The students soon found their friends and were chatting away about the festivities and their party plans for later.

David entered the room and walked quietly to a back corner, where he leaned against the wall and looked at the envelope in his hand. "David Anthony Steinman" the typed words read. He pulled the folder out and opened it. There was his name again in Old English-style writing. He passed his fingers over the letters as he stared at it. He could feel the edges and bumps of all the swirls and swashes the letters made. Closing the folder, he slid it back into the protective envelope, then looked around the room. *That's it*, he thought, *high school is finally finished*.

As caps and gowns were removed, his former classmates began to leave to meet up with their parents. David watched from his corner and waited and after a few minutes, a security guard came to speak with him.

"If you don't mind, Mr. Steinman, we're just gonna have you wait here until most of the other students and their families have gone, just so there won't be any kind of problems or issues. That way we can avoid any traffic jams and such. You understand, don't you?"

"Yeah, I understand," David said. The security guard thanked him and walked away, leaving David alone once more. He reached up and took the cap from his head, running his fingers through his hair to straighten it.

"Perfect," he heard a small voice say. He looked up to see Sheila Summers grinning at him and he laughed a little in response. "Congratulations, Mr. David Anthony Steinman."

"Thank you, and congratulations to you, Miss Summers."

"Thank you! Is your family having a party for you?"

"Oh, I'm sure they've got something planned," David answered.

"Well, I thought they might, but if by chance they don't, you're more than welcome to join me and my family at our house for a graduation party."

"All my brothers and sisters are in town and I really want to visit with them, so I'm not really sure that I'll have time to go anywhere tonight, but thank you anyway for the invitation, you were sweet to think of me."

"Oh, that's okay, I understand," Sheila assured him, "I just didn't want you to be alone on your graduation night." She paused for a moment. "Well, my mom's waiting so I gotta go. Good luck!"

"You too," David said as she started to leave.

"Bye David."

"Bye Sheila." David stood alone and waited as the room slowly emptied. He sat down on a nearby chair and leaned over, resting his head on his fists for a few minutes.

"Hey, you okay?" David looked up to see Murray standing beside him.

"Yeah, just a little worn out."

"Well, it's no wonder, with all this 'Pomp and Circumstance' going on," Murray commented with a sly grin. David rolled his eyes and groaned. "Bad joke, huh?"

"Very bad!" David laughed.

"Come on, kiddo," Murray nodded toward the door, "let's go home."

CHAPTER 16

David leaned his elbows on the hard metal railing that followed the aisle in front of the upper balcony seats. He looked out over the arena and watched as the stage hands and various members of the road crew worked diligently to ready the arena for that night's show. His mind filled with memories of all that he had done over the last couple of years. As incredible as it had all been, he couldn't shake the feeling that he had missed something important.

"Hell of a view, isn't it?"

David looked to his left and saw Murray standing at the top of the stairs. "Yeah," he replied as he looked back out over the expanse before him. Murray walked over and joined him at the railing. The two men stood quietly for a while as the hustle and bustle below them continued. "Murray, what would you say if I told you I didn't want to do this anymore?"

"You mean touring?"

"Not just touring," David clarified. Murray glanced over at him, then looked back out over the arena without answering. "I've been thinking a lot about it lately. We've been on the road since graduation and everything is moving so fast. I really haven't had a chance to stop and think about what I want to do with the rest of my life. When I hear about all the things people are involved in – all the good they're doing, all the people they're helping – it makes singing and dancing for a living seem so trivial and unimportant." He looked at his friend. "I don't mean to sound ungrateful, I'm not, I'm extremely grateful for everything you've done for me Murray." He looked down at the stage below them. "It's just that I can't help wondering if there's something else out there for me."

Murray stood for a few moments as he took in everything David had told him. He had wondered when the day would come when David would want to venture out into the world on his own. What they had accomplished together had been amazing, but he knew it would someday come to an end and when it did, he would have to let David go.

"A few years back, there was a young lady who came to one of my auditions and she sang a song for me with so much depth and tenderness and emotion… it just took my breath away.

When I asked her why she had chosen that particular song, she told me her father used to sing her to sleep with that song when she was a little girl. It really struck a chord with me and now whenever I start thinking that what we do is unimportant and trivial, I think about what that song means to Casey." Murray paused, remembering the moment. "The way I see it, if only *one* line from only *one* of the songs we've put out there touches at least *one* person's heart that deeply, then it's important to *them*, and everything we've gone through to bring that song out into the open so it can be heard was worth it." Neither of them moved their gaze from the happenings below.

"I can't tell you how to live your life, Dave, that's something you have to decide for yourself. If you feel you need to move on to something else, then move on. I have no doubt you'll be successful in whatever you choose to do. Just remember, if you ever decide to come back to this, I'll be here for you."

Murray paused a moment before heading quickly down the concrete steps and leaving David alone once more. David turned just as Murray disappeared around the wall of the stairwell. He sat down in one of the many empty seats, draping his leg over the chair arm and laid his head back as thoughts raced through his mind. Did he need to move on to something else? If he did, where would he go, what would he do? Should he leave the music behind him – could he leave it? – and what about Casey, would she be willing to leave with him, or would they have to end their relationship and go their separate ways? His heart ached at the thought.

David glanced around the arena, feeling miniscule in its vastness. He thought of all the people who would soon occupy the uninhabited seats that surrounded him. Could the songs he sang really be as important to them as Murray suggested? Did they really make a difference in the lives of the people who heard them? He closed his eyes and laid his head back again, trying desperately to quiet his mind.

"David…" The young man stirred slightly at the sound of his name. "David…" the voice said again.

He felt a gentle hand on his shoulder and turned slowly to see who was there with him. Through blurry eyes he saw the figure of a tall man with features similar to his.

"Papa?"

The man smiled warmly. "Hello son." David sat up straight and held his hand up to shield his eyes against the glare of the bright house lights. He looked again at the man standing before him.

"Is it really you, Papa?"

"Yes son, it's really me."

David felt confused. "But it can't be... how can it be you?"

"Do you remember the letter I wrote to you Davey? I told you I would always be with you as long as you kept me in your heart."

"Yes sir, I remember."

"Then you shouldn't be so surprised to see me here now." David was speechless as his father sat down in the seat next to him. He looked into Daniel's eyes and saw all the love and kindness he remembered seeing as a child.

"I've missed you Papa," David told him as his voice waivered some.

"I've missed you too, Davey."

"Why did you have to go?"

Daniel reached over and wiped a tear from his young son's cheek. "That's not important now. What's important is why I came back. I know there is something that has been weighing heavy on your heart."

"Yes," David answered.

"Talk to me son. Let me help you."

"I... I don't know what to do now, I don't know where to go..."

"You're unsure of which road you should travel in your life?"

"Yes," David confirmed, "I love what I do—honestly, I do—and I love all the people around me, but lately I've felt that I should be doing something else, something more important... something more tangible."

"Yes, I've felt the conflict in your heart."

"You have?"

"I live within you David; I feel everything you feel."

"Then tell me what I should do Papa."

"You already know what to do Davey, you've always known, from the very moment you were born, you've known."

"I don't understand, how could I know?"

"David, everyone one of us is born into this life knowing exactly who we are and why we are here. All you have to do is quiet your mind and listen to the voice within you."

"Your voice?" David asked.

"No," Daniel replied, "your voice. It's the voice of your soul Davey. If you quiet your mind and listen, then the answer will become clear." David tried hard to comprehend what his father was telling him. "I have to go now," Daniel told him as he stood up from the seat beside his son, "I am so proud of you Davey."

"No, Papa, please don't go!" David begged him. "Please stay with me!"

"Oh, Davey, I'm always with you," Daniel told him as he gently touched his son's chest, "remember?" He turned and began walking away as David watched through tear filled eyes.

"Papa wait, please!" Daniel stopped and turned to face his youngest child. "I love you Papa."

Daniel smiled at him. "And I love you Davey." He blew a kiss to David as he turned and continued his way.

"Papa! Papa, come back!" He watched as his father vanished in the distance. "Papa…" David mumbled quietly, "Papa…" As he opened his eyes, he found himself alone and engulfed by darkness. Suddenly he remembered the conversation that had just occurred. He sat up quickly and looked around him, but his eyes found nothing; he was alone. He sat back in the seat and tried to make sense of what had just happened. "It was a dream," he said out loud to himself, "it was just a dream." He stood up and glanced over the railing at the workers who were still milling about to finish their preparations for that night's show. *They must be testing the lighting*, David thought. He squinted through the darkness to find Murray and glancing up toward the stage, he noticed that it was complete. The workers had departed, and one solitary microphone stood alone in the center of the bare stage. A single white spotlight shone on the exact spot where the microphone stood. He wondered why it had been placed there, since that wasn't the normal stage setup for his show.

"You already know what to do Davey, you've always known."

He turned quickly to see who was whispering to him, but he saw no one.

"If you quiet your mind and listen, then the answer will become clear."

Once again he spun around to find the voice that whispered through the darkness and again, he saw no one. He waited to hear more, but no more came. He glanced over the railing at the members of the road crew, but no one was there. It was as if everyone had suddenly vanished. Slowly he looked up at the stage again, the solitary microphone still standing alone in the spotlight just as it had been before. David stared at it as the whisper came again.

"The answer will become clear."

David felt a calmness come over him. "This is where I belong," he said out loud to the darkness, "this is where I was always meant to be."

Before he could think another thought, the house lights flooded the arena with a bright white glow. He looked around at the crew members as they hurried to finish their tasks.

"David…" a voice called to him.

He turned quickly. "Papa?"

"David!" the voice called again. He looked down and saw Murray on the stage waving to him. "Dave, would you come down for a sound check please?"

David waved back to him and Murray put the microphone back on its stand. He watched Murray talking to several of the stagehands as they worked diligently to prep the stage. He wondered how they could have changed the sets so quickly. David stood and pondered what had transpired in front of him. *It was a dream, but I'm awake, so how could it have been?*

"Hey, are you coming down?" Casey asked from the stairwell.

David looked out over the arena again as he began to smile. "Yeah, I'm coming." He took Casey's hand as they descended the stairs.

CHAPTER 17

Casey took a sip of the hot tea she had ordered from room service as she sat on the bed reading. She and David had been traveling from city to city in order to promote David's upcoming concert tour. While David was away with Murray at one of the many personal appearances that had been scheduled, Casey decided to spend the evening enjoying some much deserved quiet time alone in her hotel room, but she couldn't keep her mind on her book. As much as she tried, all she could think about was David. Over the last several weeks, her feelings for him had become more intense. It was more than just knowing he loved her, she needed to feel his touch on her skin, to feel his arms around her.

Casey was startled by a light tapping on her door. She lay her book down on the night stand and slipped on her robe. Looking through the peep hole, she could see David standing on the other side. Casey felt her heart flutter. She wanted to open the door and throw herself into his arms, she wanted to tell him how happy she was that he came to see her and it took everything she had in her to keep from squealing with excitement. She didn't want to be like the fans that were always clamoring for his attention, she wanted him to see her as a mature woman. As Casey stood trying to catch her breath, David tapped on the door again.

"Casey?" he asked in a low voice. She stood for a few seconds trying to think of what to do. Taking a couple of steps back, she answered in as calm a voice as she could muster.

"Just a minute." She walked slowly back to the door. "Who is it?"

"It's me, David."

Casey closed her eyes and bit her bottom lip, opened the door slightly and looked out at him. "Yes?"

"Hi," David said quietly.

"Hi."

"Were you sleeping?"

"No, I was just reading a little."

"Oh, good."

"Did you need something?"

"No, I was just wondering..." David's voice trailed off.

"What?"

"I was wondering if you were still awake, I'm a little wired, I thought maybe we could talk for a while, but if you're going to bed, we can talk tomorrow."

"No, no, now's fine."

"Okay." He waited as he and Casey stood at the door. "Is it okay if I come in?"

"Of course." She opened the door so he could pass through. She hid her face behind the door, kicking herself for not inviting him in. She admired him for a couple of moments after he entered the room. He was dressed in a light blue button-down shirt and dark blue jeans with a dark blue sport coat and black suede oxford shoes. Casey thought how smart he looked when he dressed up. She closed the door and sat cross-legged on the end of the bed. "So, how did it go?"

"It was okay," David replied as he sat in one of the chairs near the sliding doors that led to the balcony, "you know how those things are, you smile and shake some hands, take a few pictures, kiss a few girls."

"Really?" Casey smiled as David blushed.

"You know what I mean."

"Yeah, I know."

"All of the people were really nice though."

"That's good. Sometimes they can be kinda pushy."

"Yeah, sometimes." David laid his head against the back of the chair and closed his eyes.

"What?" she asked, sensing there was something on his mind.

"I still don't understand it, why are they so thrilled to see a guy like me?"

"They like you."

"They don't even know me," he countered, looking up at the ceiling, "all they know is that I can sing and, maybe dance a little, but they don't know *me*."

"I liked you before I really knew you."

David looked at Casey. "And now?"

"Now I love you." Casey stated. David blushed again as a smile crossed his face.

"I guess I'll never understand it." He stood up, walked out

onto the balcony and looked over the city as the lights sparkled against the darkness of the night sky. Casey walked out and stood beside him at the railing. She shivered as a breeze blew past them and without speaking, David moved behind her and wrapped his arms around her, laid his cheek against the side of her head and closed his eyes. When he inhaled, he could smell the coconut scent of her shampoo, it was one of the little things he loved about her. He opened his eyes and stared out across the night.

Casey felt glorious. With David's arms around her, she felt safe and secure. She secretly wished that they could stand on this balcony forever, just like this. In her heart, she needed nothing else in the world, just David. Another breeze blew by and Casey shivered again, and David held her a little closer.

"Do you wanna go in?" he asked.

"I'm okay." For right now she didn't want to move, she just wanted to stay right there in his arms, letting him protect her from the world.

"Come on," he said as her took her by the hand and led her back into the hotel room. "It's really cooling down tonight," David closed the sliding glass door. Casey walked over and picked up a blanket, wrapping it around her shoulders. "I knew you were cold."

"I wasn't really cold until you let go of me," she smiled. David rubbed his arms a little to get the chill off as he reclaimed his seat by the balcony doors. Casey sat on the edge of the bed closest to him. "Wanna share my blanket?"

"No," he laughed, "I'm good." Even though he had a slight chill on the outside, he felt warm on the inside—Casey made him feel that way. He looked over at her and smiled to himself. "Am I keeping you up?"

"No," she answered quickly. Maybe too quickly, she thought. She tried to calm herself down some. She didn't want to seem forward, but she didn't want David to leave just yet. "I'm not really tired anyway."

"As long as I'm not intruding."

"You're never an intrusion." Casey tried to sound nonchalant, but she was sure it wasn't working. David stood up and walked over to the vanity counter and studied his reflection in the mirror for a few moments as Casey watched him.

"Don't you think it's odd?"

"What's odd?"

"Well, three years ago no one even knew I existed. Now my voice is coming out of stereo speakers across the country and people are paying hard earned money to see me, of all people, get up on a stage and sing and dance. Not to mention the fact that my picture is plastered across the bedroom walls of teenage girls from here to the other side of the globe." He looked harder at the reflection staring back at him. "I'm the same person now that I was then, nothing's changed… it's just odd." Casey walked over and stood behind him, laid her head against his shoulder and looked into the mirror at him.

"But you're not the same David. You're older, more mature, more experienced. You know more about the world, about life. You've traveled to new places and met new people. You're not the same person you were three years ago," she concluded, "you're better." David turned around to face Casey and leaned on the counter behind him. She wrapped her arms around his middle as he lay his cheek against her head and closed his eyes. He knew Casey was speaking from her heart and he knew she was right; he had changed, and he felt stronger and more confident than he ever had in his life. He had been able to accomplish all the things Murray and Claire said he would, but when he looked in that mirror, he could still see that insecure, lonely fifteen year old boy he used to be, he still knew what it felt like to be made fun of and to be single out, he still remembered how much it hurt to not be accepted for who he was and he wondered why it was so different now. Casey leaned back and looked up at him.

"I love you, David." He couldn't understand her love for him, either, but he accepted it.

"I know, I love you." He hugged her close to him, he loved the feeling of her, and he never wanted to let her go. Casey leaned back again and looked into David's eyes. He couldn't help but give in to the urge to kiss her. He moved toward her and pressed his lips gently to hers. As they moved back from one another, he gazed into her big brown eyes and once again, the urge came over him and he took her face in his hands and brought her toward him. His tongue found hers and they lingered for several seconds before David backed away suddenly, his heart beginning to quicken.

"What's wrong?" Casey asked with a concerned tone.

"I think I should go."

"Why?"

"Really Case, I... I should go back to my room." He moved away from her and walked toward the door, but as he reached for the doorknob, Casey's voice stopped him from turning it.

"Please don't leave David." David closed his eyes and waited. He wanted to stay, indeed he felt he *needed* to stay, as much as he needed oxygen.

"Casey…" He felt her hand on his back.

"Stay with me." David turned around to face Casey for a moment, then he leaned his back against the wall by the door and looked away from her. He loved Casey with all his heart. She was so beautiful, so pure to him, and he didn't want to take that away from her, but at the same time, he needed to be with her. Casey could see the indecision in David's expression. She walked over to him and laying herself against his body, she could feel his need for her. Casey looked up to meet David's coffee-colored eyes and he kissed her again, this time deeper and more passionately, inhaling as deeply as he could so as to take in her scent. As his tongue entered her mouth, he pulled her closer to him. Casey inhaled suddenly as David's impulsiveness stole the breath from her. He stopped just as suddenly, not wanting to hurt her.

"I'm sorry."

"Don't be."

David gently brushed the hair back from Casey's face. "I should go."

"Stay."

"It's not right."

"Does it feel 'not right'?" He looked into Casey's eyes and could see she felt as he did, that she wanted him just as much. He lay his head back against the wall.

David closed his eyes as Casey began softly kissing his neck. "Casey..." She could feel his body giving in to her. As she continued lightly kissing him, her hands found their way to the buttons of his shirt and David inhaled deeply as he reached up to stop her. "Casey..."

"I need you, David," she finally admitted, "Please don't be afraid, I'm not." He didn't say anything, but she was right, he was afraid. Both he and Casey were new to this and he knew once it was done there was no going back, but he also knew Casey was the only person he wanted to share this moment with, she was the only woman he wanted to give himself to. He kissed her softly on her cheek, then walked a few steps away from her. Casey watched him as he took off his sport coat and laid it on the chair, then slipped his shoes off and pushed them aside. She went to him, embracing him from behind and laying her face against his back, then slowly moving around to face him.

As David stood silent, she began unbuttoning his shirt. She stood looking at his smooth, bare chest, amazed at the beauty of the man before her. She raised her hand to touch him, but stopped short, knowing as well as he did that there was no returning from this. She had lied to David—she was just as afraid as she knew he was, but her need was greater than her fear. She looked to him and David returned her gaze, swallowed hard and then nodded, giving her permission to touch him.

As Casey's fingertips made contact with his chest, David shivered. He had waited so long for this moment, for the first touch of a woman's hand on his body. Knowing Casey was that woman made it the most wonderful moment of his life. He felt Casey's soft hands as they moved across his skin, touching every inch of him from shoulder to shoulder and as her hands moved up, she put her arms around his neck and kissed him again. Stepping back, Casey reached down and untied the belt of her robe and David watched in wonder as she let it slide off her shoulders to the floor, revealing the long silk night gown beneath it.

His eyes moved down her body from her slim neck to her shoulders. He could see her full breasts moving as she breathed, then her small waist and the slight curve of her hips. He could tell she wore no panties under her night gown, and he felt an overwhelming need to be near her, to hold her, to kiss her. He stepped closer to her, reached up and took her face gently in his hands. Casey smiled softly, then nodded to give him permission as he had for her.

Suddenly, the fear that David had been trying to hide came to the surface and he pulled his hands away. As he stood trying to decide what he should do, Casey took his hands in hers and gently returned them to their previous positions. He caressed her slender neck, then watched his fingers as they followed the shape of her shoulders, the look on her face seeming to beg him to continue. He leaned over and began kissing her neck, the taste of her skin heightening his need as he drew her toward him and Casey ran her hands under David's shirt and down his back; he arched slightly at her touch. Casey moved a step away, raised her hands up and slowly slid David's shirt off. He shivered again as a chill ran up his spine. Moving the small straps of her peach-colored negligée off her shoulders, she slowly lowered it to reveal her breasts to him. David felt weak. Casey's eyes met his as she stepped closer to him and nodded again.

David's hands shook as he began retracing her neck and shoulders, then continued down her body. As he reached her breasts he paused, and Casey lovingly guided David's left hand until it cupped her right breast. David felt a small rush come over him. He reached up tentatively and caressed her left breast in the same way. Casey shyly turned her eyes from his and it was then that he saw the fear she had tried to deny. David pulled her to him and held her tight, her body warm against his bare chest.

"I love you Casey, no matter what, I love you. This doesn't have to go any further, I'll still love you." He paused for a moment. "I'll always love you." David released his embrace as Casey looked up at him.

"Please make love to me David," she pleaded as a tear silently rolled down her cheek, "I need you so much." Casey lowered her arms and let her night gown fall to the floor. David was speechless as she stood exposed before him. He took Casey in his arms and kissed her as his hands followed the sinuous outline of her naked body. He couldn't believe this was happening and at the same time, it couldn't happen fast enough. Casey unhooked the buckle on David's belt, then unbuttoned his jeans. David felt the zipper on his pants open. He pulled from their kiss and stepped back toward the wall. Casey moved to him and held him, then ran her hands down his back and into the waistband of his briefs until she grasped the tight muscles of his buttocks. David arched again as her hands followed their path back up to his shoulders. They kissed again, then Casey rested her head against David's chest. She could feel him breathing and heard the rhythm of his beating heart.

As they stood quietly, Casey felt David's hand on hers. She glanced up at him and for the first time since they had met, he looked helpless to her.

"Casey..."

"Yes?"

"Casey..." He couldn't find the words to express what he felt, but Casey somehow knew.

"Can I touch you David?"

David moved Casey's hand slowly down his torso, letting her continue on her own as she neared his waist. Casey slid her hand into the front of David's pants and felt his manhood. As she grasped him in the palm of her hand, she felt David's entire body go weak.

"Casey Lee..." he whimpered as his head rolled back and his eyes closed. Casey kissed David's chest as she continued to caress his lower region, then taking him by the hands, she led him to the bed and began to remove the remainder of his clothes. David stopped her momentarily as a sudden rush of embarrassment came over him. She waited as his fear quickly passed and he allowed her to continue. As David stood naked before her, Casey leaned in toward him and inhaled his scent as he had hers. She ran her hands lightly across the muscles of his chest, over his shoulders and down his arms, then back up his arms, over his shoulders again and down his rib cage to his hips and thighs.

"Hold me David." As David embraced her, he could feel the sensation of her bare skin against his, the warmth their bodies created together and once again her sweet fragrance overtook him as he buried his face into her shoulder. Casey could feel his organ becoming firmer as they pressed against each other. She slowly pulled David down onto the bed and guided him to lie down next to her, wrapping her arms around him and kissing him ardently. David could hardly resist her advances and tried to be as kind and gentle as he felt he should be, as he instinctively began to explore the various regions of her body. He moved his hand down to her breasts where his fingertips found her erect nipples, then past her flat stomach until he reached the soft mahogany mass that surrounded her most private parts. As his hand began to caress her womanhood, Casey breathed in suddenly and looked at him in amazement.

"I'm sorry, did I hurt you?"

"No," she smiled at him, "you're fine."

"You're sure?" Casey nodded that she was and David began tenderly kissing her neck and chest. Moving to her breasts, he took her nipple in his mouth and began sucking it gently. Casey trembled as the sensation surprised her. She could see David enjoying her and as he did, she ran her fingers through his soft, thick hair. As his lips moved back to her mouth, she took in his tongue… suddenly David sat up on the side of the bed, breathing heavily.

"David? David, are you okay?"

"Casey, are you sure you want to do this?"

"Yes."

"I mean are you *really* sure?"

"David, what's wrong?"

"That's just it, nothing's wrong, everything is right, it's perfect."

"And that's bad?"

David turned his head and looked at her directly. "Casey, just tell me this is what you really want, tell me that tomorrow you're not going to regret what's happening right now."

"David, this is what I really want, and I don't regret any of it." She sat up, kissed him and laid her hand on his cheek. "Is this what *you* really want?" David looked into Casey's loving face.

"I've never wanted anything more in my entire life. I love you Casey, with everything in my heart and soul, I love you."

"Then make love to me David, please make love to me." As they lay back on the bed together, David moved above her. Casey felt small as she lay beneath him. David once again started kissing her face and upper body and sucking her firm breasts. She could feel the weight of his body beginning to press down and the stiffness of him as he neared her opening. When he entered her, she closed her eyes and inhaled deeply. Casey wrapped her legs around him and pulled him closer as their bodies joined together.

David was enticed by the moist warmth of her that enveloped him as he moved in and out and found himself increasingly unable to hold back the unyielding pressure that was building inside him. He prayed it would last, that this wondrous experience wouldn't be over too quickly. Casey embraced him tightly, her hands gripping the sweaty flesh of his torso and holding fast as their rhythm began to escalate. The tidal wave of desire that Casey had been trying to suppress for so long began to surge inside her. It became stronger and stronger with every push of David's body against hers until the sensation finally overtook her and her entire body tensed as she cried out in ecstasy.

"Oh David! David!"

As she climaxed, her muscles tightened around him. His mouth found hers and their tongues met, tangling around each other. Casey sensed his member swelling inside her, as her own arousal began to strengthen a second time. The need inside him was now more insistent, compelling him to push faster and harder than before, driving him to keep on even though he was almost totally exhausted.

"Casey... Casey!" he moaned between panted breaths. Casey held David's body as closely as she could. "Ooooh Cassandra!"

"Come to me David, come to me!"

With a few final hard thrusts, David's body shuddered and shook, and his muscles grew rigid as he exploded inside her. At the same time, her orgasm reached its pinnacle and they came together. She heard him moan again as all the strength left him, then the heaviness of his weakened body and as he lay against her trying to catch his breath, he whispered in her ear.

"I love you Casey Lee... oh, how I love you."

"I love you, David."

CHAPTER 18

As David breathed in, he could smell the light fragrance of coconut in Casey's hair and the warmth of her body next to his, every inch of her skin as soft as rose petals. He lay there for a short time with his eyes closed, thinking that maybe if he opened them, this would all turn out to be just a wonderful dream and he would be alone in his own bed. When he did open his eyes, he found the room still dark and realized that morning had not yet broken.

As he lay there next to Casey, he tried to take in all that had happened in the last several hours, hardly believing what had transpired, even though the proof was there beside him. He felt a tingle move through his body as he thought about making love to Casey and longed to be with her again, but she was sleeping so peacefully that he didn't want to wake her. He tried to go back to sleep, but he just couldn't quiet his mind, so he lay as still as he could for a while in the silence. As he watched, he noticed the morning sneaking in and causing long shadows across the far walls of the room… it was still early, he could stay a little longer. He closed his eyes again and lost himself in the thought of Casey McCallister.

As David awoke for the second time, he found the room flooded with daylight. Casey was still asleep and hadn't moved. David leaned over slightly to see the clock on the night stand—it read eight-thirty a.m. Murray was supposed to pick him up at nine o'clock, so like it or not, he had to get up. He slid out from under the covers as lightly as he could so he wouldn't wake Casey and as he stood, he noticed the imprint of himself on the bed next to her nude body—he liked that. He tucked the blankets in around her to keep her warm and then turned to sit on the side of the bed.

Slipping his feet into the legs of his jeans, he pulled them up as he stood from the bed and fastened them. After buckling his belt, he reached for his shirt, slipped it on and buttoned it. Then he picked up his shoes, shoved his socks into them and grabbed his jacket from the chair. He started to leave, but when he reached the door he stopped and looked back at Casey, still sleeping soundly. It didn't seem right, leaving this way, even though he knew he would see her later that afternoon.

As he stood wondering what to do, he noticed a notepad on the table near the door. He set down his jacket and shoes and after scribbling a short message on it, he laid the notepad on the pillow next to Casey. He retrieved his clothes and opened the door as quietly as he could, slipped out, and hooked the 'Do Not Disturb' sign on the doorknob. When he turned around, he found himself face to face with a member of the hotel's housekeeping staff. The young woman's jaw dropped as she immediately recognized him and David raised his finger to his lips, smiled and walked away. She watched him as he hurried down the hallway and slipped the keycard into his own hotel room door, then opened the door and went inside. As the door closed behind him, he leaned on the doorframe, smiled to himself and wondered what kind of sordid tales he would be involved in when he read the tabloids tomorrow. He dropped his shoes on the floor, threw his coat on the bed and headed for the shower.

As Casey emerged from her sleep, she was surprised to see that it was already nine fifteen. She lay still for a minute or so, then thought of David. She reached back to verify that he really was there and that she didn't imagine the whole night, but as her hand touched the blanket behind her, she realized she was alone in the bed. Casey rolled over and sat up, pulling the covers around her bare body and looked over at the pillow beside her. Upon seeing the notepad, she picked it up and slowly read it out loud:

"Love you, see you later... David P.S. Wow..."

Casey smiled as she held the notepad to her heart—it had been real, everything she remembered about the night before had truly happened—they had made love and it had been wonderful. Casey laid her head on David's pillow and as she breathed in, she could still smell his cologne. She pulled the covers up over her shoulders, wrapped her arms around the pillow and pictured him in her mind.

She could remember every moment of their experience together—how he was so caring and loving, yet so strong. She could remember the way he felt, how he tasted. She remembered the things he said and how he called out her name as the rush overtook him. She remembered seeing in his eyes how much he wanted her, how much he needed her and she remembered how his warm breath felt on her face, how passionate his kisses were and how it felt to have him inside her. She closed her eyes as she was reminded of the sensation and breathed in the lasting scent of his cologne again, then rolled over to face the ceiling. She took a deep breath and sighed heavily.

"I love you David, oh, how I love you," she said aloud to his memory.

CHAPTER 19

"Did you see Casey this morning?" There was no answer to Murray's question. "Dave?" Still no response. "David!"

"What?"

"I asked if you saw Casey this morning."

"No, she was still asleep when I left," David replied without thinking.

"How do you know she was asleep if you didn't see her?"

"I saw her last night and she said she was really tired," David answered, trying to cover, "since she didn't call me this morning, I just assumed she was still sleeping." David turned his head quickly toward the window of the limo.

"What's wrong with you this morning?"

"Nothing."

"Nothing?"

"Nothing."

"Well, you better get your mind together, we have a lot to do today."

"I know," David said, but he couldn't shake the memory of what happened between him and Casey the night before. The feeling of her stayed with him and the sound of her voice echoed in his head... 'Come to me, David.'

"David... David!" Murray raised his voice a little as he shook David's arm. David jumped and looked at him. "Where are you today?" David pulled his mind back into the moment.

"Murray, do we have to do this today?"

"What do you mean?"

"Can we reschedule these interviews?"

"Are you serious?"

"Yes, I'm serious, can we reschedule?"

"Dave, these interviews have been scheduled for over a month!"

"I know and I'm sorry, but there's just something I have to do."

"Well, I can try..." David didn't wait for the rest and as the limo stopped at a red light, he opened the door and jumped out. "Dave, wait! Where are you going?" Murray yelled after him, but he was gone. "Fantastic," Murray sighed to himself as he dialed a number on his cell phone, "just fantastic."

David ran as fast as he could back several blocks to the hotel and as he ran up the steps in front of the building, he passed a small group of fans that had gathered outside. When they saw him they started to scream his name, but he didn't stop. He went straight through the doors, ran to the elevator and pushed the button. As he waited impatiently, he noticed some fans in the lobby, obviously hoping for a glimpse of him. He looked up at the indicator above the elevator.

"Come on, come on!" he urged under his breath.

"You're David Steinman, aren't you?" David turned to find the group of fans standing behind him. He smiled at them. "We love your music!" one told him.

"Thanks."

"We have tickets to your show."

"Can we have your autograph?" they asked excitedly. At that moment, the elevator doors opened and though he hated to let them down, he only had one thing on his mind right now.

"Tell you what, if you come back around dinnertime, I'll have some pictures for you." He stepped onto the elevator. "See you around five, okay?" As the doors closed, he could hear them screaming. He took a relieved breath and blew it out.

"Floor, sir?"

"Hmm?"

"What floor, sir?"

"Oh," David thought for a moment. He knew the fans would be watching to see what floor he was stopping on. "Um... eight."

"Yes sir" A few moments later the doors opened again. "Eight, sir."

"Thank you." David handed the man a few dollars, stepped off the elevator and waited until he was gone. Then he headed for the stairwell and climbed the remaining flights up to the eleventh floor where their rooms were. He ran down the hall until he reached Casey's door, stopping for a moment to catch his breath before lightly knocking.

Inside the room, Casey had just put on her robe and was about to take a shower when she heard the tapping on the door. Assuming it was housecleaning, she went to the door and opened it, surprised to see David on the other side.

"David?"

"Hi," he panted.

"What are you doing here? I thought you had interviews this morning?"

"I asked Murray to reschedule."

"Speaking of Murray, where is he?" she asked, looking out into the hall.

"I left him in the limo."

"You what?"

"We were stopped at a light, so I got out and came back here."

"David..."

"Casey, I had to see you."

"But David..."

"Can I come in?"

"Yes, yes," she answered, opening the door for him. "Why are you sweating?"

"There were some girls in the lobby, I didn't want them to know what floor we were on, so got off on the eighth floor and came up the steps."

She looked at him wide-eyed. "Let me get you some water." She turned toward the sink, but David turned her back toward him.

"I don't want any water. I just want you." David pulled Casey to him and kissed her passionately. Afterwards, Casey looked at him somewhat startled, stepped back and turned from him. "Casey, I'm sorry, I didn't mean to..."

"It's okay," she interrupted, "you didn't."

David sighed. "I just couldn't stop thinking about you... about us... about last night. I had to see you again." Casey stood silent. David stepped up behind her and leaned his face near her ear, burying it in her soft dark hair. "I need you, Casey Lee." Casey closed her eyes and smiled as a tingle rushed through her. Casey Lee—she loved it when he called her that. He pressed his body lightly against her back as she untied the belt of her robe and let it fall just below her shoulders, exposing the bare skin. David kissed them gently.

"Casey, last night was the most perfect night of my life. I

don't really know how to explain it, but it felt..."

"Like we were one person?" she asked, finishing his sentence. She turned to face him. "I felt it too." Casey laid her hand on David's cheek, *He has such a sweet face,* she thought.

"Case, I've never felt anything like that before, everything in me wanted you," he confessed to her, "it still does." He leaned forward and kissed her soft lips, then, as he moved back from her, Casey let the front of her robe fall open, showing him her naked body. She moved toward him, embracing him and kissing his neck as she had the night before. David closed his eyes and felt the breath leave him as Casey invaded his soul once more. "Cassandra…"

He bowed his head down and searched out her mouth, then tasted the inside of it with his tongue for a long while as his hands memorized every curve of her being. She could feel the firmness of his desire as he pulled her close to him, then moved his mouth to her breasts as he knelt in front of her. Casey could feel the wetness between her legs increasing as his need became stronger, his arms encircled her waist as he laid the side of his face against her stomach. She held his head in her hands.

"You know this has changed us forever," he said to her.

"I know." Casey moved away from him as she closed the robe around her, walked over to the sink and splashed some cool water on her face. Still on his knees, David sat back on his heels and watched her. All he could think about was making love to her, all he wanted was to hold her, caress her, kiss her, feel her near him. David stood up and walked over to Casey and standing behind her, they looked into the mirror at themselves. "No one can know," she stated.

"What are you talking about?"

"David, we can't tell anyone about this, your career is just getting started, a scandal could kill it."

"What scandal? We love each other Casey, we want to be together. How is that a scandal?"

"I don't want to be the one to ruin your life David." Casey started to walk away from the mirror, but David stopped her and holding her by the shoulders, he looked at her directly.

"Casey McCallister, *you* are the reason I have a life… *and* a career. *You* are the reason I get out of bed every morning. *You* are the reason I show up at rehearsals and the reason I walk out onto that stage at every show. *You* are the reason I feel like singing every day, don't you see that? If you weren't here, then I wouldn't be here, and if it *ever* came down to a choice between you or my career, then to Hell with my career. There is nothing in this world more important to me than you." He swallowed hard as Casey looked into his eyes. "I love you Casey Lee, you're a part of me, there's no way I can deny it. You've stolen my heart and you own my soul. Without you," he stopped to choke back the emotion he knew he couldn't hide, "without you, I cease to exist… you are my *life*." As he spoke, Casey began to cry. She hugged him around the neck and held him tight.

"Oh David, I love you," she cried, "I love you, I love you, I love you!" David held her to him.

CHAPTER 20

The daylight coming through the window caused parts of the slightly tarnished brass picture frame to shine. David touched the glass, his reflection superimposed over the face of the man in the photo. The features of the man were similar to his own—the rounded jaw line, the gentle eyes—traits handed down from generation to generation. Memories of the few short years he spent tagging along at his father's side flashed quickly through his mind. He tried hard to remember as many details as he could, but being the young boy that he was during those years, he was sure there was a lot he had forgotten.

The one thing he remembered quite clearly was his father's voice. David could still hear the man's deep smooth baritone singing as Daniel went about his daily chores. He remembered the sound of that voice reading bedtime stories to him and his siblings when they were small, or laughing heartily as Daniel played with them and the resolve in his father's voice when he spoke of something serious.

"He had such a kind face," Casey commented as she looked over his shoulder, "I wish I could have met him."

"He would've liked you," David replied as Casey sat down at the table.

"How long has it been?"

"Ten years ago this week." They sat in silence for a few minutes as Casey observed him.

"What happened that day David?"

"What?"

"What happened the day your father died?" David stared at Casey and she could tell he was retreating from her. He didn't like to talk about that time in his life—it was just easier to leave it as far in the back of his mind as he could—but the details were as fresh as if it had all happened yesterday. He turned his eyes toward the window. "I'm sorry, I shouldn't have asked you such a personal question. I know it's a painful memory for you, you don't have to talk about it if you don't want to." She stood from her chair, touched his hair gently with her fingertips, then leaned over and softly kissed the top of his head.

"We were sitting at the kitchen table," David began in a distant voice as Casey took a step toward the doorway. She stopped and stood quietly beside him. "I had just finished my breakfast. Papa and I had been talking about different things, I don't remember what exactly, just everyday stuff. I put my dishes in the sink and put on my jacket, grabbed my books. I gave Papa a hug goodbye and started to leave, he reminded me that his band had a rehearsal that afternoon and to come straight home from school…" David paused a moment and smiled at the memory. "Papa always took me with him when they rehearsed." Casey sat down again as he continued.

"He said, 'I'll be waiting here for you.' I promised not to forget, told him I loved him and went to school. Later that afternoon when I got home I noticed a lot of cars parked outside, when I went in the house, I saw my sisters crying and everyone was kind of quiet. Before I had a chance to ask what was going on, Danny said he had to talk to me, so we went out and sat on the front steps. He said he had some sad news," David paused again as he took a deep breath, "then he told me Papa passed away that morning."

Casey listened intently, trying as best she could to keep her emotions from showing.

"I just looked at him. I told him that couldn't be true because I had talked to him before I left for school." David swallowed hard. "He said Papa had been sitting at the table working on some music and he must have put his head down to rest a bit. That's where Mama found him."

As strong as Casey tried to be for David, she couldn't stop a few tears from showing. She quickly blinked back the others as David went on.

"I still didn't want to believe him, I just kept saying it wasn't truc. I told him Papa said he would be waiting for me when I got home. He finally looked me straight in the eye and said, 'David, Papa's gone." I shook my head and kept shouting "No! No!" The club where Papa's band rehearsed was just a few blocks away so I ran as fast as I could to get there. I was sure when I walked in I would see him there, waiting for me just like he said he would be, but when I went in all the guys in the band were just sitting there and they all had the same look on their faces as my family had. I asked them where my father was and they all just stared at me. I screamed at them, "Where's Papa?" One of the guys shook his head and said, "I'm sorry, Dave, I'm so sorry." That's when I finally accepted that it was true." David's bottom lip quivered, and he closed his eyes as Casey gave into her emotions and let her tears fall.

"I didn't know what to do, so I just started running. I ran and ran and ran. I had no idea where I was going, I didn't even know how much time had passed, but by the time I stopped, it was starting to get dark. Somehow I ended up in the park near the amphitheater where Papa's band had played a few times, I walked up the steps onto the stage and laid down on the concrete, put my head down and just cried." David stopped long enough to wipe his tears on his shirt sleeve. "I have no idea how long I was there – probably just a couple of hours – but it felt like a lifetime. After a while I heard a noise and I saw Mama standing there; I could see the tears on her face in the moonlight. I just sat there. She reached out to me and I ran to her and we just stood there on that empty stage crying in the dark." He picked up the frame and looked at the picture again, "I can't believe that was ten years ago." David glanced over at Casey, "I'm sorry. I didn't mean to make you cry."

"It's okay."

"I've never told anyone that story before," he admitted to her.

"Not even Murray?" David shook his head. "Well, I'm glad you told me," she said with a soft smile.

David reached over and tenderly brushed away her tears. "So am I."

CHAPTER 21

The black car drove through the gates of the cemetery and David grew uneasy as the memory of Daniel's funeral poured into his mind. No one knew he was here; he had left the house without saying a word to anyone. He had something on his mind, and he wanted desperately to talk to someone about it, so he came here, to talk to his father.

David did his best to compose himself as he got out of the car and asked the driver to wait at the entrance for him. He turned and looked out over the hillside. The sun was just beginning to come out from behind the clouds and the morning fog had a chill to it. David pulled his jacket around him and tilted his face a bit to shield his eyes from the brightness.

The dew from the grass made his shoes wet as he stepped off the road and began walking across the manicured lawn. A short distance later he stopped in front of a moderate sized black marble headstone. He stood for a minute without looking at it directly, then took a deep breath and let it out slowly as he looked up at the engraving. 'Daniel Joseph Steinman Sr.—Beloved Husband and Father.' David's eyes became blurry with tears and he felt a lump growing in his throat.

"Dammit..." He turned away. He quickly wiped his hands across his face, took another deep breath and tried to rein in his emotions… he needed to do this. He turned back around to face the marker.

"Papa, I need to talk to you." The stillness of the cemetery made it seem as if his words were hanging in mid-air and he glanced around to make sure he was alone. "Papa, I need your advice." Suddenly he felt silly, talking to the air. He thought about getting back in the car and going home, but he couldn't move; he felt compelled to stay and finish this seemingly imaginary conversation.

"I love her Papa. I've never loved anyone the way I love her. I'm not sure how to explain it, but I figured you would understand. She's the most beautiful creature I've ever seen and when she dances… she's like an angel. When I'm around her I forget about everything else – I even have to remind myself to breath – and when she goes away..." David stopped for a moment as the thought of Casey overwhelmed him, "when she goes away I count every second until she comes back again. I want her to be in my life forever Papa. I want Casey to be my wife."

All at once David felt a familiar calmness come over him. He closed his eyes and felt the tears on his face. He knew he loved Casey and wanted to be with her, but he wasn't sure how to tell her that. Now he knew. He stepped closer to the headstone, reached out and gently rubbed his fingertips across the letters.

"Thank you Papa," he whispered with a gentle smile. David walked back across the lawn toward the road. As he reached the pavement, he turned and looked back toward his father's grave. "I love you." At that moment, a soft spring breeze whirled around him and he smiled again. David followed the road until he reached the car and after climbing inside, he asked the driver to take him home.

CHAPTER 22

Since rehearsal had finished early, Casey decided to spend some time in the garden behind the studio. As she looked over the many colorful blossoms, she thought how they reminded her of people, each one beautiful in its own special way. She leaned over the railing, closed her eyes and drew in their sweet fragrance.

"What are you doing out here?" David asked as he joined her on the patio.

"Just enjoying the flowers, what are *you* doing out here?"

"Me? I was looking for you."

"Well, I guess you found me then." She looked at him and smiled playfully.

"Yeah, I guess I did."

Casey looked up at the night sky. "It's such a clear night, isn't the moon beautiful?" David looked up at the moon shining above them, full and bright, its light giving a romantic glow to the entire garden. "David?"

"Hmm?"

"I said isn't the moon beautiful?"

"Yeah, it is."

"Are you all right?"

"I'm fine," David replied without moving his gaze. He had never noticed before how enormous the moon appeared to be, or the brilliance of its light—details that seemed insignificant to him just twenty-four hours ago began to stand out, like how the moon looked, the scent of the flowers, or how Casey's long brown hair moved lightly with the warm night breeze.

"Hello, are you in there?" Casey asked.

David looked over at her. "I'm sorry, did you say something?"

"Yeah, I did," Casey laughed, "I said it looks like you could just reach up in the sky and pull the moon down."

David looked back at the heavens. "You know, I would give you the moon if I could."

"That's so sweet," Casey swooned, nuzzling closer to him, "but I think it looks better where it is."

"Well, since I can't get you the moon, would you settle for one of the stars?"

"What?" Casey looked at him, not quite understanding what he meant. David turned toward her and opened his right hand. In his outstretched palm was a small black velvet box. Casey's eyes widened and her mouth fell open as she realized what was happening. "David…"

"Take it." Casey's hand began to shake as she reached up and took the small box. David waited impatiently as Casey stared at it for what seemed to him like an eternity. "Well, go ahead, open it."

Casey looked up at him, then back at the box, and feeling as if her heart would stop at any moment, she slowly raised the lid. Inside was a slender gold band on which was mounted a sparkling star-shaped diamond, several smaller diamonds ran down the band on either side of the star. Casey's eyes filled with tears as she stared at the ring.

"Casey, you've been in my thoughts every second of every day since the moment I knew you existed… it's almost as if I took my first breath in that instant. I'm lonely when you're not with me and when we're together, I am happier than I have *ever* been. I love you Casey, and I want to spend the rest of my life with you." Tears welled in Casey's eyes as David took the ring from its box, knelt on one knee and took her hand in his. "Will you marry me Casey?"

Casey could feel her body trembling. She had imagined that one day she and David would get married but thought of it as only a fantasy. Now here she was standing in the moonlight as he professed his love for her.

David stood up and spoke to her face to face. "Cassandra," he said as she looked into his eyes, "will you marry me, will you be my wife?"

Casey paused for a moment and then smiled at him. "Yes," she answered softly, "I would love to be your wife."

David returned her smile and carefully slipped the ring onto Casey's left hand. She couldn't help but notice how it glistened in the moonlight.

"It's beautiful David."

"I had it made especially for you." Casey looked up at him, leaned over and kissed him tenderly, then wrapped her arms around his neck.

"I love you David," she whispered, as David held her close to him. Glancing toward the heavens he mouthed a silent 'Thank you.'

CHAPTER 23

After dinner, David went out to the porch and sat on the long concrete banister. Casey sat beside him, leaning her back against his shoulder, her legs stretched out along the length of the banister and her ankles crossed. They stared out across the darkened lawn for a short while without talking. In less than twenty-four hours, they would be taking the biggest step of their lives—marriage—and both had pre-wedding jitters, although neither one would admit that to the other.

"Everyone did a great job tonight with the rehearsal dinner," Casey commented.

"Yeah, they did," David agreed.

The air went still again, with only the occasional chirp from a lonely cricket sounding through the darkness.

"Today sure went by fast," Casey observed.

"Yeah, it did," David answered and again the silence returned and lingered for several minutes.

"Tomorrow's gonna be a busy day," she began a third time.

"Yeah, it is," David echoed.

Each of them privately pondered the upcoming events of the next day. All the plans had been made—venues secured, menus created, attire chosen, invitations sent—and now the only thing they had to do for all of it to come together was to show up.

A light summer breeze blew past them and Casey pushed a few rebellious strands of hair back, tucking them behind her ear. Lightning bugs flitted about, their glow piercing the night here and there, if only for a split second.

"David?"

"Hmmm?"

Casey hesitated a moment. "Do you love me?"

"That's a silly question."

"Do you?" The pair looked at each other.

"Casey, you know I do."

"Why?"

"Why what?"

"Why do you love me?"

"For a lot of reasons."

"Such as?"

"You want me to list them?"

"David…"

"Casey, I love you because you're *you*," he offered. Casey sighed, his vagueness leaving her unsatisfied. "I'm sorry, Case, I don't know what you want me to say."

"I just wondered what it was that made you fall in love with me. I mean, there are hundreds of girls just like me in the audiences at every show we do, you could have just as easily fallen for one of them."

"No."

"No?"

"No."

"Why not?"

"Because… they're not like you."

"Yes, they are."

"No, they're not, you're… different."

"I'm different."

"Yes."

"What makes me so different from them?" she asked.

"They're fans," he answered.

"So was I before we met."

"Casey…"

"Well, I was, I bought your CD, I had your poster on my bedroom wall, my friends and I used to dream about meeting you – even marrying you – we did all the things that all your other female fans do."

"But you're *different*."

"*How?*"

"Cassandra…"

"David…"

He breathed out heavily. "I don't know how to explain it."

"Just say it."

"Okay, but I don't know if it's gonna make any sense."

Casey sat up and turned around to face him. "Just try."

"Well…" he began, then paused a moment to get his thoughts together, "when you look at me, you see me; when I talk, you hear me; when I touch your hand, you feel me…"

"And those other girls don't?"

"No." David noticed the puzzled expression on Casey's face. "I told you it wouldn't make any sense."

"Then help me understand."

"When they look at me, they see their favorite singer, a rich and famous superstar—but you see me; they listen to my songs and hear my voice—but you hear me; they shake my hand and touch my clothes—but you feel me. You don't pretend to like things just because I do, you don't do everything I tell you to do… come to think of it, you don't do *anything* I tell you to do," he said with a light laugh, "You're an independent woman with your own thoughts and ideas. You know I'm not perfect and you don't expect me to be. If I act like a jerk, you call me a jerk."

"You love me because I call you a jerk?"

"Yes."

"Okay…" Casey seemed even more perplexed by his attempt at an explanation.

David turned and addressed her directly. "What would you do if I yelled at a waiter for getting my order wrong?"

"I'd tell you to stop acting like a spoiled brat!"

"You see? That's why I love you."

"But David…"

"Casey, if I went to dinner with any one of those hundreds of girls that go to my concerts and buy my CD's and hang my posters on their walls and I acted rude or obnoxious, they wouldn't say anything about it. They would just assume I should be treated a certain way because of who I am, but you wouldn't let me get away with that, you wouldn't think twice about putting me in my place."

Casey smiled. "You're right, I wouldn't."

"And you've done that since day one," he told her, "that's why I love you."

"That's why you love me?"

"Yes, that's why I love you. You accept me just the way I am. You don't see a superstar or hear a great singing voice or shake the hand of an image, you see and hear and feel the real person… David… *me.* You don't care if I sing, you don't care if I dance, you don't care if I ever step out on another stage… you only care that I am happy and healthy and here, with you… and when I look at you, I see everything that's real and genuine in my life."

"You really do love me, don't you?" she asked softly.
David touched her cheek affectionately. "Yes, I really do."

CHAPTER 24

David paced back and forth in the small room that stood just outside of the main hall of the church. Even though the wedding wasn't until two o'clock, he had been at the church since nine that morning and dressed since noon. He wanted to make sure that out of all of the days in his life, this is the one that would be perfect. A knock at the door caught his attention.

"Come in."

"David?" Rose peaked her head in the doorway.

"Hi, Ma," Rose stood and looked at her son. Tears came to her eyes and a smile to her face as she thought how grownup he looked.

"Oh, Davey," she cooed at him, "you look so handsome."

"Thanks, Ma."

"I can't believe you're getting married. My tiniest bird is finally leaving the nest," she smiled brightly at him.

David rolled his eyes. "Ma, please, do you have to make it sound so dramatic and final?" He paced back and forth as Rose watched.

"David, what's wrong?"

"Nothing's wrong."

"Something's wrong."

"There's nothing wrong, Ma," he insisted.

"Yes, there is," she countered.

"Why do you think something's wrong?"

"It's a simple process of elimination, either you're trying to wear a hole through the carpet, or something is bothering you," she reasoned, "now stand still and talk to me."

"I'm fine Ma, really."

"You always were a terrible liar." David rolled his eyes again and shook his head as he continued to pace until Rose had finally had enough. "David Anthony, will you please stand still for five minutes!" The firm tone of her voice immediately brought his constant strides to a halt. She walked over to him and sighed. "Tell me what's on your mind, son."

"I don't know," he said, "I guess I'm just a little anxious. I want this to be the perfect day for Casey, I'm sure I'm gonna screw it up somehow."

"David, all that matters is the two of you are here and you love each other, everything else is just decoration. Twenty years from now, when you look back on this day, you won't remember the flowers or which relatives showed up or if the caterer made enough chicken. You'll only remember how much in love you and Casey are and the moment you pledged your love to one another. That's all you should remember because that's all that really matters anyhow."

David looked at her lovingly. "Do you think the caterer made enough chicken?"

"David Anthony!" Rose scolded him. She took him in her arms as they laughed.

"Well, I was coming to help you get ready, but I see Ma's already taken care of that," Danny said from the open doorway.

"I had nothing to do with it," Rose confessed.

"You mean you did this by yourself?"

"I think at the very least, I can dress myself."

He stood and admired David for a few moments. "You look great, little brother."

"Thanks."

"Well, since the two of you seem to have a handle on things here, I'm going to go check on the bride." Rose leaned over and kissed David on the cheek. "Remember what I said."

"I'll remember," he assured her.

"Take care of your brother, Daniel."

"I will, Ma," he laughed as she hurried out of the room. David walked over, opened the window slightly and leaned on the sill as a cool spring breeze blew through. He closed his eyes and inhaled as deeply as he could. "You okay, D?"

"I don't know," David admitted, "one minute I'm fine and the next, I'm sure I'm gonna pass out." Daniel let out a small laugh. "It's not funny Danny, that's all I need is to pass out in the middle of my own wedding."

"Sit down, D," Daniel instructed.

"I can't, I'm too anxious."

"David, sit down." David moved to a chair near the window and sat on the edge of the seat. "Man, you can be so stubborn sometimes."

"Sorry."

"Don't worry about it."

"I don't know what's wrong with me, Danny."

"Are you having second thoughts?"

"No, no, nothing like that."

"Cause if you are, now's the time to say so."

"Danny, I want to marry Casey more than anything I've ever wanted in my whole life. I know we're doing the right thing." He paused for a few moments. "Maybe I'm just worried about the chicken," he said, half to himself.

"What chicken?" Danny asked, even more confused than before. David saw the curious look on Danny's face and started to laugh.

"Nothing, never mind."

"Okay," Danny laughed along with his brother.

Rose knocked on the door and opened it slightly. She peaked in and saw Casey's mother.

"Okay if I come in?" she asked.

"Absolutely!" Cadence McCallister welcomed Rose into the dressing room and embraced her. Isn't this exciting? I can't stop smiling!"

"Neither can I!" Rose chimed back. When she looked over at Casey she was taken aback.

Casey stood in front of the mirror straightening her gown as Rose and Cadence walked over and stood on the opposite side of her. The three women stared into the mirror.

"Casey, you are gorgeous!" Rose complimented enthusiastically.

"You really think so?"

"Yes!" the two mothers said in unison as all three began to laugh excitedly.

"Rose, have you talked to David yet?" Casey asked.

"Yes, I have."

"How is he, is he nervous?" Rose turned away silently and Casey became concerned. "Rose, is he okay?"

Rose smiled at her. "He's fine, Danny's with him." Casey let out a sigh of relief. "As a matter of fact, he's worried about you."

"Me?"

"He wants to make everything perfect, he's afraid he'll do something wrong and ruin the day for you."

"He could never do that," Casey assured Rose, "My world has been perfect since the day I met David, this is just icing on the cake." They all smiled at each other. "Okay, I have to ask, how does he look?"

"He looks so handsome!" Rose replied, "I can't believe it myself, he's just suddenly so grown-up." Rose started to tear up as she thought about her youngest child. She sat down in a chair near the mirror and Cay went over and sat in the chair next to her. She reached out and took Rose's hands in hers.

"I know how you feel," she said, "I'm losing my baby, too." The two women embraced each other again.

"Stop it, you two! You're gonna make me cry!" The two women laughed and tried to pull their emotions together for the sake of Casey's makeup. "Just think," Casey said as Cay and Rose joined her at the mirror again, "in about one hour we will all officially be family."

Danny was trying to keep David as relaxed as possible as they sat talking about anything that came to their minds. They heard a light knock on the door and looked over just as Patrick entered.

"How is everything going in here?" he asked them.

"Good," Danny replied. They both looked at David and waited.

"Good," he answered. He turned and stared out the window and Patrick gave Danny a worried look; Danny shrugged.

"I just wanted to check on you and see if everything is on schedule, do you have any questions, Dave?"

"No," David said without turning around. Patrick and Danny glanced at each other again.

"So, you're ready to get married then?" David sat silent for a moment, then faced Patrick. "Are you okay little brother, do you want me to go over the ceremony with you again?" Patrick asked.

"No, I'm fine."

"You seem a bit nervous. Are you sure you're all right??"

David took a deep breath and let it out slowly. "I'm good," he replied with a little more confidence.

"Okay, then, I'm going to see if the womenfolk are ready, then we can get this thing started." He turned and left the room as David looked back to the window.

"You're not planning an escape route, are you?" Danny laughed.

"No," David smiled back, "I was just thinking about the first time I met Casey." He paused for a few moments.

"Love at first sight, eh?"

"I'm not sure if it was or not, but I can't remember a time when I didn't love her." Danny knew what David meant, since he felt the same way about his own wife.

"You've got nothing to worry about."David looked at him doubtingly. "Trust me, D, everything is gonna work out just fine." David let out a small sigh and nodded in agreement. He did trust Danny with all his heart, and he knew Danny wouldn't lie to him, if he said everything would work out, then it would. Danny walked toward the door.

"Where are you going?" David asked, suddenly jumping up from his chair.

"Calm down," Daniel laughed, "I'm just going to the bathroom, I'll be right back." David felt foolish for acting so skittish, but he couldn't help it.

"David?" He turned and saw Adam McCallister behind him. "Can I have a few minutes?"

"Sure," David answered, "come on in." Adam stepped through the doorway and the two men stood silently facing each other for a few awkward moments. "So..." David said, trying to break the ice.

Adam cleared his throat. "I, uh... I wanted to talk to you..." He paused as David waited patiently. Adam glanced at David then walked over and looked out the window. "David, I wanted to say..." Again, his voice trailed off as he tried to gather his thoughts. Turning to face the young man, he began again. "Son, I thought we should..." but his strong voice stopped once more. David wasn't sure what to expect and he could feel his hands shaking. He put them behind his back so Casey's father wouldn't notice. Adam relaxed a little and smiled to himself. "You know, I came in here wanting to say something very profound and wise, but the only thing I can think of to say is..." he paused as he looked at his future son-in-law, "thank you."

"For what, sir?"

"For loving my daughter as much... *almost* as much... as I do." David smiled nervously. "Well," Adam said, as he tried to curb his emotions, "I have a date with a beautiful young lady at the front of the church in a few minutes, so I'll see you later?" David nodded and Adam left quickly. The door latch clicked shut and David slowly sat down in the chair again as Adam's words repeated in his head.

Patrick knocked on the door of the ladies dressing room and heard a familiar voice from the other side of the door.

"Who is it?"

"It's not David." The door opened and Rose peered out. "Hi, Ma," Patrick grinned at her.

"Hi sweetie, come in." She opened the door for him.

"Hello ladies!" Patrick stopped when he caught sight of Casey. "My goodness, you are beautiful."

Casey blushed. "Thank you."

"My little brother is one lucky man." He walked over and took Casey's hands in his. "We couldn't ask for a better match for David, you really are exactly what he needs in his life Casey."

"I'm the lucky one, Patrick."

"I think David would disagree with you." They smiled and embraced each other. "Well, I came here to see if you all are ready to get started." The three women looked at each other.

"Casey, are you ready to marry David?" Cay asked her daughter.

"I've been ready for a long time!" Casey beamed.

"Okay, let me get the guys in place and we'll be ready to roll!" As Patrick left the room and headed down the back hall of the church, he heard a collective squeal from behind him. He laughed to himself. "Women." When he reached David's dressing room, he knocked on the door and stuck his head in. "It's show time!" He disappeared quickly, leaving the door slightly ajar.

David stared at the doorway and Danny grew concerned as he noticed a little of the color drain from David's face.

"Ready, D?" David didn't respond. Danny stood up and walked over, then reached down and touched his brother's shoulder. David looked up at him. "Are you ready?" David nodded that he was and started to stand, wobbling a bit. Danny reached out to support him as they stood beside each other for a moment. "Dave?"

David looked up at his brother, then stepped away from Danny and went over to the mirror. Looking over his reflection, he straightened the knot on his crimson Euro tie, smoothed out the matching crimson vest and brushed off the black cutaway jacket of his tuxedo, then took a deep breath.

"I'm ready," he proclaimed. He turned and looked back at Danny. "I'm ready." Danny motioned toward the door and David walked through it, Danny followed shutting the door behind them.

Even though the chapel was a moderately large building, it had a homey feel to it. The deep-colored cherry wood of the pews and the rich, deep red of the carpet made for a welcoming atmosphere. The families of the bride and groom had made sure that everything had been decorated to the nines with red and white roses and candles glowing on both sides of the alter. A white runner had been laid along the center aisle for the bride's entrance.

Patrick walked out into the main hall of the church and stood up on the altar in front of the congregation. He began to speak to the group, trying to raise his voice over the low murmur of the mingling crowd and after a couple futile attempts, he glanced over in Murray's direction. Murray patted his hip with his right hand and Patrick nodded in remembrance. He reached under his robe and switched on the battery pack for the microphone he had been fitted with for the ceremony. Once again he attempted to get the crowd's attention.

"Excuse me, ladies and gentlemen," he announced as everyone began to quiet down, "if you all will kindly take your seats, we'll be starting in just a few minutes, thank you."

CHAPTER 25

Casey stood in the vestibule of the church holding her bouquet as her maid of honor straightened the train of the bridal gown.

"Casey, you look incredible!" Brylee said excitedly.

"Thank you," Casey replied, "I'm so nervous!"

"Are you serious?" Brylee asked with an incredulous look, "All of the people you sing and dance for at all those shows and you're nervous *now*?"

"Yes!" Casey smiled back, "My hands won't stop shaking!"

"Here," a deep voice said from behind her, "let me hold them." Casey turned to see her father dressed in his tuxedo, smiling at her. Adam reached out and took his daughter's hands, he could feel them trembling. He looked at Casey's deep brown eyes and thought back to the first time he saw them. The nurse handed him the baby bundled up in a soft pink blanket and when he looked down at her, she opened her eyes and looked right back at him. It was at that very moment that she had won his heart and he had been wrapped around her delicate little finger ever since. As he admired her now, he couldn't believe this was the same child he held in his arms that day.

"Hi Daddy," Casey greeted him.

"Hi." Adam stared at Casey as he took in the moment. "Cassandra, you are beautiful." Casey's cheeks glowed with a pinkish hue.

"Thank you, Daddy." Father and daughter stood quietly for a few moments as time around them seemed to stand still.

"What happened to my little girl?"

"I'm right here Daddy," Casey told him as she embraced him.

"Ah, there she is," he joked lightly as they pulled back from their hug.

Casey smiled at him, "I'll always be your little girl."

Adam wiped away a tear and did his best to pull himself together. "So, are you sure you want to go through with this?" Casey looked at him curiously. "I mean, are you sure that he's the right guy for you?" Adam asked, winking at her.

"Yep, I'm sure."

"And there's no way I can change your mind?"

"Nope," she grinned back at him.

"Well, then," Adam concluded as he took his place at Casey's side, "I guess I should walk you down the aisle." He offered his arm to Casey. She took a deep breath and tried to relax. "Don't worry, I have it on good authority that the young man at the other end of this aisle loves you with all his heart." Casey reached up and kissed Adam on the cheek.

"I love you, Daddy."

Danny followed his brother through the long passageway toward the main hall of the church, but as David stepped through the doorway, he stopped so suddenly that Danny almost ran into him. David looked out at the enormous crowd. Every pew was filled, and people stood shoulder to shoulder in every nook and cranny he could see. He felt a strange sensation growing inside him. Danny leaned forward and whispered to him.

"Dave, go on," he urged, but his brother didn't move. Danny reached up and touched the young man's shoulder. "David, what's the matter with you?"

"Are we related to all these people?" David asked his brother. Danny looked out over the huge mass of people gathered in the church.

"Not all of them," Danny replied, "at least not yet."

David turned to look at him. Danny gave him a light-hearted smile and David turned back to face the church. He inhaled deeply and began walking again, with Danny following him up to the alter where they stood in their designated spots. When David looked out over the sea of faces again, he realized they had all focused their eyes on him. He lowered his head and closed his eyes for a few moments, then he looked over at Danny. By this time, Murray, as well as two more of his brothers had joined them. As they stood in their matching tuxedos, David thought of all the times he stood up for his brothers at their weddings. Having them here made him feel a bit more at ease, but he still couldn't shake the nervous feeling he had. As he looked out at the crowd in the church again, he felt sick in the pit of his stomach. He breathed as deeply as he could and tried to listen to the soft melody the pianist was playing, but it wasn't working.

"D, what's wrong?" Danny asked, becoming concerned again.

"I'm not sure I can do this in front of all these people," David whispered back.

"You've done concerts for thousands; this is no different."

"It *is* different, Dan, those people are strangers, this is family, this is personal."

"You can do this, D," Danny said, trying to make him feel more confident.

"I don't think so."

"You'll do great, Dave. David?" David bowed his head again and closed his eyes. "David," Danny whispered as loudly as he could without drawing attention to himself.

"I'm gonna pass out," David whispered without looking up.

"No, you're not."

"Yes, I am."

"No," Danny repeated in a firm, slow voice, "you're not." A few moments of silence went by.

"Danny, I feel kinda sick."

"Stop it David."

"I'm serious…"

"Everything will be fine." Danny tried to sound reassuring, but even he was beginning to doubt if David was going to make it through the wedding. As David stood waiting for the ceremony to begin, he could feel his own body shake with anxiety. He heard the pianist begin to play the opening chords of the wedding march.

"Danny, I'm gonna pass out."

Three of David's sisters walked down the aisle in their matching claret-red strapless dresses, each carrying a hand-tied bouquet of white roses.

"David…" Danny tried to quiet him as the bridesmaids began to file past them. Casey's cousin Brylee, the maid of honor, began her walk.

"I swear Danny, I feel dizzy."

Brylee took her spot, with the ring bearer following close behind.

"David…"

"Honestly, Dan, I really don't..."

Danny reached over and took hold of his left elbow; he could feel David trembling. He leaned toward David and whispered directly to him. "David, look." David turned to look at Danny, who gave a small nod toward the back of the church.

David looked down the long pathway that ran between the church pews. As the flower girl finished her turn, he saw Casey waiting patiently at the opposite end. She was dressed in a floor-length gown of soft white lace with long sleeves and a low-cut scalloped neckline. The close fit of the dress showed off her small waist and petite figure and the small train spread out behind her. She wore her mother's pearl necklace and earrings, which matched perfectly with the pearl buttons that fastened down the back of the dress and on the cuffs of her sleeves. She wore her long brunette hair up in a loose bun of soft curls, accented with white roses and baby's breath. Small, soft tendrils of curls framed her face. Her bouquet consisted of several deep red roses. David stood mesmerized by the sight of her.

"Oh, my..." David said in a quiet breath as her beauty rendered him speechless. As he stood staring, Casey's eyes met his and she smiled softly. The nervousness and trembling that David felt several moments before had vanished and he suddenly felt perfectly calm. Just as suddenly, the words his mother had said to him came flooding back to his mind. 'All that matters is the two of you are here and you love each other... You'll only remember how much in love you and Casey are and the moment you pledged your love to one another. That's all you should remember because that's all that really matters anyhow.'

As the wedding march played, Casey's father escorted her down the rose-lined aisle of the church toward David. The closer they drew to him, the lovelier she became. It didn't seem to be possible, but it was true. Every moment that she was in his life made her more beautiful to him. At the end of their walk, Adam kissed his daughter sweetly, then took her hand and placed it in David's. David looked down and held it gently, feeling the softness of her skin. After a few moments she gave his hand a soft squeeze and he looked into her eyes, meeting her loving gaze as they smiled at each other. For the first time in his life, David felt he was exactly where he should be – here in this church, giving his love and his life to this woman.

CHAPTER 26

"Dearest family and friends," Patrick said as he began to address the wedding guests, "on behalf of my youngest brother David and his bride Cassandra, I want to welcome you all here today and thank you all for joining us in this wonderful celebration of their love.

"I was 25 years old when David was born and I knew from the first time I held him that he would be a very special young man. As he grew, David and I had many chances to speak with each other about various things and during one of these discussions, David told me he often wondered if it was true that there was someone for everyone, that God had created a special 'someone' just for him. He wondered if he would ever find that 'someone' and in response to his questions, I reminded him of the passages in the Book of Genesis when God took a rib from the man and used it to make a 'helper' who was just right for man. This is why a man leaves the home of his parents and joins the woman as the two are united as one.

"I told David when the time was right, God would bring him and his 'someone' together. He never mentioned this again until the day he and Casey told us they were engaged. He took me aside and said he remembered the conversation we had many years earlier and that what the Bible verse had stated was true. The Lord had made a 'helper' that was just right for him. So we have gathered here today to join them as they 'unite into one'. Please bow your heads as we pray.

"Dear Lord, we ask that you hear our prayers for Cassandra and David as they stand before you on this day and pledge their love for each other. May their lives always be a testament to the reality of that love, Amen."

"Amen," the congregation repeated.

"Our family has always used music as a means of expression, so today we would like to honor David and Casey with two special songs." As one sister assumed her place at the piano, one of the brothers picked up his guitar and sat on the stool beside her. The crowd listened as the siblings took turns singing for the bride and groom. After they returned to their seats, Patrick addressed the gathering again.

"David and Casey have each written something special to express their love for each other here before you today. Casey? "

Casey turned to David and smiled softly as she unfolded a small slip of paper. David could see her hand shaking ever so slightly as she held the note; he reached over and took her other hand. She inhaled deeply and held his hand firmly as she began to read.

"David, I used to lie in my bed at night and stare at the poster on my wall of the young man with the handsome face. I used to talk to him and tell him all my secrets. I used to listen to his tender voice as he sang love songs that I was sure were meant just for me. Sometimes, when I felt daring and extremely optimistic, I would dream of this day and try to imagine what it would be like to stand here with him. Now, I look into the eyes of the man I love every day. I talk to him and tell him all my secrets. I listen to his tender voice as he sings love songs meant just for me. And now, standing here with him today, I realize this day is more wonderful than I could have ever imagined it to be. I have always loved you David and I always will. You are my dream come true."

Casey lowered the paper and looked into David's eyes and he gave her hand a gentle squeeze as he blinked back tears. Patrick put his hand lightly on David's back.

"David?" David glanced at Patrick and then at Casey. He reached into the inside breast pocket of his jacket and retrieved his own small piece of paper.

"Casey, there aren't too many things in this world that I can guarantee will happen. I can't guarantee that the sun will always shine or that the flowers will always grow. I can't guarantee that things will always work out the way we planned or that people will always be nice to us. I can't guarantee that I'll always sing the right notes or remember all the right dance steps, but I can guarantee that I'll be there to keep you warm when the sun doesn't shine and to help you plant new seeds when your garden won't grow. I can guarantee that I'll be there to comfort you when our plans don't work out and to protect you when people are mean and unkind and I can guarantee that the sound of your voice will always be the sweetest song I'll ever hear and the life we share together will be a dance that I'll never forget. I love you Casey."

David folded the paper and placed it back into his jacket

pocket, then took Casey's hands in his. They looked into each other's eyes as Patrick continued.

"Cassandra and David, I want you to take a moment and look at the hands you are holding as you take these vows today. These hands that you give freely to each other as you step out in faith and enter into marriage are the hands you will turn to for both strength and tenderness throughout your lives together. Remember also, that there are many other hands that you can reach out for when you find yourselves facing difficult times together. Please don't be afraid to ask for a shoulder to lean on when it's needed. The love of your family and friends surrounds you today as it will always."

"Cassandra Lee, have you come here today to give your heart to David Anthony?"

"I have."

"Do you promise to stand by him in good times and in bad, to care for him in sickness and in health, to support him through the laughter and the tears and to share with him your joys and your sorrows?"

"Yes."

"Will you be loyal to him, encourage him, respect him and be compassionate toward him? Will you be his friend and companion and accept him as nothing more than the man who stands before you now with all his strengths and all his weaknesses?"

"Yes."

"Do you promise to cherish him, honor him and love him for the remainder of this life and beyond?"

"Yes."

"Do you, Cassandra Lee, take David Anthony to be your lawfully wedded husband?"

"I do," Casey placed the ring on David's finger. Patrick turned to his brother.

"David Anthony, have you come here today to give your heart to Cassandra Lee?"

"I have."

"Do you promise to stand by her in good times and in bad, to care for her in sickness and in health, to support her through the laughter and the tears and to share with her your joys and your sorrows?"

"Yes."

"Will you be loyal to her, encourage her, respect her and be compassionate toward her? Will you be her friend and companion and accept her as nothing more than the woman who stands before you now with all her strengths and all her weaknesses?"

"Yes."

"Do you promise to cherish her, honor her and love her for the remainder of this life and beyond?"

"Yes."

"Do you, David Anthony, take Cassandra Lee to be your lawfully wedded wife?"

"I do." He slipped the gold wedding band onto Casey's finger. The couple smiled lovingly at each other, then looked to Patrick, who was beginning to become emotional. Patrick dabbed the tears from his eyes and pulled himself together as best he could.

"Please bow your heads and pray with me. Dear Lord, Cassandra and David have come here today so that they may end their separateness and begin their new life together. We ask you to bless them Lord and to help them make the most of those blessings. We also ask Lord, that you help them when trials arise, give them the courage to face the unknown and help them to find humor and joy in every situation. We ask these blessings for Cassandra and David and that you will keep them in your favor for all the days of their lives. Amen.

"Cassandra and David, starting right here and right now, where there was only one there will be two. The warmth you find in each other's arms will shield you from the cold. The light you find in each other's eyes will illuminate the darkness and the love you find in each other's hearts will chase away the loneliness. Your two souls have joined to follow one path through life. Are you ready to begin your journey?"

"Yes," the couple answered in unison.

"Ladies and Gentlemen, it is now my pleasure to present David Anthony and Cassandra Lee as husband and wife. Here's the part that David has been waiting for all day," Patrick said with a mischievous grin, "Little Brother, would you like to kiss your bride?" The crowd in the church let out a collective laugh. David smiled and nodded his head as he looked at Casey.

"Yes, I would." He pulled her toward him gently and kissed her as a rousing cheer rose from the congregation. David and Casey couldn't help but laugh.

CHAPTER 27

Casey stared at the gold ring on her finger as the newlyweds sat quietly in the back seat of the limousine. She slowly turned it round and round as David watched her.

"What's the matter?" he asked her, "Don't you like it?"

"It's the most beautiful ring I've ever seen," Casey answered without looking up. David looked down at the ring on his own hand. He knew that they were just simple gold bands, but they held so much meaning for both of them. As he sat back and turned his eyes to the passing scenery, Casey gently slid her hand into his and rested her head against his left shoulder. They sat silently as the car traveled toward their celebration.

Daniel and Murray arrived at the reception site within minutes of each other and met up in the lobby. The manager of the establishment came out to greet them.

"Hello, gentlemen!" he said as he offered his hand. Murray shook it in response.

"Hello, Mr. Thomas. This is Daniel Steinman, David's oldest brother," he said as he introduced the two men. "Daniel, this is Mr. Harold Thomas, he runs this gigantic place."

"Very nice to meet you, Mr. Steinman."

"Likewise, Mr. Thomas and please, call me Daniel. There will be many 'Mr. Steinman's' here tonight and it can get confusing." The three men chuckled together.

"As you wish, Daniel," Mr. Thomas replied. "I trust everything went as planned this afternoon?"

"The wedding went off without a hitch," Murray answered.

"Well then, the happy couple will be arriving soon. Let's go inside and I'll show you everything." Mr. Thomas turned and headed down the main hall as Murray and Danny followed close behind. He led them through a large set of ornate wooden doors and into a dimly-lit room where the reception was to be held. As the doors swung open, Mr. Thomas stepped aside so the two men could enter ahead of him.

The reception hall was spacious and beautiful. The tables were covered with red linen table clothes and all of the chairs were draped in white linen with a red sash wrapped around the back and fastened with a bow. In the middle of each guest table sat a small arrangement of red and white roses with a tall white taper candle in the center.

Across the wall opposite the main entrance on a raised platform was the head table where the bride and groom and the wedding party were to be seated. The table and chairs were dressed with the same linens and settings as the guest tables. A beautiful arrangement of red and white roses ran along the front center of the table directly in front of the bride and groom's chairs. A large dance floor was located on the same level as the guest tables, centered between the head table and the main doors and to the right of the dance floor was a large stage area. Along the left wall was placed a long counter where bartenders were busy setting up for beverage services and above all of this hung several large crystal chandeliers that sparkled like diamonds, giving the entire room a rich romantic glow.

While the band warmed up on the stage, a supervisor stood with clipboard in hand checking over the room as various servers and attendants scurried around trying to make sure everything was in perfect order before the guest's arrival. Murray and Danny stopped in the doorway trying to take it all in.

"Holy mackerel!" Murray said as he stared out into the room.

"Wait till Dave sees this!" Danny said to Murray. Mr. Thomas saw the shock on their faces and immediately became concerned.

"Is there a problem, gentleman?" he questioned. Murray and Danny continued gazing at the room. "Did we forget something?"

"Oh, no, no," Murray stammered, "everything is beautiful."

"Daniel?"

"It's perfect Mr. Thomas, thank you."

"Good, good," Mr. Thomas said as he sighed in relief, "now, if you'll follow me please, I just have a few last-minute details to discuss with you." Mr. Thomas turned and headed back down the hallway toward his office. Murray and Danny looked at each other silently, then looked back at the room as they turned to follow him, a room attendant closed the doors as they left.

Soon the guests began to arrive and one by one, couple by couple, family by family, they entered the reception hall. Inside, the attendees were asked to sign the guest book and then were escorted to their tables where name cards marked their individual seats. As they sat, they chatted about the wedding ceremony and got better acquainted with each other. Servers moved in and out of the rapidly accumulating crowd with trays of various hors d'oeuvres.

When the car carrying the newlyweds neared the reception hall, David asked the chauffeur to continue driving for a little while. He could feel his new wife looking at him.

"I just want these few moments to last a little bit longer."

Casey held his hand a little tighter and cuddled up next to him on the seat. The driver took them on a scenic ride past the park, then down near the river where he found a secluded spot to park so the conspicuous long black car wouldn't be easily seen.

"I'm gonna get out and stretch my legs a little. You two don't mind if I leave you alone for a while, do you?" David sat for a second, then smiled as he told the chauffeur they would be fine. "By the way," the driver said as he got out, "you might want to roll the window down, it's really romantic here." He looked in at David and Casey. "Nice and quiet and private." He winked at them and smiled. "See you in about fifteen minutes." He closed the door and they watched him through the window as he walked several yards away from the car. The pair realized they were alone with each other for the first time since their special day had begun. David smiled and shook his head.

"What?" Casey questioned, but David looked away. She laid the palm of her hand lightly on his cheek and David turned his eyes back to hers. "Tell me."

"You're just so beautiful."

She paused a moment as her face became rosy and warm. "You look really nice."

"Thanks."

They sat with each other for a few minutes without talking. Even after all the time they had spent together over the last few years, there was an awkward feeling between them now. Neither one knew what to say to the other.

"Do we have anything to write on?" Casey asked.

"I'm not sure," he said as he started looking around the back seat of the car. He managed to find some cocktail napkins in the mini-bar as Casey pulled a pen from the small clutch purse she was carrying.

"Turn around so I can use your back." David did as she asked and Casey laid the napkin against his shoulder. He could feel the smooth glide of the pen as it moved across the paper.

"There," Casey said as she finished; David turned back to face her.

"What is it?" he asked her.

"I wanted to write my name."

"Write your name?" Casey nodded. "Kind of an odd time to sign autographs, isn't it?

"I guess, but this one's for you."

"For me?" Casey smiled and nodded again. She held the paper napkin out to him; he took it from her and unfolded it and as he read what she had written, his smile widened. 'I Love You, David Steinman. Forever and Ever, Mrs. Cassandra Lee Steinman'. He leaned toward her and kissed her tenderly.

"Thank you."

"You're welcome."

"No, I mean for marrying me."

"Thank you for asking." Casey leaned toward him and David closed his eyes as their lips met again.

"You truly are exquisite." They sat lost in each other until they heard a faint whistling in the distance. As the sound got closer, they realized it was the chauffeur trying to warn them that he was returning. When he reached them, he stopped, leaned his back against the side of the car and cleared his throat as David and Casey looked at each other. "Ready?" he asked her. Casey nodded that she was. David reached around her and touched the button that controlled the window. "Excuse me, driver?" The chauffeur turned around, pretending to be startled.

"Yes sir?"

"We'd better get going."

"Oh, yes sir," the man answered, "right away." He opened the door and climbed back into the front seat. After fastening his seat belt, he started the engine and put the car in gear.

"By the way," David began. The driver turned to look at

him.

"Yes sir?"

"Thanks."

The chauffeur smiled and winked at them again. "Anytime, sir."

David held Casey's hand and tried to relax as they traveled steadily in the direction of the reception hall. The phone in the limousine buzzed and the driver picked up the receiver and spoke to the person on the other end.

"Hello? Yes, everything's fine, we just hit some traffic on the highway, but we're almost there now, we're just a few miles out." He paused to let the caller speak. "Let me ask them, hang on." He lay the receiver across his shoulder and spoke louder so his passengers could hear him. "Sir, they said there are a lot of photographers and such out front of the building, they said I should drive around to the service entrance in the back."

"Um... tell 'em..." He paused and looked at Casey.

"Yes sir?"

"Tell 'em we'll meet 'em at the front door." Casey's eyes sparkled as she smiled at him.

"Yes sir!" the chauffeur said happily. He repeated the message to the caller and hung up the phone. "I told them we'd be there in about ten minutes. Security will be waitin' for you."

"Thank you."

"My pleasure, sir."

After driving for several minutes, the chauffeur made a right turn and headed down the main thoroughfare of the city. As they got closer to the site of the reception, they started to see the flashing red and blue lights of police cars and officers in the street directing traffic. They could see more officers attempting to keep the sidewalks in front of the building clear of onlookers. To the immediate left and right sides of the entrance, two large groups of photographers and reporters had gathered to await the couple's arrival. When the car reached the traffic cop at the intersection, the driver rolled down his window.

"Where are you headed?" the officer asked.

"To the Steinman reception," the driver answered. The officer directed him to drive down the right-hand lane toward the front of the building. As the car pulled up to the curb, security guards and police officers posted themselves around it and lined the red carpet that led through the crowd and into the lobby.

"Gee whiz," David laughed, "look at all of 'em. You'd think the president was coming to town!" Casey and the chauffeur laughed along with him.

"Are you ready?" the driver asked them.

Casey looked to David's apprehensive eyes as he glanced out the tinted rear windows of the limo, she could feel his hand shaking in hers.

"Well?" Casey asked. David couldn't keep the smile from spreading across his face as he watched her eyes dance with excitement.

"We're ready," he answered.

"Okay," the chauffer said as he unbuckled his seat belt, "here we go!" He got out of the car and headed around to open the back-passenger side door. While they waited, David took a deep breath and blew it out slowly.

"You're not nervous, are you?"

"No, of course not," David replied unconvincingly. He paused for a moment as he glanced out at the massive group of photographers. "You're sure you don't want to sneak in through the back door?"

"David!"

"Just checking."

As the car door opened, David could already see the flashes from the cameras going off. He straightened his vest and tie, and then slid across the seat to exit the car. As he stepped out, a large crowd of fans that lined the opposite side of the street screamed to him. He looked over and waved, then looked back to the car. Casey slid over to the edge of the seat and took David's hand as she stepped out carefully onto the curb. The couple stood together by the car as the cameras around them clicked off picture after picture. Their names echoed around them as photographers and fans alike called out to them.

"Over here!"

"This way, please!"

"We love you, David!"

"How about a kiss!" someone yelled out.

Casey turned to David and smiled. "How about a kiss?"

David looked into Casey's warm chestnut-brown eyes. Somehow, in that instant, the crowds were gone, and it was just the two of them. He gently wrapped his arms around her waist and kissed her deeply. As the kiss ended, there was a deafening cheer from the crowd. David leaned his forehead against Casey's and closed his eyes.

"I'll never get used to this," he confided to her and she laughed a little in response. David stepped back and looked at her. He felt the softness of her skin as Casey lay her palm on his cheek. They began walking along the red carpet toward the front door of the reception hall.

"Show us your dress!" a photographer called out.

David gave her a 'go ahead' look and Casey moved a couple feet away from him to show off her gown. As she modeled for the crowd, the photographers yelled out for her to turn this way or that way. David stood alone with his hands in his pockets watching her. He was seemingly forgotten about, as Casey's loveliness overtook them all. He didn't mind though, he was perfectly content to let her take the spotlight, on *any* stage. As the flashes from the cameras continued, Casey turned to find David. When her eyes found his, they exchanged smiles and David stood for a few seconds, mesmerized by her. Casey reached over and took his arm as they neared the front entrance, stopping only for a moment to give a final wave to the crowd before disappearing into the building.

CHAPTER 28

The door latches clicked shut as the newlyweds continued through the lobby and into the long hallway. When they reached the door of the banquet room, a security guard stopped them and asked them to wait outside in the hall. He disappeared through a side door then reappeared a few minutes later.

"They're getting ready to announce you," he told them. As they waited patiently, they could hear Murray as he addressed the wedding guests.

"Good evening, ladies and gentlemen." The crowd began to quiet down and take their seats. "First off, the families of the bride and groom and I would like to thank everyone for coming to share this wonderful occasion with us. We would also like to thank Mr. Harold Thomas and his staff for the hard work and effort they have put toward this reception and I'm sure you'll agree, they have done an excellent job in making this the most beautiful room we've ever seen. You have gone far past our expectations Mr. Thomas." After a small round of applause, Murray continued. "I have had the pleasure over the last few years of working very closely with David and Casey. I knew by watching them work together there was chemistry between them, however, I must admit that I really didn't see this coming," Murray paused as light laughter rose from the audience, "but David has surprised me again and again and this time is no exception. I have stood on many stages and introduced David and Casey to thousands of people, but never have I introduced them as I am about to tonight. Ladies and gentlemen, if you will kindly turn your attention to the main doors on the opposite side of the room, at this time it is my honor to introduce to you the new Mr. and Mrs. David Anthony Steinman!"

The guests stood and applauded as attendants pulled the two large doors open to reveal David and Casey standing on the other side. As the couple stepped over the threshold into the room, their eyes opened wide. They looked around at all the flowers and candles, the china and silver shining on the tables and the shimmering crystal chandeliers that dangled from the ceiling above it all.

"Oh... my..." Casey began.

"Wow..." David interrupted. They both stood oblivious to

the cameras snapping away in front of them as their eyes continued to survey the room.

"It's..."

"Wow..."

"David..."

"Wow..."

"Yeah... wow!" They both began to laugh.

"Mr. and Mrs. Steinman?" a voice said to them, but they were too caught up in the moment to hear it. "Excuse me, Mr. and Mrs. Steinman?" the polite voice said again. Still there was no response from the couple. The man stepped closer and addressed them again. "Pardon me, Mr. and Mrs. Steinman?" The two looked in his direction. "Would you follow me please?"

The man smiled, then turned and headed into the crowd. They followed the attendant through the maze of tables and up the few steps to the head table where the rest of the wedding party was waiting for them. Murray spoke to the crowd again as David and Casey took their seats.

"Now that we're all here, we can get down to business. I don't know about all of you, but I am famished and since dinner is on David, I suggest you try one of everything!" As the crowd began laughing and applauding, Murray looked over at David, smiled and pointed at him as if to say "Gotcha!" David smiled back at Murray and shook his head. "If you'll all take your seats please, they're about to start serving. Thank you."

The guests scattered to their respective tables as servers filtered out into the room. After delivering small salads and bread baskets to each of the many tables, they hurried back to the kitchen to prepare for the next course. As the rest of the salads were being served, David's brother, Patrick was handed a microphone and stood to bless the meal.

"Folks, if you'll all please join my family and me in a short blessing," Patrick said as he bowed his head, "Father, we'd like to thank you for all the blessings You have given us today—the beautiful day, the good food, the wonderful company of our family and friends and the opportunity to share this glorious occasion with David and Casey. We ask that You bless this meal and all the people here with Your love and keep them in Your Heavenly favor. Amen." There was a short pause as everyone finished the blessing. "Well," Patrick concluded, "bon appetite!"

The sound of forks and knives against china dishes mingled with muted voices as the guests ate and chatted with each other. Casey immediately began to devour her food, while David sat with fork in hand wondering if he could get away with not eating the salad. Looking at the little bowl full of dry purplish-green leaves, bean sprouts and crumbled blue cheese, he thought how this was unlike any salad he had ever eaten before. He moved the bowl's contents around with his fork and saw what looked like a cherry tomato. He gently pushed his fork into it and raised it to his lips, sniffing at it before placing it into his mouth, just to make sure it *was* a tomato.

"This is really good, isn't it?" Casey asked him. He looked at her and nodded in agreement. Casey took another bite and looked over at David again. "Aren't you hungry?"

"Yeah, I'm just not in the mood for salad."

Casey watched him for a second before going back to her meal. David stirred the salad ingredients around once more and then laid his fork on the table beside the bowl. Soon the attendants returned to collect the salad bowls. As the main course was placed in front of him, David stopped the server.

"Excuse me."

"Yes Mr. Steinman?"

"Um... what exactly is this?"

"Tonight, we are serving roasted pork loin with rosemary and whole grain mustard sauce, roasted rosemary potatoes and creamed spinach." David looked at the plate. "Is there anything else, sir?" the server asked politely. David looked up at him.

"No, thank you," he smiled. The waiter nodded and returned to the kitchen. David sat and watched the other servers shuffle plates around the room and as one of the women passed behind him, he called out to her.

"Excuse me, Miss?"

The woman stopped short and turned to him. "Yes Mr. Steinman?"

"Are you serving anything else tonight besides the pork loin?"

"Yes, sir," she answered. David's spirits rose a little. "We are also serving pan roasted bass with tomato and herb cream."

"Oh."

"Would you rather have the fish? I'd be happy to exchange it for you."

"No, no, I'm fine, thank you."

"You're welcome," she smiled as she left him. Once again he heard the knives and forks against the plates as everyone enjoyed their meals. David picked up his fork, but didn't eat anything.

"Are you feeling okay?" Casey whispered to him

"Yeah, why?"

"Cause you're not eating." David shrugged, he didn't want to tell Casey that he didn't like bass and he *hated* rosemary seasoning.

"My stomach is a little queasy, just nerves I guess."

"Relax, the hard part is over, now all we have to do is eat, drink and dance the night away!" She smiled at him happily, kissed him on the cheek and went back to her food. David placed the fork back on the table and sat back in his chair.

"Would you like some water Mr. Steinman?" one of the waiters asked, startling him.

"Yes, please."

"Is your food satisfactory sir?" he asked, noticing David's untouched plate.

"It's great. I'm just not very hungry."

"Would you like me to remove your plate?"

"Please," he replied. The waiter quickly picked up the plate and headed back toward the kitchen. David sighed. He hated lying to people, but he didn't want to hurt their feelings, everyone had worked so hard to make their wedding day perfect for them, he didn't want to let something as small as dinner overshadow those efforts. *Well, there's always the cake*, he thought.

From a few seats away, Murray watched as David's dinner vanished into the kitchen and he knew something was up. When he saw the same waiter return with a fresh pitcher of water, Murray waved him over. He inquired as to why David sent his food back and the waiter relayed what David had told him. Murray whispered something to the waiter, who nodded affirmatively.

"Right away, sir," he replied and walked off in the direction of the kitchen once more.

As the guests finished their dinners, the empty plates were taken from the tables and replaced with full glasses of champagne engraved with the couple's names and wedding date. At the same time, Murray stood and began to speak.

"Folks, now that we've had a delicious meal, I believe the Best Man has a few words he would like to say." Murray handed the microphone to Daniel. As Daniel stood, David looked anxiously at Casey.

"Don't worry," Casey whispered to him.

"Hello everyone, for those of you whose acquaintance I have not yet had the pleasure, my name is Daniel Steinman and I am David's eldest brother. I am also his best man and as such, I am required to make a toast to the bride and groom." Daniel smiled in David and Casey's direction. "My brothers and sisters and I were very excited when David was born—the sisters, because they had a new baby to fuss over and the brothers, because it evened the score at ten and ten." Laughter rose from the tables as David smiled. "As he grew older, we made a lot of memories together and I'm sure David will agree, as the youngest he put up with a lot of— forgive me, Ma—crap from the rest of us." Once again, there was laughter.

"We have shared some very happy, joyous times and we have shared some very sad and even heartbreaking times. Throughout all those times, we have watched as our baby brother grew into the fine, upstanding young man that sits here today. We are very proud of the person David has become. He's kind and generous, trustworthy and honest, intelligent and funny, passionate, caring and loving. He's the kind of friend everyone wishes they could find and the kind of brother everyone asks God for." Daniel placed his hand on David's left shoulder, and David closed his eyes as his emotions began to overtake him. "And now, after all this, he's gone and surprised us by doing something totally unexpected; he's gone and fallen in love with a beautiful young woman named Cassandra and somehow convinced her to be his wife." A round of applause and a few hoots and whistles came from the crowd. Casey reached under the table and held David's hand.

"So, in light of this current development, I ask you all to join me in raising a glass to toast David Anthony and Cassandra

Lee. May they always have happy times and smiles, may they always be surrounded by people who love them, may their lives always be filled with music and laughter and may they always see in each other's eyes the love they see today." Daniel raised his glass toward Casey and David as the gathering followed suit and a tear rolled down David's cheek as Daniel finished the toast. He felt Danny's hand squeeze his shoulder lightly. David slid his chair back and stood to face Danny. As they looked at each other, David's emotions got the best of him and his tears fell freely, and Danny smiled at his little brother as the two siblings embraced tightly. Stepping back from their embrace, Danny took David's face in his hands. "I love you, D." David was so overcome with emotion that he couldn't speak. Danny held him again as the guests stood and applauded.

"Can I have one of those?" The two men turned to see Casey beside them. David stepped back a little as Danny and Casey hugged one another.

"Welcome to the family, sis!" Danny said to her.

"Thank you, Danny!" Casey returned, blotting away her own tears with a handkerchief. The dinner music resumed as the three of them tried to regain their composure. A low murmur began to rise as the guests began to mingle again. David wiped his face with a linen napkin and pushed in his chair.

"I'm gonna go find Ma," David told Casey, "wanna come with me?" She nodded as David took her hand and led her past the head table, then down the few steps to the main floor. When they reached the bottom step, they were met by several friends and well-wishers. David and Casey shook hands and kissed cheeks as everyone took pictures and hugged them. Amongst the many people surrounding them, David managed to find two of his brothers just ahead of him, and he waved at them, trying his best to be seen in the crowd, but to no avail.

Guest after guest continued to offer their congratulations as the couple graciously accepted each one. David noticed a third brother facing him and took a chance for one last attempt at a rescue, waving his hand above his head, he tried once more to get their attention. Finally, the three men noticed their brother's signal in the large crowd, just as David and Casey were about to be swallowed by the blob of people that had accumulated around them.

"Uh oh, I think we're needed," one said, "Come on, guys!" They headed toward David and Casey. "Excuse us folks, but we need to borrow these two for a few minutes." The three siblings made a protective circle around the bride and groom and escorted them out into the open.

"Thanks," David offered, "where's Ma?"

"This way." They led the couple to where Rose and the McCallisters were sitting. David snuck up behind Rose and placed a kiss on her cheek and Rose beamed when she saw him.

"Davey!" she said as she hugged him tightly.

"Hi, Ma," he smiled and sat down next to her.

"So, are we doing better now?" David nodded yes. "No more nerves?"

"No, but there is one thing bothering me."

"What's that?"

"I thought we were having chicken." Rose looked at him scornfully. "Sorry," he giggled, "I couldn't resist." Rose's expression softened. As she looked at David, he could see her eyes glistening with the hint of tears. "Mama…"

"Shhh," she stopped him, placing her finger over his lips and giving a small shake of her head.

"Ladies and Gentlemen," a voice from the stage said over the speakers, "at this time we would like to invite the bride and groom and their parents to the dance floor."

"*Now*?" David looked toward the voice.

"Yes, now," Rose replied. She dabbed her eyes with her napkin. David sighed heavily. "David Anthony, don't you want to dance with your mother?"

"Well, yeah, but..."

"David, come on!" Casey urged. He looked up at her and then back to Rose.

"You should always do what your wife tells you David," she winked at him and they smiled together. David stood and helped Rose with her chair before following Casey's family to the dance floor.

"Ladies and gentlemen," the voice spoke again, "please welcome Casey and her father, Mr. Adam McCallister, in their father-daughter dance." Adam walked to the middle of the dance floor with Casey on his arm. About halfway through the song, Cay was invited to join her husband and daughter. "And now, ladies and gentlemen, please welcome David and his mother, Mrs. Rose Steinman in their mother-son dance. David escorted Rose to the center of the dance floor.

"You know, you really are a great dancer," Rose complimented him as they danced. David blushed as he laughed and when the dance ended, David hugged her close.

"I love you Ma."

"I love you too, baby." Rose and David moved apart just as Casey and her parents walked up to them. Adam took Casey's hand from his arm and Rose took David's hand. Cay joined them as together they placed Casey's hand in David's.

They stood for a few moments as Adam looked at his new son-in-law. "You'll make sure she's safe?" he asked softly, his eyes moist with tears.

"Yes sir, I'll take care of her." Adam smiled at his daughter, then offered his arm to the ladies and escorted them from the dance floor.

"Ladies and gentlemen, it is my pleasure to present Cassandra Lee and David Anthony in their first dance as husband and wife," the voice from the stage announced. A single spotlight focused on the newlyweds, making them the center of attention. David smiled and shook his head.

"What's so funny?" Casey smiled back at him.

"You've always got me out on a stage somewhere."

Casey put her arms around his neck. "That's because I don't want to be out here alone."

"You never will be." He wrapped his arms around her tiny waist. She looked into David's face and knew he meant what he said. She closed her eyes as their lips met, then David laid his check against hers. "I love you Casey," he told her as the first measures of the song began. He gazed into her eyes as they moved together. The music started to build, and David felt a happiness in his soul that he hadn't felt in a long while. He surprised Casey as he suddenly twirled her around the dance floor. The guests applauded as the couple gracefully moved together and Casey allowed David to lead her as she lost herself in the music.

At the start of the second verse, David took Casey in his

arms and held her close. As they stared at each other, Casey saw a playful look in David's eyes. Hearing the music begin to build again, Casey gave David a sly smile. He spun her around, then back close to him. Together they circled the dance floor, letting all the passion they had for each other show to those around them. As the music slowed near the end of the song, David twirled Casey once more, then took her in his arms and slowly dipped her. He raised her up to face him as the last strains of the song faded and the crowd roared with applause. Casey looked at David in amazement, her brown eyes sparkling. He smiled at her, sweat glistening on his brow.

"What was *that*?" she asked incredulously.

"What?" he shrugged. Casey gave him a 'you know what' look. "Oh, that, I just felt like dancin'." He smiled devilishly as he took her in his arms and spun around with her.

"David Steinman!" Casey held tight to him. David laughed out loud at her reaction, then stopped and looked deep into her eyes. His heart was overflowing with love for Casey McCallister and he kissed her fast and deep so as not to miss the moment.

"Ladies and gentlemen, the newlyweds would be honored to have you join them on the dance floor," said the stage voice. The applause subsided as the guests began to pair up. The band played a soft melody as Casey and David held tight to each other. David leaned into Casey and pressed his face into the soft skin of her neck. As he inhaled, he recognized the scent of the soft musk perfume she always wore. They swayed slowly to the music and he thought of their first dance together in the studio several years back. He remembered how he had hurt her feelings and how close he came to losing her forever… he held her closer.

"Never again," he whispered; Casey looked at him.

"Did you say something?"

David smiled softly. He pulled her to him and kissed her. Casey took a deep breath in as David's lips continued down her neck to her shoulder. She held on to him tightly as a tingling sensation ran down her spine. She pulled back from him, knowing if he continued, she wouldn't be able to resist him. Casey reached up and smoothed the hair around his face, then placed her cheek against his, closed her eyes and said a silent prayer. *He's perfect, Lord, thank you.*

CHAPTER 29

David followed Casey back to the tables and the two sat down to rest a bit.

"Well, either you've been holdin' out on me, or I'm a damn good teacher, which is it?" The pair turned to find Claire grinning at them.

"Claire!" Casey stood and hugged her tightly.

"Hi sweetie!" Claire greeted her as she kissed Casey's cheek. "You look ravishing!"

"Thank you!" The two women stared at David and waited.

"So, which is it?" Clair asked. David looked at her for a moment, then remembered her initial question.

"Well, you didn't think I came up with that on my own, did ya?" The ladies laughed.

"Good answer, now, give me a hug!" She stepped back a little and looked David over, straightened his tie and smoothed his jacket. "You clean up nice!" Admiring the two of them, Claire felt tears welling up in her eyes and David and Casey smiled to each other. Claire blinked as a tear ran down her cheek and Casey felt a lump in her throat.

"Claire, stop it!" she pleaded.

"I can't help it, I can't believe these two beautiful people are the same two scared kids from just a few years ago." The two women embraced each other again and cried together.

"Are you crying *again*?" Murray asked as he joined them. Claire looked over at him as he handed her his handkerchief. "Here." Claire dabbed at her eyes so as not to mess her makeup and David repeated the gesture so Casey could do the same.

"How do I look?" Casey asked him.

"Same as always," David told her, "gorgeous." Casey rolled her eyes at him as he laughed, and he leaned over and kissed her cheek. The four continued to socialize until their conversations were interrupted once again by the voice from the stage.

"Ladies and gentlemen, we ask that you please clear the dance floor for the next few minutes. It's time to cut the cake! If the bride and groom could join us once again, please..." the voice trailed off. David heard the announcement and turned to Casey who was talking with some old friends.

"Casey, come on," he whispered, but she didn't hear him. "Case," he whispered a little louder. He waited as the women continued talking and laughing together. David was trying to be as polite as possible, but it was getting harder to do. Hearing that it was time to cut the cake reminded him of how hungry he was and how much he had been looking forward to this moment. He decided this situation called for a drastic measure on his part. Standing directly behind Casey, he placed his hands on her shoulders and poked his head into their conversation.

"Would you ladies excuse us for a few minutes, please, we have a cake to cut."

"The cake!" Casey said as her eyes widened, "I forgot all about it!" David nodded.

"Are the bride and groom still present?" the stage voice inquired jokingly as the guests laughed.

"David, they're waiting for us!"

He nodded and pointed toward the dance floor. Casey turned and hurried in the direction of the voice as David tagged along behind. The couple emerged from the crowd just as the room attendants wheeled the wedding cake into the spotlight. They took their places behind the cake table and waited as the official photographers steadied their cameras and prepared to capture the moment for posterity.

David stared at the white butter cream-frosted four-tiered cake with red roses cascading down the side and a cake topper that read 'C & D'. He was sure that it was going to taste heavenly and even though his mouth was watering and his stomach rumbled, he resisted the urge to scoop up a finger full of frosting. As they went through the motions of cutting the first piece together – cameras flashing, guests cheering – all David could think about was that first bite. He picked up the small piece of cake from the plate and turned to Casey. Slowly, each fed a piece to the other and as the cake melted in his mouth, David felt himself relax some. *Finally,* he thought, *food!* Again, the cameras flashed around them and Casey leaned over and kissed him.

"This cake is delicious!"

"I know! I just want to eat the whole thing!" Casey laughed. David swallowed his bite and licked the frosting from his fingers. As they spoke, the room attendants began to wheel the cake back to the kitchen.

"Casey, where are they going?" he asked anxiously.

"They're going to cut it up and serve it to everyone."

"Do we really have to share it?" he asked, half joking and half serious.

"Don't worry, my love, I'll make sure you get a huge slice," she told him as she kissed him again. Then she hurried off to rejoin her friends. David watched as she disappeared into the crowd, then looked down at the small plate he was still holding in his hand. Rubbing his finger across it, he salvaged what was left of the icing, stared at it for a few seconds and with a defeated sigh, he stuck his finger in his mouth and licked it clean. Somehow, he knew he had seen the last of his own wedding cake.

Murray found David among the crowd of family and friends and put his arm around David's shoulder.

"Can I talk to you for a few minutes?"

"Sure," David answered. He excused himself from the group and walked along with Murray. "What's up?"

"I got you a wedding gift, but I wanted to give it to you in private," Murray explained. David stopped walking.

"Well, why didn't you say so? Wait a minute and I'll go get Case..."

"No, no, this gift is just for you."

"For me?"

"Don't worry, I got something for Casey, too. The two began walking again as Murray led the way into the kitchen.

"So, what is it?"

"I knew it was the perfect gift for you, but I wasn't really sure how to wrap it."

"Murray, you know I don't care about that."

"I'll tell you what, why don't you sit down here for a minute and I'll go get it." Murray guided David to a chair by the table and started to leave the room, then stopped and turned back to David. "Oh, and you gotta close your eyes."

"Murray," David began to complain.

"Come on, Dave, just close your eyes for a minute, I really wanted it to be a surprise."

"All right, all right," David replied with an exasperated sigh. He sat in the chair with his eyes closed while Murray stepped out of the room. As David waited, the quiet of the room began to bother him.

"Murray? Murray, where are you?"

"I'll be there in a minute!" Murray called back to him. David could hear people moving around him and he wondered what kind of gift it was that couldn't be wrapped and required more than one person to bring it into a room, the suspense was killing him.

"Murray, what's taking so long?"

"Geez, will you just relax for a minute? I'm almost ready." David waited as patiently as he could for a couple more minutes. Finally, the moving he had heard around him stopped and the room grew quiet. "I think it's all here."

"Can I look?" Murray purposely didn't answer in order to keep David in suspense as long as possible. He looked at the others in the room and held a finger to his lips asking them to stay quiet. "Murray?" Still there was no answer. "Ackerman!"

"Okay, you can look." David slowly opened his eyes, not sure of what he might find. To his surprise, he saw Murray standing across the table from him, flanked by Mr. Thomas and his chefs. Sitting on the table in front of David was a silver platter upon which sat the biggest cheeseburger David had ever seen. He could see that it was loaded with his favorite toppings and mayonnaise oozed from its edges. Beside the burger was a mound of steaming hot French fries and next to the platter on the table was a gravy boat filled with brown gravy. The table had been set with a knife, fork and napkin, and a small candelabra with two taper candles burning in it stood nearby. A smile grew across David's face as he surveyed the table.

"I hope you like it," Murray told him, "I had it custom made just for you." David looked up at Murray and Mr. Thomas. "Gotcha!" Murray laughed. Mr. Thomas and his crew began to laugh and applaud.

"It's exactly what I wanted, thank you."

"Thank you, Mr. Thomas," Murray said, "you and your staff are the best in the business." Mr. Thomas nodded in gratitude and left the room with his chefs in tow. Murray sat down on the chair across from David and watched as David stared at the food. "What are you waiting for?"

"So, I can really eat this?"

"What are you talking about? Of course, you can eat it."

"I mean, no one's gonna take it away and cut it up into a billion pieces and pass it around the room?"

Murray laughed. "That really was a fantastic cake." He glanced at David who gave him an irritated look. "Eat it before it gets cold." David sprinkled the fries with salt and black pepper, then grabbed the gravy boat and doused the entire pile. After cutting the enormous burger into quarters, he began devouring the meal as Murray sat quietly watching and shaking his head.

"How did you know?" David asked while chewing a chunk of cheeseburger.

"Don't talk with your mouth full."

David chewed a few more times and swallowed. "How did you know?" he asked again.

"Well, I saw the waiter take your dinner plate before anyone else had finished, so I knew you didn't eat and I know you only got one piece of the cake."

"One *bite*," David corrected.

"One bite of cake, I figured you had to be hungry."

"That's why I pay you the big bucks," David smiled as he shoved a fork full of gravy-coated fries in his mouth. He sat back in his chair and closed his eyes as he chewed. "This is *so good*!"

"So, how's it feel to be a married man?" Murray asked. David grinned as he wiped his face with his napkin.

"Were you really surprised that we got married?"

"A little," Murray admitted, "I knew back when Casey started working with us that you were falling for her, but I didn't think you had the nerve to ask her out, let alone ask her to marry you."

"Thanks!" David laughed. Murray laughed with him while David poked at the remaining fries on the platter.

"You really love her a lot, don't you?"

David pushed the fries around in the puddle of gravy. "Yeah…" He smiled as the thought of his new wife filled his mind. David stabbed a couple of the fries with the fork and looked up at Murray. "You want some of this?"

"No, thanks," he replied with a shake of his head as David filled his mouth with fries again. Murray leaned back in the chair and waited while David finished his meal.

ENCORE

David sat quietly at the table in his dressing room staring at his reflection in the lighted mirror. He had lived this scene countless times during the last decade, so much so that on occasion he had trouble separating the blur of days in his mind. He thought about all the cities he'd traveled to and all the stages he had performed on, about all the songs he had sung, all the people he had met and he knew he owed it all to Murray Ackerman.

His mind flashed back to the night of his very first show. He recalled the letter his mother had given him, closing his eyes as his father's voice echoed around him. 'Follow your heart'… 'Always believe in yourself'… 'You are going to accomplish great things David and I'll be there to share them all with you.' He looked into the eyes of his reflection as a single tear traveled slowly down his cheek. "Thank you, Papa." A knock on the dressing room door startled him.

"Come in," David called out as he quickly wiped the tear away.

"Hey," Murray said, popping his head in the door.

"Hey."

"'Bout ready, kiddo?"

"Yeah, just about."

"Dave, what's up?"

"Nothin'," David assured him, "I was just thinkin' about things."

"Now that'll get you into trouble!" Murray joked.

"Yeah, I know," David laughed, then he paused. "Murray, do you remember that first concert we did?"

"How could I forget it? You were so scared."

"I was terrified."

"I honestly didn't think you'd go through with it, but you went out on that stage and gave it your best shot."

"I'm glad I did," he admitted, "it was because of that show that I finally figured out where I belong." David turned to face him. "You know Murray, I don't think I've ever thanked you."

"For what?"

"For being a pest," David laughed as Murray smiled, "for not taking 'no' for an answer, for introducing me to the most beautiful girl in the world, for bringing music back into my life, for waking me up, giving me a reason to want to live again…" His voice softened as it trailed off.

"Dave, you don't have to…"

"Ackerman…" The two men stared at each other for a few moments, both attempting to control their emotions. "Thank you."

Murray smiled at him. "You're welcome… ready to go?"

"Yeah," David said with a deep breath. He stood from the dressing table and headed out into the hall. Murray followed him as they walked down the long corridor and into the wings of the stage. He gave a signal to the stage manager when they reached the top of the steps and as the house lights dimmed and the band began to play, David could feel the energy and excitement of the crowd. He felt the familiar butterflies in his stomach as Murray handed him the microphone.

"Still scared?" Murray asked.

"Yeah."

"Still wanna do this?" he teased.

"Yeah."

"Well, then…" Murray took a step back and motioned with his hand, "the stage is yours, my friend."

They shared a smile as David turned and stepped out into the spotlight…

~ ~ ~ ~ ~ * ~ ~ ~ ~ ~